Also by Mike Holst

**A long way back
Nothing To Lose
No Clues in the Ashes
Justice For Adam
The Magic Book**

Best Wishes

Mike West

BACK from the ASHES

Sequel to *No Clues in the Ashes*

MIKE HOLST

iUniverse, Inc.
New York   Bloomington

Back from the Ashes

iUniverse books may be ordered through booksellers or by contacting:

iUniverse
1663 Liberty Drive
Bloomington, IN 47403
www.iuniverse.com
1-800-Authors (1-800-288-4677)

Because of the dynamic nature of the Internet, any Web addresses or links contained in this book may have changed since publication and may no longer be valid. The views expressed in this work are solely those of the author and do not necessarily reflect the views of the publisher, and the publisher hereby disclaims any responsibility for them.

ISBN: 978-1-4502-5727-5 (pbk)
ISBN: 978-1-4502-5728-2 (ebk)

Printed in the United States of America

iUniverse rev. date: 9/16/2010

Acknowledgments

To Glenda Berndt goes my heartfelt thanks for all of her talents and work on this story.

To my wife Kitty, who makes me get it right, in everything I do, once again thank you.

To the men and women I served with in the fire service. Although this story is from my imagination it would not have existed without you and the ordeals we went though. You my friends, like the fires that are seared into our memories, will never be forgotten.

AUTHOR'S NOTE

The insidious deeds of David Bennett come alive once more in this sequel to *No Clues in the Ashes*. To those of you who haven't read the first book, I encourage you to do so before taking this literary trip into the dark world of this man. Your journey will be so much richer knowing what preceded this story.

In *No Clues in the Ashes,* we met David Bennett and Mike Flanagan. Adversaries? Yes, to put it mildly. Flanagan was an up-and-coming firefighter, on the Minneapolis Fire Department, when he suddenly changed careers and went into arson investigation. A near-death experience at a fire had been the final straw that propelled Mike into it. Then he met David Bennett, a chemical engineering student turned serial arsonist, who had discovered the perfect way to set an almost undetectable fire. After a long, and mostly futile, attempt to catch and stop this maniac of a man, Flanagan caught up to him in an elevator in Minneapolis with a firebomb that David could not diffuse. Bennett went to a fiery end—or so they thought.

Now, in this story that takes place ten years later, David Bennett is back in business. He is the most callous and relentless psychotic pyromaniac that Chicago has ever experienced. He has no conscience and no moral compass. He is driven by an unrelenting desire to burn down the city of Chicago after his near-death and failings in Minneapolis, and his defeat at the hands of Mike Flanagan. Here in this city, far from Minneapolis, Flanagan and his department, David has developed a new strategy that could prove to be catastrophic for the city of Chicago.
Enjoy the story
Mike Holst

Fire can be one of the most comforting things we can enjoy or one of the most frightening things we can experience. Man has learned to use fire over the years for both good and evil. Man is the only creature that dares to create fire and use it for his own satisfaction because he, and he alone, has learned how to control it.

CHAPTER ONE

September, 1975

THE BLACK FORD CROWN VICTORIA had been idling softly for over half an hour at the end of the small, suburban Chicago cul-de-sac. Just the soft whoosh of the fan blades and belts, and a gurgle of fluids under the hood, could be heard in the still night air. A dark wet spot of condensation had formed on the cold asphalt under the warm exhaust pipe, and another had formed under the middle of the car hood. It was just a subtle reminder of the early morning chill in the Chicago suburb. Outside of the confines of the automobile, the darkness seemed to envelop everything into a murkiness that made it hard to distinguish where something ended and something else began. The dark night actually made the night air heavy and unyielding, and brought on a hint of claustrophobia, not knowing what was lurking there. The darkness also masked all color and clarity, turning the outside world into a realm of black and blacker.

The lone occupant in the car leaned against the driver's side window, his softly exhaling breath fogging a spot on the glass with each respiration. In the gleam of the dash lights, his right hand could be seen on top of the steering wheel and a cigarette glowed softly from between his nicotine-stained fingers. Those same fingers were engaged in a constant, nervous tapping motion; his other hand lay quietly in his lap.

A W-beam metal guardrail, with a yellow and black dead-end sign bolted to the middle of it, was the only thing between the car and the steep hillside that descended behind it. The hillside was barren, covered only with scrub brush, tall dead grass and an occasional stunted evergreen. Paper and plastic bags were intertwined in the brush and scrub trees, giving the whole area an unkempt look. The grade was very steep—over forty-five degrees. It continued down about a hundred feet and then leveled out into the shoulder of a busy freeway. The last thirty feet or so was bathed in dull yellow sodium lights, on poles placed alongside the freeway.

On the other side of the freeway was another guardrail made of cable and posts. Then the terrain fell off once more, down another fifty feet, into an industrial area where about fifteen buildings formed a factory complex reminiscent of an army camp. The buildings connected to each other in various ways and were haphazardly arranged. It was almost as if they had been built, one after the other, as an after-thought or part of a giant Lego game. An eight-foot chain link fence, with three strands of barbed wire on top slanted outwards, extended around the perimeter of the entire complex. At one end of it, the two-lane gated road was shut, but not locked; the chain meant to secure it hung loosely from the side of the gate. It was the only way in and out of the complex.

Lights were on in scattered sections of all of the buildings, and fifteen or twenty cars were parked in the lot closest to the first building inside the gate—the only two-story building you would find.

All of the buildings in the complex were constructed of the same yellow brick with black, metal-framed glass windows, and were all more glass than brick. The glass in the windows of all of the buildings except the first building, which obviously was the administration building, were opaque, as if they had been painted over. In the administration building, the windows were cloaked with blinds and a few green plants were visible, giving the offices a homey, lived-in touch.

Two large smokestacks and a water tower stood like quiet sentinels behind the first building. A thin cloud of smoke, visible in the parking lot lights, filtered out of one of the stacks and drifted north, away from the complex toward Lake Michigan. The name **ATLAS** was stenciled, in large black letters, on the side of the silver water tower. A red strobe light on top flashed on and off, reflecting off the smoke cloud that drifted over it.

It was cold in the damp October air that came off Lake Michigan, which was only a mile away. Off to the east, the lights of downtown Chicago glowed against the low cloud layer and the top of the Sears Tower seemed to disappear in the clouds like Jack's fantasy beanstalk.

Below, however, the streets of downtown Chicago were still very much alive with lights, cars, and hundreds of people still refusing to acknowledge that nighttime was fast fading away and soon it would be another day. Car horns honked, engines raced, tires squealed in protest, and somewhere, a few streets away, the sounds of sirens were slowly fading away. It was just another Friday night in the Windy City.

A large white number was painted on the side of each building in the factory complex. A gray, mostly windowless square metal building with twin smokestacks positioned alongside of it, separated the administration building from the rest of the complex. It was lit up on one end by what seemed to be a single-lamped fixture over a small steel door. The lights inside of Building 3, an adjoining building, had not changed in amount or intensity since he had parked the car.

The man reached up and adjusted the rear view mirror to watch the darkened homes on the street behind him for activity, but it was dark and quiet. There was just a mongrel dog walking along, marking his territory by peeing on mailbox posts, and then he quietly disappeared between two houses.

The window in the car slowly lowered about halfway and a cigarette butt flicked out on the asphalt, landing in a shower of sparks. He lowered the window down more to listen but nothing of interest came to his ear, just a few other dogs barking and the noise from the traffic racing by on the freeway below him. With the silence came the cold air and he raised the window back up.

For a second it seemed that the faint lights in Building 3, the one he had been watching, appeared to flicker and nearly go out. Then, a wisp of smoke came out of one of the windows that had been left partially open at the top. It had started. The pill had gone off where he had left it in the wastebasket yesterday—a miniature version of the firebombs he had made back in Minneapolis. He no longer needed to make a big fire, the sprinkler system would see to that.

David sat up straighter in his seat. His hands were shaking as he lit another cigarette and blew the first puff out the window. His left hand resumed its position back on the top of the steering wheel; his right hand went back in his lap. He shifted slightly, sliding down a bit as if to appear less conspicuous.

Suddenly, he could hear a bell that had gone off somewhere in that same building he had been watching, and he leaned forward over the steering wheel to see better. For a minute, the bell's clanging was the only distraction, and then he saw the shadow of someone running across the parking lot from Building 5 with what appeared to be a fire extinguisher in his hand. The man struggled with his keys for a moment, then opened a door in the side of Building 3 and disappeared inside. A moment later, the building was engulfed in fire from one end to the other. Most of the windows blew out in a large whoosh, and then the only sound was of tinkling glass falling everywhere on the dark asphalt outside the building. The frame of the still-standing building, now minus its windows, looked like an angry metal skeleton enveloped in fire. The fire spread quickly to the roof and the burning asphalt made a billowing cloud of black smoke that was barely visible against the even blacker sky.

David, who had perked up with the explosion, sat back in the seat again and took another long drag of his cigarette. His right hand, still in his lap, seemed to be actively massaging something in the folds of his clothing. His face had a look of serene pleasure on it. He was behaving like a dog scratching a sensitive spot inside of his ear, being very careful and very deliberate. This had been a long time coming and he was going to enjoy every minute of it, but it was nothing compared to what he had planned for Chicago.

At Station Thirteen, the doors of the firehouse were rising slowly, and Clint Travis was anxiously watching the gauges on the dash of Engine Thirty-eight. The bells had just rung for them less than a minute before.

Just as Clint reached for the red button to release the air brakes, Captain Bob Evers slid into the other seat and picked up the radio microphone. He turned and looked behind him at the other two men who had just closed the cab door behind them. "Hit it, Clint," he said. They were a man short tonight and that bothered him. Sometimes it was hard enough with five people.

The big Cummins diesel engine roared to life as the forty-five thousand pound fire truck came alive, pulling out on the apron and turning right toward the freeway entrance. The red strobe lights on the truck reflected off the windows of buildings they were going by, doubling their effect. The blare of the air horns was deafening as they blew through a red light.

"Engine Thirty-eight is in service to Atlas Industries—5700 Russell." said Bob Evers. It was a formality to check in with Dispatch. The people there knew they were in service the moment the overhead doors opened. As he looked in his outside mirror, behind him he could see Truck Thirteen following them. Both units were housed in Station Thirteen, along with Battalion Chief Harold Franklin, who was in service at another fire right now. He normally didn't respond with them unless it was a multi-alarm fire.

"We have you in service at 3:33, Engine Thirty-eight. Be advised that Engines Sixteen, Eleven and Truck Four will be backing you up on this call. We have several calls on this fire and it seems to be expanding rapidly. Let us know what the situation is as soon as you can."

"Ten-four, Dispatch," Evers answered. Truck Thirteen's air horns blared behind them. The huge 85-foot aerial ladder was a formidable piece of equipment, and guiding it through heavy traffic was an art in itself, but it was right on their tail.

Several cars had pulled over and stopped alongside the freeway. People were getting out and standing on the shoulder of the road, watching the fire burning and escalating below them. Workers were coming out of several of the buildings not burning and running to move cars that would be in the way when the fire equipment arrived. All of them, and the spectators above them on the freeway, were oblivious to the black sedan parked across the road, on the hill high above.

David had heard the sirens and saw Engine Thirty-eight and Truck Thirteen coming down the freeway and then exiting down the ramp into the industrial area. His breathing was rapid, his face flushed—it had been a long time since he had done this and this was his trial run. If it worked, there would be more—lots more. He was older and wiser now than the last time he was in business and he would not make the same mistakes that had left him so horribly scarred from burns.

His right hand, which had been so busy in his lap, now reached for the shift lever. The backup lights flashed on momentarily as he went through the gear selection and then the car drove slowly away. He was halfway down the block before the headlights came on and the driver's window closed.

Capt. Bob Evers had been to too many fires in his twenty-three year career. He had seen much worse than this fire at Atlas but he took each fire seriously. One of the security guards from the plant was waiting by the now-open gate. He pointed the route they should take, around to the left, as the big rigs came through the gate. Evers gave him a wave but they didn't stop. Every second counts in fire fighting. Engine Sixteen was exiting onto the ramp at the top of the hill.

The first priority would be the exposures as there was little they could do for the building that was burning. The building didn't have a lot of fire load as it was a storage building for steel supply; row upon row of racks filled with bar steel and sheet steel. They were as visible as if they had been outside in the parking lot as most of the building was now gone. The burning roofing material comprised most of the fire load.

Engine Thirty-eight set up on the far end of the fire, putting a wall of water up from its deluge gun to protect the adjacent building which it was attached to. On the way in, they had hooked up to an outside yard hydrant for a water supply. The big, four-inch supply line snaked around the corner from the truck, pulsing as if it had a heartbeat of its own as it fed the engine over a thousand gallons of water per minute. Another line was laid to supply Truck Thirteen, which had extended its ladder nozzle over the other end of the building to keep the fire out of the power plant building. Engine Sixteen's crew had gone through the office building to make sure the fire had not gotten inside the power plant building. They had taken hose packs with them and would hook up to standpipes inside the building.

Battalion Chief Franklin was now arriving on the scene and taking command. He asked for a second alarm. This would bring one more engine, another truck company, a squad company and one more Battalion Chief but, most likely, they would not be needed as the fire was fast blackening down.

The black Ford sedan drove quietly down the alley and pulled up to a wooden two-stall garage. David Bennett reached up and pushed the button on the door opener clipped to the visor. The car pulled into the garage, parking alongside a gray pickup truck. The logo on the door of the truck said, **Knowlton Alarms and Sprinkler Systems.**

He sat in the car for a few minutes while he collected his thoughts.

Everything had gone as planned. Hell, even better than planned. Were there people in that building when it exploded? Well, he saw the one guard go in. Were there others, and did he care? No, he didn't. If there were fatalities it was because they were in the wrong place at the wrong time. He did not seek to kill people but, he had to admit, it made the experience more worthwhile.

His thoughts went back to Minneapolis where it had all started eleven years ago. *How many people had died in those fires?* He didn't know and he didn't care. All he knew is that someday he would go back there and Mike Flanagan would pay for what he had done to him. For now he had other plans.

The pain he suffered daily from being nearly burned to death while crawling up an elevator shaft, while the fire below was literally cooking him, was a constant reminder. He had lain on the roof of that shaft for hours, with third-degree burns on the lower half of his body, and listened to them celebrating below over the body of that poor, homeless man he had dragged in there with him just before the doors closed.

He remembered having to crawl down those same ladder rungs hours later, with skin hanging from his legs; having to pry those elevator doors open and walk through that ramp in the early morning hours until he found a car full of clothing; breaking in and stealing new clothes to wear. He could never forget that painful cab ride to the airport and wanting to scream out from the pain.

David opened the car door and left the garage, heading for the house. He still walked stiff-legged from the heavy scar tissue on his legs. Without proper medical treatment his burns had healed into a hideous mass of scars and weeping flesh that to this day, eleven years later, still had not healed. He could not squat or bend his legs more than a few degrees. Every day was a lesson in pain that could not be ignored. Only the drugs kept him going—morphine, cocaine, and heroin—whatever he could buy.

Inside the house the message light was blinking on his machine but he ignored it. He was tired and was going right to bed. His cat, Sampson, was lying on the end of the bed waiting for him.

The fire was contained and slowly, one by one, they shut down the trucks and appliances. Clouds of wet, foggy steam still billowed over the charred remains of the building. The fire had done some damage in the connecting power building, as the huge door that separated it from the building that burned had not closed all of the way. It was held open with a fusible link that had separated, but a barrel of metal shavings had been carelessly placed against it, preventing it from sliding shut. On the upside, the sprinkler system in the power building had stopped the fire. The hose line that had been stretched, by the crew, from Engine Thirty-eight had also helped.

Bob Evers had sought out Chief Franklin as soon as he could after things calmed down. "Kind of a strange fire, Chief," he remarked.

Chief Franklin, his tired face lined with the furrows of so many bitter memories from days gone by, looked at Bob Evers and said, "What's that you say, Captain?"

"Well, when we first pulled in the fire load was gone wild, but it seemed to die down even before we got set up. Looking at the building right now, there was not a lot of fire load in that building as it's mostly racks of steel and other metal," Bob shrugged his shoulders, "for what it's worth," he said. He was tired and wanted to get out of there.

The Chief walked away from the scene, turning his back to the carnage and talking on his handheld radio.

"I need an investigator down here at Atlas," he said to Dispatch. "Captain, why don't you pack up and get ready to leave. I am going to leave the truck company here for lighting. Engine Thirty-eight and the squad company will also be clearing."

There was some static on his radio and Chief Franklin said, "Repeat please," to whoever it was.

"This is Dispatch, Chief. Investigation is on their way."

Bob Evers had gone over to the burned-out building to collect his men and equipment. He stopped long enough to draw his hand across his throat, his signal to tell Clint to shut down the pumps. Hand signals between the pump operator and others were critical because the big truck made so much noise you could hear nothing when you were standing right next to it.

Clint cut the throttle and the big diesel died down. He closed the gate valves, and the canvas hoses that had been firm and pulsing, now became limp as their lifeblood ran away.

Clint was the old man of the station and was looking at retirement in the spring if things went well. It had been a good run, and he was proud of his years with Chicago's finest, but as with all old fire fighters, time has a way of dulling the senses and it was no longer fun. There is little the old ones have not seen and done, the challenges becoming fewer and fewer.

As a rookie, Clint had received his baptism of fire on December 1st of 1958 at Our Lady of Angels. Nothing had ever topped that fire. He never forgot the sight of all of those little bodies in that burned-out school. He had been at McCormick Place when it, too, burned in January of 1967. His memory chip was full and now it was time to push "save" and shut it down. There would be no deleting anything for, like an old soldier, those memories would have to fade away with him. He was only fifty-four so that might take a while but he and Emma, his wife, had already bought a little piece of property south of Tucson. The kids were settled all over the country so Emma and he would now be free to roam.

Darrel Strickler and Arnie Hogan were preparing to leave the building. The two fire fighters from Engine Thirty-eight were rolling up the hose, draining the excess water from it and piling it outside the door. They would stack it on the platform on the back of the engine for the trip back. Once there, this hose would be run through the washer, hung to dry in the hose tower, and the truck would be reloaded with dry hose.

As he came close to the door they had come in, Darrel stopped to uncouple two sections of hose. Bent over, with his nose by the floor, he smelled it before he saw it.

It was the night watchman who had run in with the fire extinguisher. He had still not been missed because there was no one else to miss him in this part of the plant.

At first, Darrel thought he was looking at a pile of garbage because the body was right next to a trash can. It certainly didn't resemble what it had once been. The fire extinguisher that had been under his arm had exploded from the heat of the fire, adding to the destruction of the body.

Darrel whistled and Arnie looked up at him. "Hey man, we got ourselves a roast," he said.

"Shit!" Evers said as he looked down at the body. He wanted to get out of here and now they would have to hang around for the coroner. "Let's look around," he told Darrel and Arnie, "and make sure this is the only one." He called Dispatch with the news, as Chief Franklin had already cleared the scene. Franklin overheard the call but did not return to the scene. Instead, he radioed Evers and told him to expand his search, which they were already doing. He would arrange for a coroner. They should stand by to assist.

"I knew it," Evers said. "Every time this happens right at shift change and we get caught up in something."

He had little sympathy for the victim. He looked down at the charred body. The arms and legs had retracted into a fetal position. Fingers and toes were burned off except, on one foot, part of a shoe remained. The front of the skull was looking up and the teeth were grinning in some kind of a hideous grimace. The exploding fire extinguisher had disemboweled the body and the wet entrails lay spilled out on the floor.

Was this where the fire started in this trash container? If so, why did it spread so rapidly to the rest of the building? *Piss on it,* Evers thought. *Let Investigation figure it out.*

CHAPTER TWO

DAVID SLEPT WELL THE REST of the night. Most nights he would awaken several times from the pain in his legs and have to try and find another position, but nothing seemed to work for long. The next morning, he propped up his pillows and reached for his cigarettes. His cat, Sampson, was still on the end of the bed, licking himself. David clicked his tongue to try and make him come to him but Sampson just looked at him and went on licking his furry genitals. *I guess if I could do that I wouldn't come to me, either,* David thought, and he smiled at the image it projected in his mind. The room was dark except for what little light spilled in around the edge of the shades. There was just enough of it to make out the dresser and the nightstand next to the bed, and to show off the piles of clothing and magazines on the floor.

The digital clock on the nightstand said 10:55 a.m., but the illumination had been turned down so you could barely read it. David reached over and turned on the lamp; Sampson responded by jumping off onto the floor, going over and sitting by the closed door.

He was naked as he lay there smoking, on top of the grimy sheets. The sheets had been white at one time but now they were yellow, and spotted with yellow and red bloody patches from the weeping sores on his legs. He looked down at his flaccid penis but didn't linger there. His gaze became fixed once more on his legs. They looked like two pieces of rotting flesh. Scars had covered scars and, here and there, they had broken open to create even more scars. Each time, some of the elasticity of the skin left and they became more rigid and more unyielding.

Done smoking, David stuffed the butt in an overflowing ashtray and, swinging his legs around, got out of bed, went into the bathroom and turned on the shower.

Jerry Martin gunned the engine and the red Chicago squad, with **Fire Investigator** emblazoned on the door, sped northward on the freeway. He had been busy tonight and was suffering from a headache caused by lack of sleep and too much coffee. He drove carelessly, with one hand loosely draped over the top of the steering wheel, his other hand holding a cup of coffee in his lap. There was a constant stream of chatter on the department radio from fire rigs that were in service around the city. A little red light zipped back and forth on the face of the scanner radio, searching for activity and stopping on a channel from time to time. His ear had tuned out most of the noise, his mind recognizing only his own call letters and anything that sounded especially frantic.

He was tense today—the results of nicotine withdrawal. He was in day four of trying to quit a fifteen-year smoking habit that had spiraled to three packs a day. It wasn't only his health that had been suffering, but also the expense of smoking; corners needed to be cut somewhere.

Since Colleen had taken the kids and walked out on him, it was tough making ends meet and trying to keep up two households. *I wonder what she is doing right now,* he thought. There wasn't any room in his thoughts for hate. He still loved her and he knew it, *but goddamn it, Colleen,* he thought, *you sure are making things tough. I know I wasn't around very much, and I know I was a horse's ass from time to time because I was always tired and preoccupied. Yeah, I drank a lot, baby, but you drove me to that. You could have cut me some slack, baby. Things would have gotten better. I know they would have. Yeah, I was ignoring the kids, too, but how the hell is this helping that get any better, with me living on one side of the town and you on the other.*

Jerry gazed out the side window at an old lady sitting on a bus bench, bundled up against the early morning cold, dragging deeply on a cigarette. *God, what he wouldn't give for a weed right now.*

The car idled roughly while he waited for a red light to change, and the oil light flashed on occasionally, but just faintly. He made a mental note to have it checked out.

He could have whistled in to the scene and been done with it but he was tired of lights and sirens and used them only on rare occasions. His whole life had been one big emergency when you thought about it. It had started in Vietnam and had just gone on from there. Ten years in a truck company and now five years in investigation; he was still only thirty-eight years old but he felt like he was fifty-eight.

A horn beeped behind him and he looked up at the now-green light, paying no attention to the person who had so rudely interrupted his thoughts, and gunned the car forward.

The car stunk like smoke from his dirty coveralls lying on the floor in the back seat. Another mental note came to mind. *Put that shit in the trunk after this.* The back seat was covered with boxes full of files and books. Shiny gallon paint-style cans, that held specimens, were also stuffed on the seat. An attaché case on the floor held his camera and a back-up camera. The passenger seat was empty. They usually worked in pairs but Belinda was off tonight, taking care of her sick kid. Working with a woman could have its problems but he tried to stay non-judgmental, despite the little voice in the back of his head that kept saying it just wasn't right. He needed to get an attitude adjustment on that subject but he wasn't ready for it yet.

He made a right turn and was up the ramp, merging onto I90-94 heading northwest towards Skokie. *It should be about five more miles,* he thought. As he looked over at the empty passenger seat, his thoughts went back to Belinda Clayton, his sidekick. The Department had partnered her with him about a year ago. She had hired in right out of college. Sometimes Jerry thought she was over-qualified for the job in some respects, with her fancy college degrees and all, but that was where the department was heading. She had a PhD in Chemistry and a BA in Fire Science, but what she didn't have was a background in the fire service. He had called her Ms. Fancy Pants for the longest time. Oh, not to her face, but she had heard it in a roundabout way.

She hadn't always been as perfect as they all thought she was, being dedicated to the fire service, and the kid she was home taking care of tonight gave mute testimony to that. But she was a good mom and he had to give her credit for that. Living on your own after your wife has kicked your ass out is one thing, but being a single mom was something else. *Shit, he was going soft. Now he was making excuses for her.* Jerry laughed and shook his head at the thought.

Dispatch had told him *Exit Twelve B,* and here it was. He merged over one lane to the left, crowding in front of a kid in a blue pickup who quickly honked his horn and gave him the finger. *Hey, have a little respect, dirt wad,* Jerry thought, and returned the gesture.

His notepad said, **Captain Bob Evers, Engine Thirty-eight.** Jerry stuffed it back in his shirt pocket after checking the name again. He knew Evers—they had been on several calls together and once, when he was a Truckee, they had worked together on a roof fire on an asphalt plant.

The off-ramp was slippery from water that had spilled from one of the trucks. His car slid a little on the steep grade so he cut the throttle, coasted through the gate, and drove around to the freeway side of the building. You couldn't see the burned building from out front but the wet pavement left no doubt where the trucks had gone.

"Hi, Bob," Jerry spoke first as he walked up to the three men sitting on the back of the engine.

"Well, it's about time," Evers said with a big grin.

"Sorry about that, but I was over in Cicero on a bus garage fire when the call came in. Also, I'm the only guy on in the whole fucking town tonight."

"Where's your little blond sidekick?" Evers smiled.

"You know about her?"

"Seen her once at a fire in a theater. Kid's got a nice rack on her."

"Forget her rack," said Jerry. "What have we got?"

Bob gestured toward the burnt out building. "Place was burning like the Hindenburg when we got here. Had to set up out here and deck gun the place because it was so hot, but it died down in a hurry—even before we got water on it."

"Sprinkler system working?" Jerry asked.

"Yes, and that makes it stranger because there was very little fire load in there. Mostly racks of steel. Can we go now?"

Before Jerry could answer, the medical examiner's truck pulled up. An older man in a white lab coat over a dark blue suit walked toward them. "Dr. Takmoto," he said. "You have a fatality?"

"Oh, we got you a dilly," said Evers. "Hope you brought a big garbage bag."

The little Japanese doctor did not answer his comment but said, "Show me."

"Hey, Arnie! You and Darrel go help him," said Evers to the other two men who had been sitting silently on the back of the truck.

They both stood up and started for the building, with the doctor following them.

Arnie looked back at Evers and said, "Ish!"

Bob took Jerry's arm in his, like they were going to walk down the aisle somewhere. "Let's go nose around, Inspector," he said.

David stayed in the shower until the water turned cold. He thought about the fire last night and how good it felt to be back in the business again. In fact, he felt so good about it he became excited again and so he took care of it in the shower. It was the third time in less than twenty-four hours. He was getting his sexual excitement back, also.

Bennett had bought the sprinkler business from the Knowlton brothers about nine years ago. He had worked for them for about a year and a half, mostly as a service man, but the brothers were getting old and wanted out. So, with the last of his mother's money, he managed to swing the deal.

David had kept the company name. It would have been risky to get his name on anything public even though Mike Flanagan, in Minneapolis, thought he was dead. Flanagan got around and David did advertise in some fire department magazines. Chicago was not that far removed from Minneapolis. Besides, the Knowlton brothers thought it was nice and had encouraged him to do so. Every so often he would send them a check, just for using their name.

He installed fire alarms, too, but he farmed all of that work out to a sub-contractor and kept 15% off the top. Right now, the real money was in the maintenance of sprinkler systems. David, with his chemical background, had come up with some soluble oil that was more miscible than previous products. The oil kept the pipes from rusting and deteriorating. This was a big problem in sprinkler systems as, otherwise, water in the pipes had to be flushed in a constant program to keep them clean. Once treated with David's oil, they were good until they were used. It wasn't a hard sell for David and business had been good. In fact, today he had an apartment building to service in Oak Park and two other contacts to talk to.

The other big benefit to David, besides making a living, was it gave him a chance to get back into the arson business. For many years after he left Minneapolis he had walked the straight and narrow, almost afraid to burn his garbage. Petrocyclomate, David's fluid of choice that he had discovered the formula for, was not being manufactured and he had used all he had possessed back on that fateful day in that Minneapolis parking ramp.

Then the military had inquired about using it in some incendiary bombs in Viet Nam so, for a few years, a supply of it was made by a refinery in the Beaumont, Texas area. However, it proved to be too hard to handle so they scrapped the idea. The refinery was left with several hundred barrels of it in stock. Because it would eat through metal barrels, the ingredient that made it so corrosive and volatile had been purposely left out. But David knew where to get it, and get it he did.

David stumbled on it, completely by accident, through a newsletter he received from the refinery from his college days. He bought up all he could afford, no questions asked. The refinery was glad to get rid of it. Right now, he had an equipment garage where he kept all of his pipes and fittings, with over one hundred fifty glass-lined barrels stored in it, full of the now-reformulated petrocyclomate. He found out something else almost by accident. The oil he used to keep the pipes from rusting also kept the petrocyclomate from eating through the pipes and fittings. It made his plan almost perfect.

Bob Evers and Jerry Martin had walked the entire length of the burnt-out building and back again. They were standing by the outside door now, looking at the spot where the body had been found.

"I think this trash pile was where it started," said Evers, "but I'm at a loss as to what got it going like it did."

"Did you guys smell gasoline or anything?" Jerry said.

"Nothing but smoke—nothing unusual, anyway." Evers was nervous and wanted to get out of there; he was already late for breakfast.

"Well, I think I will try to take some samples, but you guys pissed enough water on this to float a crab boat, so I doubt that will show much."

Evers let the slam with the water usage pass. He had heard that before from these damn inspectors. *How did they expect them to put the fire out? Blow it out? Goddamn retards,* Bob thought. *You could always tell the ones that didn't come up through the ranks. Oh yeah, he had been a Truckee for ten years, but that didn't cut no shit with the boys in the Engine*

Companies who put the fires out. They just didn't know what it was like on a hose line in a fire.

"Anything else?" said Evers. "It's light enough now you shouldn't need our lights, right?"

"Naw, I think I'm going to get out of here, too. I'll come back later when my partner is here. She's the chemist."

Both men walked back together to the engine where Arnie and Darrel were back, sitting on the end plate of the truck. The coroner had left and it was time to call it a day or a night, whichever fit.

"Hey, Evers! You owe me some new gloves," Arnie said, as they walked up to them.

"How's that?" said Bob.

"You made me help that old Jap pick up that cooked grease ball, and now my fucking gloves stink so bad I can't wait to throw them away."

"Maybe you should stay back there on the ride back if you stink that bad," said Evers. He stepped up into the truck and slammed the door, waking up Clint, who had been draped over the steering wheel.

"Home, James," he said.

David checked the address against what he had written down—6600 York. This was the place. Now he needed only to find Harlan in Maintenance.

The perky little blonde receptionist paged Harlan for David, and he heard him tell her over the speaker he would be right up. He walked around the lobby while he was waiting and looked at the display boards that were set out to exhibit the company's many products. They sold safety products for industrial applications; there were lots of masks with different kinds of filters that washed out the air for people in bad atmospheres. David picked up a mask and slipped it on while looking towards the receptionist's desk. She was playing in her cleavage, absent-mindedly, with the eraser of a yellow pencil. When she saw him looking her way, she spun around in her chair and opened a file.

David heard footsteps behind him and turned to face a large black man in a blue suit with a nametag that said, **Harlan Christianson, Maintenance Supervisor.** Harlan was the biggest black man David had ever seen. His suit coat was open and his shirt was unbuttoned three buttons down from the top. His stomach, which was as flat as a tabletop, disappeared under a thin white belt. His chest bulged out of the green colorful shirt he had on, accented by a wide gold necklace around a neck as thick as a tree stump. He showed a set of large ivory teeth in a toothy grin and, switching his radio from his right to his left hand, extended his hand, saying, "I'm Harlan. How can I help you?"

"David Bennett. I'm here from the sprinkler company, Knowlton's." Harlan's hand dwarfed his hand, but he tried to put a little extra firmness in his handshake.

"Let's go down to the sprinkler riser room while you explain what it is you are proposing we do." Harlan's voice was deep and loud, echoing off the hallway walls as they walked through a corridor from the reception area to the plant. The noise of manufacturing was increasing with every step until Harlan opened a steel door and they were in the factory—then it erupted into a loud crescendo.

They didn't try to communicate in the factory—David following Harlan, staring at his broad backside, while they walked briskly along. Several employees glanced up from their duties as they passed. They were all dressed in white lab coats. The room they were in was not that large by industry standards. They soon went through another door into a quieter area that had some vending machines and a table set up. It looked to be a break room of sorts.

"Can I get you a coffee or a doughnut?" Harlan asked.

"I better not," said David. "But thanks, anyway."

"Well then, through here," said Harlan, and they stepped into a small room with half a dozen large steel pipes coming out of the floor and disappearing into the ceiling. There were also several electrical boxes in this room.

"What I sent out to you in my proposal," said David, "was a way to eliminate those costly flushing sessions of your sprinkler pipes. What I will do is drain your system like we do every year, but this time we would be pumping soluble oil into your pipes before we recharge them with water. This oil will keep the pipes from rusting and, hopefully, you will never have to flush them again."

David handed Harlan a small jar of oil in a bottle. "Let's get some water here and I will show you how this works."

There was a small slop sink in the corner and David filled a beaker with water from the faucet. Then, taking the jar with the oil back from Harlan, he mixed about half an ounce with the water in the beaker.

"Hold out your hand," David said.

Harlan, smiling, held out his large hand and David poured a small amount of the mixed liquid in his palm. "Rub that between your fingers," he told him.

"Slippery," said Harlan, "but does it stay mixed?"

"I'm going to leave that beaker with you for a few days and you watch it. If you're satisfied with the results, I could come back in a couple of weeks and take care of your whole system. I estimate that two barrels will take care of everything here. That's about 2500.00 dollars worth. That's the cost of one year's flushing. After that, they're on the house because you won't need to ever do it again. Every time we drain the system, we can get air into it and cause lots of problems. This will take care of all of that, too."

Harlan was still rubbing his fingers together. "What if we have a fire and the system gets used?" he asked.

"Well, we would have to recharge it, but only that zone," David answered. "You have ten zones here so, at the most, I would say three hundred bucks."

"Sounds reasonable to me," Harlan said. "I'll pass it by the boss and get back to you, but I don't see any problems."

David closed up his lab case, and smiling, said, "I can be here the day after you call me."

They left the room and walked back the way they had come. David looked at the piles of raw material lying everywhere between machines. *What a fire it will make,* he thought. *This big black ape is way too stupid to worry about. He hasn't a clue.*

He squinted in the bright sun as he stepped outside into the parking lot. This was enough for today. Tomorrow he had two places to go talk to, and one to service. That one would make thirty-three buildings that were now ticking time bombs.

There was always the chance that one of these places would have an accidental fire, which wasn't a problem, except he would miss all of the fun.

He groaned as he stepped into his truck. Something had let go in the back of his left leg and he could feel the blood running down his calf. He sat with the leg stiffly out in front of him, pointed toward the passengers side of the truck, and rested his forehead on the steering wheel.

He was going to have to spend some more time on the remote fire-starting device he was working on. The fire yesterday had been successful but it had involved him getting into the building to start the initial fire with a delayed igniter. A bomb is useless if you can't set it off without getting caught. Sooner or later, him being there before the fire would draw attention.

Harlan walked back to his office. The product made sense, but there was something weird about the man. He seemed to be caught somewhere between nervous, and agitated. Harlan had been in the business of meetings with salesmen for thirty years and he knew when someone was not being honest with him. This guy just didn't pass the smell test.

Speaking of that, he sure did stink like Bactine, or some kind of antiseptic. Walked goofy, too—like his pant legs were frozen. Oh well, he thought, *no sense shooting the messenger here, the product seemed to be legit.* Harlan made a point to call him tomorrow and place an order, despite his reservations.

CHAPTER THREE

Jerry had one more call to handle and then he would call it a day. He was going to have Belinda come over to Atlas tomorrow and follow up on things. It was mostly chemical tests that she was better at. Yeah, there was something fishy that had gone on there, but for right now he had his plate full of other things, and it was time to delegate. A wave of tension washed over him as he felt of his pocket for his cigarettes for about the one hundredth time today.

He was starting to rationalize with himself about this whole smoking thing. *No one gave a rat's ass about him, anyway,* he thought, *so why was it so damn important he took care of himself. Hell, Colleen and the kids would be better off without him. Plus, he knew lots of guys that smoked all their lives and lived to be eighty. Come to think of it, he also knew a few that didn't make it to sixty-five, but what the hell, they probably had screwed-up genes to start with and nothing would have helped them, anyway.*

Just then all of the idiot lights on the dashboard came on and the car quit. Jerry was going about forty when it happened so he nosed it down an exit ramp, coasted to the bottom and there he stopped, right in the middle of an intersection. Jerry got out and, pushing on the doorpost, managed to shove the car through the intersection and over to the curb right next to a hydrant. *Piss on the cops! If they don't have a sense of humor they can give me a damn ticket,* he thought.

Next, he called on the radio for a mechanic from the city shops and they told him two hours. Jerry was just too depressed to deal with it all. He walked down the block to a Seven Eleven and bought a pack of Camels. A dog chased him on the way and Jerry yelled at it, "Go ahead, you miserable mutt—bite me in the ass. See if I give a shit!"

He smoked one on the way back from the store and lit another when he got back to the car. *Might as well do it up good,* he thought, as he sat in the car waiting and catching up on paperwork. He looked up often as he read because he wasn't in the best part of town. The Chicago Arson Unit was hosting the International Arson Investigators Conference in three weeks at McCormack Place. It was just another thing to worry about, although most of the work that had been assigned to him had already been done.

Mike Flanagan was fast becoming an icon with the Minneapolis Fire Department. He had taken over the helm from his mentor, Gordy, three years ago. Under his direction, the Fire Investigators Unit had been transformed into one of the best in the country. Beside himself, they now had three other full-time investigators and a full-time secretary. They did some of their own lab work, worked fire prevention in the schools and aggressively pursued most criminal arson cases.

In fact, that was where he was going today—to court to testify in a case that had resulted in the deaths of two people.

At thirty-six, the years were just starting to show on him. His hair was sprinkled with a few gray hairs and he had developed a small paunch from too much of his wife, Laura's, great cooking. His oldest daughter, Cindy, was a junior in high school this year. Like her mother, a stunning woman with the same golden hair and baby blue eyes. Cindy and Laura were inseparable, and as close as a mother and daughter could be. As for Mike, he and Cindy had a lot of love and respect for each other, but somewhere down deep something had always been missing. He was her adopted father and that seemed to bother Cindy.

Their son, Mickey, was fourteen and the pride of the park board baseball program. Thin and lanky like his father had been, he was just starting to show his adolescence with a few pimples and stray chin whiskers. He was already planning on a fire department career. His dad was his hero and Mickey copied everything he did. The only difference was, when he got to the fire department, Mickey didn't want to be a fire investigator. He wanted to be the Chief, after a long and distinguished career as a fire fighter.

Then there was Cara—the baby at ten years of age, and the apple of her father's eye. Like Cindy, she had already mastered the piano. Gifted beyond her parent's wildest expectations, she was looking forward to a life of music. Unlike Cindy, she was not pretty, but rather plain looking. She had her father's reddish brown hair, freckles and skinny build. Right now, her mouth was full of braces and she was in that awkward time of life when she was no longer a little girl, but womanhood was still a few years away. Also, unlike Cindy, she was not as close to her mother as Mike would like, but Laura worked hard at it.

Laura had never gone back to work on the outside after Cara's birth. She was deeply involved in her family and her community. She was indifferent to Mike's career, although she tried to show interest from time to time. Most of her time, however, was tied up with the kids, the P.T.A., her garden club and church. If there was one thing Laura was not indifferent about, it was her and Mike's marriage. They loved each other with all their hearts and worked hard at keeping each other happy.

Mike was going to Chicago in a few weeks for a conference, where he was to be one of the featured speakers. When he returned, they were going to take a long family vacation. They were way overdue.

David sat at the kitchen table, the garage door opener in his hand. He had just finished making another modification to extend the range that it could transmit. He was going to give it a try in a few minutes.

The opener was nothing more than a switch that would close a circuit, causing a spark to start a fire in a small vial of chemical. If it worked, it would be a small thing to adapt it to the explosive devices he had made.

He set up the receiver on the table and then, putting on his hat and coat, he went out the back door to the alley and walked down to the end of the block. School had just let out and some kids walking by hollered at him, "Hey, stiff legs, you walk like a penguin!" David watched them walking away, chattering and laughing amongst themselves. He would see who got the last laugh. There was a sprinkler system in their school and he serviced it.

At the end of the block, he slipped his hand in his pocket and pushed the button on the opener, holding it in for just a few seconds. Then he turned and walked back home. Turning the key in the lock, he went directly to the table and picked up the receiver switch. The contacts had closed. A smile spread across David's face as he set the switch back down. No more would he have to get in the buildings to do his dirty deeds. It was all downhill from here.

Monday morning, Belinda and Jerry Martin met in the office for just a few minutes while going over the day's work. "We had a fire in a steel warehouse yesterday, and I think you better go out and take a look at it." Jerry said. "I didn't stay around long, but something was used in there—no doubt about it. It was a fatal fire, but the guy who died was a watchman who worked for them so I don't think he had anything to do with it."

"What's the address?" Belinda asked.

"Atlas Iron Works out on I-94 West. Are you familiar with it?"

"I'll find it." She was reading the report while she talked with him.

"Our car died so you will have to stop by the motor pool and pick up something else—and get your stuff out of the old one." Jerry looked at her over the top of the paper he was reading. "I'd go with but I need to get caught up here today."

"Yeah, you look very busy." Belinda made a ball out of the paper she had been reading and threw it at him. "I didn't want you along, anyway."

"Good," said Jerry, "I don't like you, either," he quipped, and gave her a toothy grin.

The minute Belinda went out the door, he reached in his desk drawer for his cigarettes and fired one up. He didn't need her riding his ass about smoking, too. Not right now, anyway.

The car was ready when she got to the motor pool so she headed out to Atlas right away. Traffic was heavy for a Monday morning, so it gave her time to think while she sat in the slow-moving line. She worried a lot about her daughter but last night, for the first time in a long time, she had slept through the night and that was encouraging. Being a single mom was no joyride that was for sure. One-night stands can turn ugly when you have to live the consequences, but she loved her daughter with all of her heart and things would get better. She was optimistic about that.

The yellow police tape was still strung around the building, warning everyone that it was a crime scene and to stay out. Belinda stood beside the car, looking the scene over while she put on her coveralls. Then she lifted the tape and walked underneath. At first, she stayed outside, just walking the length of the building and peering inside. The broken glass from the windows crunched under her feet. She was looking for signs that might tell her which part of the building the fire started in, but the destruction seemed to be pretty uniform. She walked back to the door the watchman had entered in and went inside. The heat had bowed the door and she had to force it with her knee.

The sun was warm coming through the blown-out windows, but the minute you were shaded, the cold came right back at you and Belinda shivered. The structure was wide open and offered little shelter.

The building seemed to still be orderly inside, although badly scorched. Some of the steel beams in the roof were warped but seemingly, not in any one place. Some of the steel on the racks on the floor had also warped. The charred remains of a desk and a forklift were in the corner—behind the door she had come in. A blackened bulletin board held scraps of burnt paper and what looked like had once been a nude calendar from some tool company, with just December left showing. A wooden chair had the back burnt off, but the seat and four legs were still intact.

A yellow chalk line marked the spot where the body of the watchman had been found. It was also where, Jerry had said in his report, he felt the fire had started. Water was still dripping from sprinkler pipes that ran on both sides of the building. Almost all of the heads in the building had opened. There was no sheen in the puddles on the floor that could be attributed to gas or fuel oil. Her meter was not picking up any petroleum odors that it could or would recognize, so she shut it off.

She just stood there looking around, and was baffled. She had no idea where to look and no idea what to look for. There was bound to be oil on the floors. After all, this was a steel warehouse. How to separate the wheat from the chaff?

By the end of October, an early winter had come to the Chicago area and snow banks were lining some roadways. It was still warm enough that the sun melted the streets clear during the day, but its strength was losing the battle to melt the big piles. They would be there until the spring solstice came once more to warm things up and wake things up. It had been a few days since it had snowed and the grimy color of the snow banks gave mute testimony to that.

David had been very busy. Not only had he sold his rust-inhibiting process to another seventeen companies, but he had installed an ignition source in about half of his accounts. By Christmas, he hoped to have them all up and ready to go. It gave him a sense of power to know that, with the push of a switch, he could turn Chicago into the greatest inferno since the Great Fire of 1871 that had killed three hundred people and destroyed much of the city. He had more potential for an even bigger fire because the city was much larger now than it was then. True, they had a better fire department now, but he was convinced they could be beaten. This time it would not be some cow kicking over a lamp in a backyard barn.

Time was a factor, but not a big one, as long as nobody got wise to him. The investigation at Atlas Fire had gone nowhere. Both Belinda Clayton and Jerry Martin had been back to the scene several times but nothing was ever found.

The second week in October, the Chicago Department had hosted the Annual Fire Investigators Conference at McCormack Place. Jerry Martin had talked with Mike Flanagan, from the Minneapolis Department, over a few beers. They had discussed several fires they had both investigated over the years and shared tips and ideas. Both men had a lot in common when it came to the fire department and they enjoyed each other's company. The similarities ended there, however. Their personal lives were as different as night and day.

Mike was happily married to a loving wife, while Jerry's wife was one trip away from the lawyer's office to file for divorce. Mike's kids were the pride of his life, while Jerry saw his as mountains of child support.

On Wednesday, the final day of the conference, Mike and Jerry saddled up to the bar for one last glass of suds and, this time, Belinda was also there. They took their beers over to a table by the window—Jerry, sitting with his back to the window, while Mike and Belinda sat opposite him. Belinda found Mike fascinating when he talked about the use of different accelerants that have been used in fires, and how they react and are detected. The talk ranged from gasoline to fertilizer.

"We had a guy years ago," Mike said, "that was using some chemical that isn't even available any more. He was a chemical engineering student who came up with the formula, and then had to scrap it because it was so volatile. He found a way to ignite it by combining it with some kind of nitrates. The bad thing was, it left no residue. We were never able to find anything at any of his fires."

"What happened to him?" Belinda asked.

"He died in one of his own fires. Poetic justice," said Mike, wiping the beer foam from his lips.

"How did you find out about this stuff?" Belinda asked.

"Just luck, and a diligent professor at the University of Minnesota."

Just then, another man from the Chicago Department approached the table, and gave Jerry a note.

"Trouble?" said Belinda.

"Wife trouble," said Jerry with a frown, and left to find a phone.

"Do you have a family yet?" Mike asked. "I mean, are you single or married?"

Belinda stirred her beer with her finger, as if to give the answer some thought, before she looked at Mike. *Was this a come-on or did he really care? Did she really care?*

"Yes. Yes, I do," she said softly. "I have a little girl that is just a baby, but no husband. It's hard to manage, but we do, and I will." She was blushing just a little as if her secret was out.

Mike was quiet for a second, remembering another woman with a little girl, a long time ago. That little girl was now a teenager and his daughter, and that woman was now his wife.

"Got a picture of her?" Mike asked.

Belinda dug in her purse and pulled out a snapshot of a dark-haired little girl. It was almost a newborn picture.

"You must be so proud of her," Mike said. "What's her name?" He said it like he honestly cared.

Belinda smiled. "I am proud," she said, slowly shaking her head. "Yes, I am. Her name is Samantha."

They finished their drinks and Jerry came back and said his goodbyes, as he had to leave. Mike looked at his watch and said, "You know what—I better getting going, also. My flight leaves O'Hare in about two hours."

Before he left, Belinda asked Mike for his business card, and asked him if it would be alright if she called him for information from time to time.

"Call anytime," Mike answered. "Information or just to talk. We're all in this together. Take care of that beautiful baby."

Belinda smiled and said, "Thank you, I will." She shook his hand softly but wanted so badly to give him a hug.

She sat there for a few minutes after he had left. The smell of his cologne was still in the air. *Where were all the single men like him?* She thought.

CHAPTER FOUR

DAVID NEEDED TO HAVE ANOTHER fire to quell the appetite he had rebirthed—not just for the thrill of it, but also to test the ignition source that he had installed in most of the buildings where he had worked on their sprinkler systems. It would be a small fire as he wanted to save the big ones for later. F-day he called it. This time it was an apartment building, situated almost on the Lake Michigan shoreline, a few miles south of Evanston. Twelve luxury units in a small, brick-faced dwelling, and the only apartment building in this upscale residential neighborhood. It sat between two large older homes with enough yard to be comfortably away from them. Right behind the building was a ten-unit garage and all the residents had been encouraged to keep their automobiles inside, as the lot was only big enough for about eight vehicles.

In front of the building was a wide, deep front yard that was filled with old, twisted, half-dead oak trees and one large weeping willow that seemed to be shedding branches all over the place. A banner in the front yard, stretched between the willow and another tree, advertised a vacancy, but it was hard to read as one of the ties had come loose and it had folded over on itself. The vacancy happened to be in the same unit, on the ground floor, that David had installed his igniter in.

The sprinkler heads in this particular building were recessed— hidden behind chrome plates about three inches in diameter. They had only been installed in the kitchen areas to save money. David had installed his igniter about three weeks ago when he had serviced the system.

The sprinkler heads worked whenever enough heat was present to melt a fusible link in the head, which held a spring in place which, in turn, held a valve closed that held the water back. The heads in this building operated at one hundred and twenty nine degrees. David had made his ignition source to respond to a signal from his transmitter. When he sent the signal to the device, it would cause an electrical circuit to close the contacts being part of that circuit. This circuit, which had a battery, would then heat an electric heating element to provide an ignition source. At the same time, the heat from the fire melted the fusible link, releasing the volatile fluid stored in the sprinkler pipes. The whole ignition thing was self-contained and powered by a small, six-volt dry cell battery, tucked up in the ceiling where no one would see it. The battery had been modified to hold enough of the fluid in a special double jacket glass vial to incinerate itself. He had burned several of them in tests, and you had to be lucky to find any part of them after the fires. David was still careful and wiped each and every part clean of any latent prints.

There had been a point, years ago, when David had felt it was inevitable that someday he would be caught. It wasn't that he wished for it, but he had been so out of control back then that he made a lot of mistakes. So much of the time he had been in a sexual frenzy and like a peeping Tom, he took a lot of risks to get as close to the action as possible. He was a brilliant person even if he was a social psychopath.

But that had all changed and he realized it. Oh, he was still a psychopath but right now, as far as he was concerned, he was on top of his game. The sexual insanity that was the reason for it all was still there, but it was much better managed. This time, all of the elements that he was going to use in this macabre game were being tested—and retested—to make sure they worked as planned.

He had very little feeling for his victims. It was something he just wasn't going to be bothered with. They were the pawns in his little game, and if they got in the way, they were expendable, and if they escaped? Well, they would live to fight another day, wouldn't they? Either way, they were no threat to him.

He hadn't worked at all today, which was Friday, but spent the day brooding over his plans to burn the apartment building Saturday night. Even with his newfound confidence he still worried that he was missing something.

There was a public beach directly across the road from the doomed building and although it was closed for the winter season, the building that housed the changing rooms and the lifeguard tower were still there, unoccupied. His plan was to use that lofty perch to watch this whole thing unfold. There was a parking lot for the beachgoers right next to it that always had a few cars in it, mostly joggers who ran the paths around the lake.

He had an impulse to go down there today just to look things over once more, but a cautionary flag was raised reminding him that, the more he was seen around there, the greater the chances he would become a suspect. So he tinkered in his garage with some more igniters. In less than a year the shit was going to hit the fan in the great city of Chicago, and he smiled thinking of it.

Belinda had been back at the Atlas site several times but there was just nothing there to be found. She had released the building back to the insurance company and the owners, and was ready to shelve the file. Business was good and there were too many other places she was needed. Besides, Jerry Martin had been missing more work than he came to so she had little help.

The Chicago Fire District was divided up into six districts and there were investigators in each district. Some of them had as many as four people, but her district had only her and Jerry. Sometimes, when they were overwhelmed, they could get help from another district, but they were all very busy so that was an outside chance at best.

Today was Friday. Tomorrow she had the day off and she was looking forward to it. She wasn't going anywhere because she had moved into a new apartment and was looking forward to unpacking the rest of her stuff and doing a little decorating. At four-thirty, she headed for home, everything else could wait.

Saturday was a great day in the Chicago area. A high-pressure area dominated the weather pattern, and a warm spell gave everyone a reprieve from the icy blasts that were to come. Joggers and moms with baby carriages crowded the paths around the big lake, trying to squeeze out just one more day of outside. The high temperature was in the sixties and the sun blazed down unfiltered through a blue, cloudless sky.

But as nighttime fell, the temperature dropped rapidly. Tonight was Halloween and a few kids were seen running from house to house, their breaths making little steam clouds and their cheeks turning rosy red. The old days of elaborate costumes seemed to be waning and some kids had done nothing more than to paint their faces, almost as if they were going to a Bears game. A few dads and mothers walked along with the little ones, sending them up to the doors under watchful eyes and then showing them where to go next.

By nine-thirty, the hoards of children had thinned out to just a few stragglers; some of them had dumped their bags at home and were coming around for seconds. Many houses simply closed up shop and shut the lights off.

No one noticed the black Ford sedan pull into the swimming beach parking lot across the street and stop. No one noticed David Bennett walk, stiff-legged, to the bathhouse and climb the stairs to the roof. He settled down in the lifeguard's perch and gazed out over the placid lake. Far out to sea, the red and green lights of a freighter blinked softly as it made its way across the big lake, back to the passage that would take it out of the St. Lawrence Seaway and, eventually, to the Atlantic Ocean.

A smaller cruiser came close to shore and the sounds of partying going on board, including the shrill laughter of a couple of women, echoed across the still waters. The inboard engine chugged softly in the chill night air, almost at an idle. Waves broke softly on the beach as they came to shore from the wake of the boat.

David slouched in the seat, trying to be as inconspicuous as possible. The back of the high wooden seat faced the road, and the apartment building behind him, so he was well-hidden. The chair was built in an Adirondack style so he could see between the slats when he turned around, but for now, he seemed to be more interested in the lake and the evening.

At about 11 p.m. he looked at his watch and then behind him. There were three lights on in the building that he could see from here. He was feeling benevolent tonight and he was trusting that most of them would make it out. The unit where the fire was going to start was dark and, he hoped, still unoccupied.

With no furniture there was not much fire load but that was all right. That was part of his plan. He would supply the entire fire load that was necessary. His hands had gotten cold and he had them in his jacket pockets, one of them wrapped around the switch that would start the whole thing going whenever he felt the time was right.

His legs were getting stiffer by the minute from the cold, and a shiver ran up his back and settled at the base of his skull.

It was a grim reminder of his persistent pain and where it had come from. For now though, it was time to do something to make him feel good. David turned and, facing the building behind him once more, pushed the button.

It took a few seconds for the element to heat up and when it happened, it wasn't a loud explosion, more like a whoosh followed by the sound of breaking glass. The fire seemed to engulf the unit it started in within seconds. It came out the blown-out windows and its angry, searching tentacle fingers reached up the outside of the building, finding the wooden decks, window trim, anything wood or plastic it could incinerate and devour. From there, the heat took out more windows, and it slithered like an angry snake up the side of the building and into the units above.

The only sounds now were burning wood crackling and somebody screaming. A bedroom window opened in the unit above the burning one, and an Asian woman dropped two small kids, in their pajamas, twelve feet to the lawn below. Neither of them appeared to be hurt but they were screaming for her to jump—holding their arms out for her. She hesitated for a few minutes and then the smoke and heat finally forced her out, dressed only in her underclothes. For a second, she reminded David of a circus acrobat. She hit the ground and rolled over several times, tried to get up, and then laid still. The kids rushed to her side, and although she raised her arms, she could not get up; so they hovered over her, crying and talking in some language no one could understand.

There were now several people coming out the back of the building and the fire alarm was blaring inside. A police car that just happened to be going by had stopped, and the two officers rushed over to help. While one of them pulled the Asian woman and her kids to safety, the other tried to get in the back of the building, but was driven back by the heat and smoke.

A neighbor, from the house next door, came running with a ladder but laid it down when no one appeared at any of the windows—and the heat was becoming unbearable.

At Station Thirteen, Engine Thirty-eight was, just now, clearing the concrete apron, heading for the fire two miles away. The call had come in forty-five seconds ago. It had been a busy night with kids lighting mischief fires in dumpsters, garbage cans and abandoned cars, while out celebrating Halloween.

Darrel Strickler and Arnie Hogan were working with a rookie, Doris Collins, and they were the fire fighters on duty. Bob Evers was the Captain again, sitting up front with Clint Travis. Clint's icy blue eyes scanned the road ahead for trouble as he guided the big rig through the crowded streets. Not only was it Halloween, but it was also Saturday night and the lake drive was always crowded on Saturday night. He worked half of a chewed-up toothpick from one side of his mouth to the other as he drove. He seemed to not be listening to anyone, but in reality, he heard everything that was going on.

"Squad on the scene says she is going pretty fast," Evers said to the fire fighters behind him on the rear seat.

"Good," said Strickler. "I'm tired of all of this chicken shit stuff we've been getting."

Doris nodded her head and smiled. She needed a few more fires to wash away the rookie stigma. She wanted to say something, but felt she might sound stupid, so she just kept still.

Arnie was busy trying to get his helmet adjusted and paying no attention to either of them. "Hunk of shit equipment," he muttered under his breath as he tried to feed the strap through a buckle.

Cory Watkins had been a cop in Chicago for nine years now. Most of the time, when they were at a fire, they took care of crowd and traffic control. But sometimes, if they got there before the Fire Department, they would do what they could to get people out of the building. They had found this fire before they heard about it. In fact, they were the ones who had called it in.

Cory had seen his share of fires but this one seemed to be blowing up in a hurry. Every time the fire got to a new area it was almost like it was being reenergized by some other source. It would flare up in intensity and then gradually die down to what would be normal for the fire load in the area.

He had given up on trying to get inside. They would just have to hope everyone got out that was inside.

"How's she doing, Bert?" he said to his partner, who was sitting on the grass trying to comfort the woman who had jumped.

"I think she jammed her backbone," he said. "She couldn't move when I first got here, but she seems to be coming out of it. Maybe you want to go get a blanket for her from the car."

The two children sat beside them, not saying anything, just concerned about their mom.

"Not much else we can do," Cory said. "I think I hear the Fire Department coming now."

David had remained expressionless for a few minutes but, slowly, a slight grin broke out. At first, the woman who had jumped caught his attention with her screams but then, looking upstairs and to the right, he saw a sliding patio door open partway. It looked like someone was trying to open it wider, but it seemed to be stuck. It closed for a second and then opened again, but not as wide as it had been.

Ugly, gray-yellow smoke was billowing from the apartment through the partially open door and then, suddenly, there was a touch of red and yellow at the top of the opening. At the same time, a tongue of large flame appeared, then rolled out of the door and up and over the building's fascia, setting it on fire, too, as it curled inward over the roof. It was then that he saw an arm reaching out, as if it was reaching for anything to latch on to. It was pleading for something to grasp and to help pull the rest of the body out. It groped in the smoky air for a moment, fingers outspread, and then fell back into the smoke and fire where he could no longer see it.

David heard the air horns from the incoming fire equipment. It was his signal to leave. He walked stiffly down the steps to the parking lot. His left hand was in his pocket, holding his growing arousal against his body as he walked slowly to his car. No one was watching him but he was taking no chances. Everything had gone perfectly up until now, but the nosey ones would be here soon.

He turned to the left out of the parking lot and passed the burning building one last time. Right now, there was little anyone could do to stop him.

The minute Engine Thirty-eight got on the scene, it was apparent they had their hands full, and Evers called for another alarm. There didn't appear to be any life safety issues. The Asian woman on the lawn was being taken care of, and a few people had dirty faces, but no one seemed to be in any danger.

Without any exposures, the biggest question was where to start with putting out the fire. One thing was obvious—the water they had on the truck was not going to suffice, so they called for Engine Twelve, the next engine in, to lay a supply line in to them. They would also supply Ladder Six, which had arrived and was setting up its aerial apparatus to take care of the roof and upper floor fire activity.

On the upper floor, three of the six apartment units were showing some kind of fire activity in them, including the one that had been home to a handicapped man. There was no way to know if he was in the unit or not but, if he was, it was assumed he was beyond any kind of rescue attempt.

Captain Evers and the three fire fighters from Engine Thirty-eight had attacked the fire in Unit Three, which was the origin of all of the fire. They had made entrance through the patio doors and were inside right now with two, one and a half-inch lines. Battalion Chief, Norm Marks, had arrived and assumed command of the scene.

With the fire in the unit knocked down, the fire fighters from Engine Thirty-eight were amazed to find no furniture in the unit. They pulled one line out and Strickler and Evers attacked the fire that had extended to the unit next door. They were not able to make entrance but had to fight the fire from outside, through the windows, until help came from Engine Twelve and then, with three lines going, they made fast headway.

Entrance to the upper floors was now being made by Engine Forty-six, which had also arrived at the scene and was being assisted by Ladder Six.

David had arrived home and, right now, was sitting in a chair listening to a scanner tuned to the Chicago Fire Department primary channel. He would also try to catch the news on the hour on television.

Most of the time they saw and showed much more than he could see at the scene.

He was naked as he listened and played with himself. The sexual pleasure he received from this was beyond comparison. He had been with women, but they did nothing for him like this. He was still looking for that ultimate pleasure that seemed to still elude him. This fire tonight, and the one at Atlas, were just warm-ups for something big to come.

He reached over and turned the scanner off. Most of the action was over and the fire rigs were returning to quarters. He was tired and needed to rest.

He sat on the edge of the bed and, reaching out, stroked the cat's back. It was standing alongside of him, almost leaning into him, purring with contentment. David pushed it away, tiring of its attention, and he lay down on his back. He pulled the dirty sheet up to his chest and tried to sort out his thoughts.

Of the three hundred barrels of petrocyclomate he had purchased, he had used all but seventy-five. There was no hope of ever getting more. He would have to choose his targets wisely from here on in, but he could not afford to get lazy. There was always the chance that one of the buildings he had already prepared would have an accidental fire. Each day, the clock was ticking and the big day was still almost a year away. He would let it all hang out on October 8th, the anniversary of the Great Chicago Fire. How fitting that would be.

Out on the kitchen table right now was a map he had drawn, and redrawn, that showed all of the buildings that were ready to burn. He had tried to plan a map that would allow him to cruise around the route, setting buildings off as he passed them. At the same time, he needed to enjoy the carnage and the confusion he would cause.

CHAPTER FIVE

SHE HEARD THE RINGING AS if it was far away behind some kind of foggy partition. Maybe if she ignored it, it would go away. Unconsciously, she had pulled the pillow over her head to muffle the noise, but then she thought of her baby sleeping beside her and sat up, grabbing the phone from its cradle and knocking a glass of water to the floor.

Belinda hadn't had time since moving in to hang draperies, so a blanket with a Chicago Bears emblem on it had been hastily strung across the window to give her some privacy. She wore only a torn, white tee shirt and white cotton panties. The room had been hot and during the night she had kicked most of the covers off on the floor. Now, she was cold, and she pulled her knees up against her chest as she sat in the middle of the bed.

The baby in the bassinette stirred in her sleep but didn't wake, and she croaked, "Hello," into the phone with a voice filled with phlegm. Clearing her throat, she tried once more—this time more clearly.

"This is Dispatch," the female voice on the other end of the line said. "I am sorry to call you, but Jerry Martin is not answering his radio and they need an inspector at an apartment fire as soon as possible. I was told to call you."

She didn't answer right away but turned on the bedside lamp and looked at her watch. It said 1:15 on the digital dial.

"Inspector, did you hear me?"

"Yes, yes," Belinda said, running her hands through her hair and looking for her robe. "It will be a while; I need to find someone to watch my child. I will call in for the address as soon as I'm ready."

When she worked during the week, Belinda took Samantha to a daycare that she trusted, but they weren't open this time of the night. She had one place to try and fall back on—her mother. Tentatively she dialed the phone, trying to think about what she would say to her.

"Mom, look, I know how late it is but work called. I have to go in and, if you could just take her this time, I will try to line up someone else the next time this happens."

Belinda and her mother had not been on good terms since she had become pregnant with Samantha. But, whether she liked it or not, once Samantha was born and her mother realized that she had a grandchild, she had settled down.

"Bring her over. I'll put the porch light on," she muttered and hung up the phone.

Belinda's dad had left the scene for greener pastures long ago, so that was part of her mom's attitude problem.

She changed the baby's diaper, threw a bottle of formula and some food in a bag, wrapped Samantha up and was out the door into the crisp October air. There was heavy dew on the car windshield and she let it warm a minute before taking off, but not before she called the Dispatch number and checked in service to the call. Her mother's place was right on the way.

The streets were deserted, or as deserted as Chicago gets on the North Side this time of the night. Mom was waiting for her at the door and Belinda said, "Thanks, Mom. You don't know how much this means to me."

Her mom took the sleeping baby and said, as she closed the door, "Hurry back and be safe."

Engine Thirty-eight and the Battalion Chief were the only two units left on the scene when she pulled in and shut off her car. For a few seconds she sat and just took in the scene, trying to ascertain what she should do first and to rub the rest of the sleep out of her eyes. A portable generator on the back of one of the trucks rattled away, powering a few hand lights that had been strategically set up around the perimeter of the building.

Captain Evers was the one who spoke first when she left the car and approached the scene. "Where's Martin?" he asked. "That's who we called and instead we get you." He had no time for females in the department and he made no bones about it.

Belinda looked at him disgustedly. *What did she have to do to get any recognition in this department? No, she hadn't been a firefighter and she hadn't paid those holy dues they kept bringing up. Six years in college and a degree in Chemical Engineering meant nothing to them. There would come a day when her knowledge was going to make them all look silly, and she could hardly wait.*

"I have no idea where Jerry is." she said. "They did try to locate him, and being here tonight was not my idea, but it is my job, so let's work together on this and I'll get you and your boys free as soon as I can." She had almost spit out the words, "your boys" at him and he caught her tone of annoyance.

"What was burning when you got here and when was that?"

Evers was looking at the ground and hanging on to his blackened helmet by the chinstrap. He was still pissed but sensed he'd better back off on this. Before he could answer, Belinda took him by the arm and they walked away from the engine, which was still pumping and making considerable noise, to try and talk it over.

"I don't know the exact time but I'll check with Dispatch and get it for you." He brought his gaze up to meet hers and sensed that she was pleading with him to cooperate.

"There was fire in those two apartments when we arrived." He pointed to the black holes over his shoulder where the patio doors used to exist in the two units. One unit was on the ground floor and the second was above it.

"I think the bottom one was the point of origin."

"Let's go inside," Belinda said.

Water was still dripping and hanging from the ceilings where it had formed into little liquid stalactites. On the way to the unit she wanted to inspect first, she could see the walls in the hallway were black with soot, but the fire damage was only minimal. The doors must have prevented interior spread, and the fire going up the outside walls had caused most of the spreading. Plastic alarm boxes that had been mounted on the walls were pulled out in the activated position, but they hadn't melted. The carpets, soggy and saturated with water, didn't look burnt, either. There just hadn't been a lot of heat in here.

The door to the unit was charred on the inside, nearly to the point of breaching the wood but somehow, it had held. The greatest damage was in the kitchen area, but this made sense because the wooden cupboards were all there was to burn in the empty unit; initially, anyway, because as soon as the heat built up high enough, almost everything became fuel.

The sprinkler head in the ceiling was open and still leaking water. The fire department had shut it down but, being on the lower floor, it was draining out the whole system. Belinda shined her flashlight beam at it but everything appeared as if it had worked as planned.

"We didn't spend a lot of time in this unit," Evers said. "It was empty enough that there wasn't that much burning. The fire went out the kitchen windows, caught the wooden deck on fire, and then went into the unit above here. That's where the woman and the kids jumped from."

"How are they doing?" Belinda asked.

"She screwed up her back but the kids were fine. They transported all of them over to St. Luke's if you want to talk to them."

She scribbled some notes, not saying anything to Evers about wanting to talk to them or not, and then said, "Let's go upstairs."

The unit upstairs had extensive damage and there were a few wisps of smoke still coming from the insulation in the roof joist area. All of the ceilings had been pulled down and much of the contents had been thrown out the windows. The worst damage seemed to be in the kitchen area again, but that would make sense because the fire had come in the patio doors directly across the room. Once again, the sprinkler head had been activated.

"Were the sprinklers going when you came into these units?" she asked Evers.

"Yep. All three units that were burning had them going. Didn't seem to do a hell of a lot of good, did they?"

Belinda didn't answer him, but he had a point, and it was puzzling her. Normally, sprinklers in apartment buildings controlled a fire before it ever got big enough to spread.

"Where was the other unit that burned?" she asked.

"Across the hall. Poor bastard in his wheelchair didn't have a chance."

"There was a fatality?"

"Sorry, I thought you knew." Evers shifted his feet nervously. "The coroner left with him just before you got here."

"You do know the policy says when we are called on any fatal fire, the body is not to be moved until we get here."

"Hey, talk to the Battalion Chief. It was his call, not mine. I have to get back to my men, so if you need anything else just call." With that he left, going down the short hall and outside.

Clearly agitated, she scribbled down some more notes.

Crossing the hall again, she noted the lack of fire damage in the hallway. *The fire had not come this way, that was for sure. Had there been more than one fire?*

But, entering the other unit and playing the beam from her flashlight on the kitchen ceiling, she could see how the fire arrived; it had followed the sprinkler pipe. The hole in the walls between the units was twice as large as the pipe and had not been plugged.

Belinda leaned against the wall as she tried to absorb what she had seen so far. *There was no doubt someone had set this fire,* she thought, *but how, and why did it spread so crazily from unit to unit?* She was in over her head. Maybe Martin was home now. Belinda tried both his home phone and cell phone but there was still no answer. Maybe she should call the office and see if she could get help from another district. This could be more than a fire investigation. Hell, it could be a murder investigation, too, but the last time she had suggested calling for outside help, Jerry had been all over her for that.

She took char samples from the apartment where the fire had started, to be checked for flammable liquids, and three rolls of film. As for now, she was going to secure the building and get a fresh start when she found Martin. If they were going to ask for help from other districts, Martin could make the call. She was tired and stunk like smoke and needed to get home.

David awoke the following morning, as rested as he'd been in a long time. Not only rested, but self-confidant that he had the Chicago Fire Department right by the short hairs. In just short of a year they would write about the second time Chicago burned. He lay in bed smoking, and thinking about some things he could do to make things even more difficult when the time came.

They called it the Windy City, and that was no cliché. The winds came off the big lake on a regular basis and, if there was one thing that would be an asset to a conflagration, it would be a stiff wind. He had seen pictures on television of the allied incendiary bombings in Germany during the war. That's what he imagined Chicago would look like when the time came.

A sarcastic smile spread over his face and he reached down and rearranged his growing erection in his shorts. *My, how this made him happy; time to get the paper and read about it.* He slid out of bed and padded to the front door to retrieve the paper. He had an hour before his first appointment at a fiberglass factory. *Hell,* he thought, *fiberglass might not need a lot of help to be a good fire!*

Jerry Martin had been so drunk the night of the fire he had never made it home. He had slept in his car in front of his old house. He had had some aspirations about going in and talking some sense into his ex-wife but he passed out before he got that far. Now, with daylight shining on him through the car windshield, he had come to his senses and decided to go back home.

His hands were shaking so bad he could hardly light the last cigarette in the pack he had. He pulled into a diner and went in to get some coffee to go, grabbing a glance at the daily paper on the way out.

The headlines were bold with a statement from President Carter. He threw it aside and the metro section fell partway out, far enough for him to see the heading, **"One Dead in Chicago Apartment Fire on the North Side."**

He read a few paragraphs into the story and, at last, there was the address—4216 Lake Drive. *Shit, that was in his district and he was on call last night.* Jerry reached for his cell phone but it was dead. He pulled into a convenience store and parked next to an outside pay phone. He flipped open his black book for Belinda's number and punched the numbers in.

Belinda was just stepping out of the shower when she heard two things with her foggy, sleep-deprived brain—the phone ringing and Samantha crying. She wrapped a towel around her and picked up Samantha and the phone at the same time.

"Hello," she said, meekly.

"Hey, kid, did you read the paper this morning?" Jerry started.

She didn't answer his question, but said, "Jerry, where the hell were you last night?"

"Sorry, kid. I got a little blasted and slept in my car. Why? Did they call you out?"

"Yes, they called me out, and you know that I don't know shit about what I am doing over there so it would be nice if you could give a little help!"

"Do we still have the scene?" he asked. *He was not going to get in a pissing contest with her; he could feel her anger over the phone.*

"Yes, I did manage to do that."

"I'll go over there right now and look around, and then get with you later today, if that is alright."

"Fine," she said, and hung up the phone. She had been so engrossed in the conversation with Jerry she hadn't noticed that her towel had slipped away, and Samantha was helping herself to breast milk. The baby's tiny hands were cradling her swollen breasts as she worked hard for the warm fluid they held. She sat down on the edge of the bed and finished nursing her, running her fingers through the baby's soft silky hair. It felt so good to feed her, knowing that the body that had created her was still nourishing and sustaining her life.

It was hard to try and work, and be a mom. She thought back to her senior year in college and Hal. They had gone together for almost two years and they were so good together. He was big and strong, handsome, athletic and smart. He had come from a wealthy family that lived in a big house on the east side, close to Lake Michigan. She was poor and had come from an alcoholic mother who lived in a rat-infested apartment close to downtown. Her mom lived off her meager pension, and life existed only from one bottle of cheap gin to the next. She had been dry now for a few years and seemed straightened around.

Hal's parents seemed to like her at first but, as time went on, it became more and more obvious that they were hoping the relationship didn't last. They had wanted someone with a little more blue blood than hers for their son.

Hal seemed to defy them on that issue, however, and the future still seemed bright. That is, until that one fateful night when they made love all night on Hal's living room floor. They couldn't get enough of each other, and their frenzied lovemaking was more than the condom could take. Enough of Hal's seed managed to escape that thin sheaf of safety to find a tiny egg, which would split and become Samantha.

Hal was not ready to be a father and insisted that she get an abortion, but she would have no part of that, and now she had no part of him, either. He no longer called or seemed to care.

Belinda was lucky to get her job with the fire department, but it was her second choice. Her first was to be a chemist—anywhere that she did not have to put up with a bunch of egotistical males who saw her only as someone to bed down with. But those dreams would have to wait for another day; right now she needed a paycheck.

The baby slept in her lap, full and happy, her mouth still making little sucking motions. Belinda lay softly back on the bed, pulling Samantha with her and curled around her, lying in a fetal position. Then the weariness caught up with her, and she fell back to sleep.

Jerry Martin was sitting in the parking lot behind the apartment building, looking at the boarded-up windows ringed with black soot. His hands still shook from last night's drinking session, and threatened to spill the fresh cup of hot coffee he cradled in his hands. He had to quit trying to drown himself in this sea of self-pity. His marriage was over and he had to accept it and get on with his life. His kids needed him to be a respectable person and as good of a father as he could be under the circumstances. He had failed the department last night and he had failed Belinda.

He left the car and raised the yellow tape over his head, walking toward the back door, which was closed and locked with a department lock. Jerry recognized the master lock draped through a hastily-installed hasp. Fishing in his pocket, he found his keys and unlocked the padlock.

It was eerie and deathly quiet inside. His shoes squished in the carpet and he tried to stay away from the sooty walls. His flashlight beam bobbed around as he tried to follow the path of destruction back to where it had all started. That was Fire Investigation 101. Find the source and identify it and then determine what it was that started it. Fire rarely travels downward so this basement unit he was going to first had to be the culprit.

It helped so much to talk with survivors and witnesses at a fire.

Even the men and women from the fire department helped a lot but, right now, they were all gone and he was on his own. He coughed and cleared his throat, spitting out a gob of brown-tinged, tobacco-based phlegm. His hand had gone to his pocket for his cigarettes but they were all gone; now would be the best time for him to get back to the straight and narrow. He had had a good start on quitting, but he had been weak. But, just because he had stepped backwards a second didn't mean he couldn't go forward again.

Jerry stepped into the nearly empty, charred-out unit. He scratched his neck and ran his hands through his hair. *Did it all burn up? Did they throw everything out? The place was empty; fires need fuel to sustain them.*

He walked to a window that had not broken out and looked outside. He didn't remember anything lying outside the windows. He cleaned a spot on the window with his elbow, but the lawn was empty. Going back in the kitchen area, his light swept the room and then settled on the hole in the ceiling where the sprinkler head was located. *No way—no way should there be this much damage in an empty, sprinkled unit. Maybe the sprinkler system hadn't worked. It had to be dry. Yeah, that's what happened. The system was shut down and some disgruntled former renter with a key had gotten in and splashed a little gasoline around.*

He had seen this happen before.

Belinda's fitful dream was so real that her face went through a whole catalog of twisted emotions. *She was back at the fire and they were working shoulder-to-shoulder, combing the ashes for any clue. She was the student and he was the ever-so-deliberate teacher, pointing out every clue in the fire's behavior. He was so methodical that she felt like he was reading the whole thing from a script. That somehow, he knew just what had happened here, and now he was going to share it with her. So sure of himself, but yet so careful to document everything as they followed the path of the fire, leaving nothing unproven.*

The scene changed suddenly and although they were still in the middle of the burnt-out room, he paused from the non-existent agenda he seemed to have followed up to now and, putting his hands on her shoulders, turned her face to his. Her eyes were drawn like magnets to his eyes. She sensed that the fire investigation was over for the time being, and they were entering a new dimension in their relationship. His hands went to her back and strong arms pulled her to him. She seemed so powerless to stop any of this. But how did he get here and why did he come? He had told her to call if she ever needed any help. Why, after one brief conversation and one small offer of help, did she feel this strongly about this man?

It was the combination of the baby crying, and a seemingly relentless knocking at the door, that brought her back to the real world. Startled, Belinda sat up and grabbed for her robe—realizing suddenly that she was naked, her bath towel now lying under her on the bed. The clock said 12:30 p.m.—she had slept for four hours.

Hurriedly, she slipped on her robe and, picking up Samantha, headed for the back door. Through the window she could see it was Jerry Martin.

CHAPTER SIX

David Bennett had taken the map of the downtown Chicago area that he'd been keeping, and put stickpins wherever he had altered the sprinkler systems in buildings to become likely infernos. He had started assembling this battle plan a while back—like a good general draws up his plans—and he had been keeping it handy, under his bed. Right now, he was fastening it to his bedroom wall with a couple of pushpins, where he could dwell on it and look for flaws so he could make the necessary adjustments.

He had, initially, stayed on the South side of Chicago where he lived. His thinking was, when the firestorm hit, he needed to overwhelm a fire district. Yes, they would send reinforcements from other districts but that all took time, and time was good when it came to spreading fires.

With any luck at all he would be ready for action by the first of the year. He would have loved it if he could have pulled it off on October 8th - the anniversary of the Great Fire of 1871. But that date had come and gone and he'd not been anywhere near ready. Still, it wasn't too far in the future to wait until next year for it to happen, but the risk of one of these building having an accidental fire and triggering the sprinkler system was always there. He had run his tests and, so far, had gotten by with it, but it would be pushing his luck to think that, sooner or later, someone was not going to catch on.

Today he was going to be working on a building close to the downtown area. They manufactured plastic toys and it had seven zones in its sprinkler system. The zone he would be filling with petrocyclomate was the plastic storage warehouse. It would make for quite a fire. It would also use up all but thirty barrels of his remaining stock.

"Did you say that the fire department turned the sprinkler system off?" Jerry was sitting at the kitchen table holding Samantha while Belinda slipped some clothes on. The little girl was smiling at him and holding one little fist in her mouth. Her tiny feet kicked at Jerry's stomach while he held her in his lap. *When was the last time he had held one of his own kids when they were this small,* he thought. He couldn't remember holding them. He did remember when his own kids were this little, however, but that had been a while back and now they hated him just like their mother hated him. What a crazy, mixed-up world it was.

"Hang on a moment, I can't hear you," Belinda hollered as she brushed her teeth. "I'll be right with you." She had put on a department tee shirt and blue jeans. Her long black hair was in a ponytail, tied together with a red silk scarf. Her face showed the effect of too little sleep, with bags under her eyes she hadn't had time to smooth out.

"This ain't a bad place, kid," Jerry said, looking around. "Is it bigger than where you were?"

Belinda was changing the baby's diaper on the tabletop and she looked up, a little perplexed. She was not in the mood right now for a social call.

"It's not bigger, but it's nicer. Getting back to the sprinkler system you had asked about—yes, Captain Evers shut it down."

"Belinda, doesn't it seem odd to you that the fire could spread that much, no matter what started it, with the sprinkler system in operation?"

She picked up the crying baby and bounced her while patting her back to quiet her down. "I did think that, yes. I also saw how it spread from that bottom unit up the outside of the building, and through the hallway following the pipes. There were some clear code violations there during construction."

Jerry shrugged his shoulders. "Building was twenty-five years old," he explained. He had no idea what she was talking about, but didn't want to appear stupid.

"Look, Jerry. Let's go back there tomorrow and check things out together. We're supposed to be a team, and you're supposed to be the leader, but you haven't..." her voice trailed off.

He didn't make any excuses for his absence even though he knew what she was getting at. He was standing and nervously playing with the bill of his cap. "See you at the office in the morning," he said.

He closed the door quietly behind him. He was hoping she wouldn't turn him in for last night, but he didn't dare ask her not to.

Maybe he would stop and pick up a six-pack to take home and relax a little.

On Friday morning, Belinda and Jerry were both in the office early. The coroner's report had come back on the fire victim in the second floor unit. His name was Steve Isakson. He lived alone in the apartment—despite the fact that he was severely disabled from an auto accident and was confined to a wheelchair. As Belinda studied the report, she was thinking about how horrible it must have been to be trapped in a fire, unable to help yourself escape. She turned the sheet over and read the cause of death. All it said was, "severe burns." The smoke hadn't gotten him first, he'd burned alive. She shuddered. She would never get used to this kind of stuff.

For some reason, she hadn't heard much about the fatality in the fire from the fire officer on the scene. They weren't supposed to move the body until the fire investigators were on the scene and authorized it. There would be no pictures, either. What a mess this was turning out to be. If she and Jerry determined that this fire was set, and it sure looked that way, then this was also a murder investigation and they would have to turn it over to the police department.

Later that day, Jerry had gone over to the Central Record Keeping Agency and poured through some old reports. This fire had him perplexed, but it wasn't the first time he'd felt that way. That's what arson investigation was all about, solving a mystery.

This fire, and the one at Atlas, had some similarities. In both cases the sprinkler system, which was pretty much fail-proof, had not put the fire out. He was trying to see if there had been any other fires that had acted this way that he may, or may not have, known about. This room held the records for all of the fire investigations that had taken place in Chicago over the years, not just his district. Right now, he was in the cold case files and there were literally thousands of them. *It would take a legion of people to pour over all of this stuff,* he thought. Frustrated, Jerry returned the files he had opened to their boxes and left.

Maybe he would go back to the apartment building and take another look without Belinda. Sometimes he just worked better alone.

Today, David was loading up pipe from his warehouse on a flatbed trailer. He had to get it over to a site on the Northeast side, where he had been awarded a contract to outfit a newly-constructed office building with sprinklers. He looked around his warehouse for all of the fittings and couplings they would need. He subcontracted all of the physical work out except the actual charging of the system with oil and water. That was his business and his alone.

In the back, in a dark corner of the building, sat the remaining barrels of petrocyclomate—the wonderful discovery he had made almost ten years ago at the University of Minnesota. Slowly, he counted the barrels. This was the end of it, but if he was careful it would be enough to do what he intended to do. Meticulously, he examined the barrels for leaks, but found none. The barrels were glass-lined but all it would take is a small crack and the fluid would eat its way through the steel barrel in a few days. Only the emulsifier oil he added would keep it from eating through the pipes in the sprinkler systems; it didn't mix with water unless it was first mixed with the oil.

In the other corner sat all of the empty barrels he had used up. There were still some traces of the chemical in them, but he was working on a plan to get rid of all of them as soon as his work was done.

David looked at his watch. Enough of this, he'd better get these supplies to the building site.

Jerry walked out of the package store with a brown bag containing a twelve-pack of his favorite beer, and a fresh pack of cigarettes in his hand. He would have a can right now on the way over to the fire site, and then save the rest for tonight. Tomorrow was Saturday, and he had the kids for the weekend, so he was going to have to behave himself. He inhaled deeply from the cigarette and then chased it with a long draw on the can of beer he had slipped into a Coca Cola can wrap. Beer and smokes went together like salt and pepper. They just complimented each other so much and made him feel so good. He looked at his watch. He had a couple of hours of daylight left. Jerry called Belinda at work on his cell.

"Fire Investigation, this is Dorothy."

"Hey, kid, this is Jerry. Belinda around?"

"Yeah, hang on, Jerry. She's around here someplace."

"Hi, Jerry. Where the hell are you? You had an appointment at two this afternoon. Did you forget it?" Belinda pulled the blinds apart to look at the smog-filled Chicago skyline.

"Appointment with who?" Jerry asked, almost angrily.

"Some guy from Knowlton to go over some sprinkler plans."

"Shit! I got tied up in records and forgot all about him. I hope you handled it."

"Yes, but that's the last time. I do have work of my own, you know. Jerry, are you smoking again?"

"What makes you think that?" Jerry said, looking at the smoking cigarette in his hand, and then dropping it by his feet and grinding it out.

"I can tell by the way you breathe, but just so you don't have to lie to me, let's drop the subject. What do you want?"

"I'm going back over to the fire site from the other night, and then I'm going home. Have a nice weekend, kid."

"You, too." Belinda hung up the phone. *The guy could be the best fire inspector in the state if he could just reign in his bad habits*, she thought. Damn, she forgot to tell him about the spooky guy from Knowlton. He had seemed very nosy about the apartment fire. Most guys who put in sprinkler systems didn't want the details of the fire; they just wanted to know how their system worked at the scene. Oh well, Jerry was right, it was Friday and she needed a nice weekend—time to call it a day.

CHAPTER SEVEN

WHEN JERRY GOT BACK OVER to the burned-out apartment building he was feeling a lot more relaxed. He'd drunk three beers and it was just enough to help him relax, but not dull his senses that much. He unlocked the padlock and walked back inside where the fire appeared to have started. The windows had all been boarded up so it was very dark inside, but his flashlight played carefully over the ceilings and walls. The air was still strong with the smell of smoke and soot, and water that had frozen and thawed still dripped from the ceiling. Jerry tried to stay out of the droplets, but one caught him right in the eye as he looked up at the exposed sprinkler pipes. His eye clouded over and burned. He rationalized that it was the oil they added to the water in the pipes, to keep the pipes from rusting, that he was feeling.

Turning quickly away, he dug into the wood trim in the apartment with his pocketknife. No matter where he dug, the char seemed to be about the same depth. *So unusual for it to be like that,* he thought. *Fires start someplace and then they spread. They don't just appear everywhere unless some kind of flammable liquid was spread around first. Even then, there are always trailers or areas where the liquid pooled or ran.*

His light went back to the leaky sprinkler head. *Why didn't that appliance stop the fire in its tracks? It was extremely rare for fires to win in a sprinkled building. It just didn't happen unless the water was shut off or there was some kind of an explosion that compromised the system.*

Around the pipe, next to the leaky head, there was a metal band—much like a hose clamp. *Why was that there? It didn't look like it served any good purpose.* Maybe he would have to ask the people who put the sprinkler system in what that was.

For a brief moment, Jerry thought about removing the clamp and taking it with him, but he didn't have a stool or ladder, and he would also need a screwdriver. He had one in the car, but it was getting late. It was Friday night, and those other beers in the car were beckoning to him. On Monday, he would call the sprinkler people and have them meet him back here. There was probably some easy explanation.

His cell phone was ringing so he set his flashlight down and answered it.

"This is Jerry Martin."

"Jerry, this is Dispatch and they want you over to the old railroad depot on Chelsea Street. Somebody set several fires inside the depot."

He looked at his watch. *Damn* it, he thought. *Just when he was thinking about having a quiet evening at home, and if they already knew someone had started some fires, what the hell did they need him for? Call the cops.*

"Okay, I'll stop on my way home," he mumbled into the phone, and flipped it shut. Maybe if he had a smoke and a beer before he left he would feel better.

David had come from the meeting with the fire inspector with a bad taste in his mouth. *First of all,* he thought, *he hated women in those kinds of authority positions. Not that she hadn't been nice to him, but they were all so smug when they talked to you, and always made you feel like you were trying to do something you weren't supposed to be doing. Damn it, he was just trying to get a permit to put sprinkler pipes in a building. She had gotten all defensive when he asked about the fire the other night up by the lake—like it was private or something. Didn't he have a right to know what had happened? After all, it was his sprinkler system that was in that building.*

Now David had some decisions to make. He had enough petrocyclomate for two, maybe three more buildings. The building he was working on right now would be one of them, but then he had to pick up another job or two, and fast. So far, the only fires were the ones he had set, but the chance of an accidental fire was always there and that would ruin his plans. They all needed to burn on the same night.

Belinda got home from work that Friday night and decided she and the baby had been cooped up too long—she needed to get out. She showered and put on blue jeans and a fresh top. They went out for supper and then over to her sister, Diane's, for the evening. Her big sister was always good to talk to. With her mom being a hopeless drunk,

Belinda looked to Diane for mentoring and guidance. After all, she was a successful heart doctor and would do anything for her little sister except babysit. It wasn't that she hated little kids—she didn't. She loved Samantha when Belinda was there but, when she was eighteen years old, she had lost a baby she was babysitting for. It was a SIDS death and she never got over it. Even today, at thirty years old, she would not allow herself to get into a relationship with any man. She had a firm rule—no babies, not anyone else's and, surely, not one of her own.

The two sisters sat in the living room of Diane's posh, North Side apartment, drinking wine and giggling about old times, when Belinda's cell phone rang. It was Jerry Martin. What did he want? And no, she wasn't going to go with him to some smoky scene tonight.

For a moment she thought about not answering it but finally she flipped open the phone and said, "What, Jerry?"

"Hey, kid, you got time to talk?" the slurry voice on the other end of the line said.

For a few seconds she said nothing. She was tired of this. Every time he got drunk he would call her just to talk about something.

"Jerry, I'm on my own time right now and I don't want to talk to you for that reason, and also because you've been drinking again! You should be calling for some help with your addiction instead of calling me. I can't help you, as much as I would like to. God knows I have tried."

She waited for him to reply but he broke the connection and the phone went dead.

"Trouble?" Diane said.

Belinda looked shaken. "Yes, you could say that," she finally murmured. "That was my partner at work. He's a very bright man and I enjoy working with him, and for him when he is sober, but he has to get some help because he's dragging us both down."

Diane's face showed concern but she offered nothing back.

"We have a difficult problem right now that needs to be addressed. We have had two fires in the last few weeks that seem to have been set. Both of them resulted in people losing their lives. Usually, with fires like this, we are able to find out what was used in the fires, but for some reason there seems to be no trace of how they got started and why they spread so fast."

Again, Diane didn't know what to say. She knew her sister so well she could usually finish her sentences for her but, when it came to this mysterious business of investigating fires, it was all Pig Latin to her. "I'm sure this person will slip up somewhere," she finally said. "That's how we all get caught when we live a life of crime."

Belinda had to digest that a little before she commented back. Diane seemed to be incriminating everyone. Finally, she dismissed it as just a general answer that really didn't mean her or Diane.

For the rest of the evening, they ate a bucket of wings Belinda had brought, and drank a bottle of wine—even though she wasn't supposed to drink when she was nursing Samantha. When the subject came up, she said with a giggle. "Maybe it will help her sleep. God knows I could use a good night. Beats putting it in a baby bottle, we both get the benefit this way." They both had the giggles now.

Jerry was lying on the living room floor. He had knocked the phone that was beside him out of its cradle, but he was too blitzed to hear it. The floor was littered with empty beer cans with ashes on top of them where he had deposited his cigarette butts. The television was showing some monster movie, but it could have been the Bears game— he wouldn't have known the difference right now. When he'd finished the twelve-pack, he stumbled to his bedroom, brought back two-thirds of a bottle of Jack Daniels and laid back down in the mess. Right now, it was gripped in his right hand, resting on its side on the floor. What had been left in it was spilled on the threadbare rug, but most of it had found its way down his throat first.

Jerry was semi-conscious and, every so often, he would scream at Noreen for all of the bad things she'd done to him. She had ruined his perfect life by leaving him and taking his kids away. He didn't think about the reasons she left him, such as what he was doing right now. He was too pissed off to think about that.

"Noreen, you selfish bitch," he screamed once more. Then he vomited all over himself and, mercifully, passed out.

Saturday morning, Noreen bundle the boys up and headed for Jerry's. As much as she hated the way he acted, and had come to realize they couldn't live together, she still loved Jerry. He was the boys' father and they needed him in their lives. Ryan, who was six, seemed excited about going to his dad's for the weekend. They always got to go out to eat and watch whatever they wanted to on television. Their dad was just like a big buddy. Both boys had their extra clothes and pajamas in their backpacks. Todd, who was four, was whining about forgetting his new game he wanted to show his dad.

The traffic was light for a Saturday morning, and Noreen had made good time as she rounded the corner to the apartment building. She felt some guilt about Jerry having to live in such squalor, but he had brought it on himself, had he not? Maybe she would stay for a while and have a cup of coffee with him, just to show him her heart was in the right place. She had brought a box of doughnuts from home.

Noreen parked in the parking lot next to the city car Jerry was allowed to take home. Had she looked on the floor on the passenger's side, she would have seen all of the beer cans, but she was carrying Todd to keep his feet dry and had Ryan hanging onto her coattails. It had rained last night and then froze, and the parking lot was like a skating rink.

A young black man coming out of the building, held the door for her so she wouldn't have to buzz Jerry's apartment to get in. She entered the elevator with the boys in tow, and pushed the button for the seventh floor. *I hope he's up*, Noreen thought, looking at her watch. It was eight-thirty.

The hallway on the seventh floor was incredibly hot, despite the fact someone had opened the window on the far end—right next to Jerry's door, and she could hear traffic on the street below. The boys had run ahead and were pounding on his door. Somewhere, a television was playing loudly and she realized, as she approached, that it was in Jerry's apartment. Across the hall she could smell bacon cooking and hear people talking.

Noreen pulled the boys out of the way and told them to quit pounding on the door, somewhat puzzled that Jerry hadn't answered. She knocked once more, and then reaching down, tried the knob. It was unlocked.

When the door opened, Noreen knew immediately that something was wrong. She could smell the vomit and see Jerry's feet on the floor. He had fallen over on his left side—away from her view and facing the couch.

Noreen grabbed the boys and told them to stay in the hallway, but Ryan had already seen his dad's prone body and was crying loudly. Todd, sensing his brother's grief, was also starting to cry. The lady across the hallway, hearing the noise of the boys crying, opened her door against the chain. "What's the matter?" she asked. Noreen was trying to calm the boys down and keep them out in the hallway.

"I'm Jerry's wife, and these are his boys. Something's not right here." She indicated with a nod of her head, in the direction of Jerry's apartment. "Could you watch the boys for a second?"

The neighbor took the chain off and ushered the boys, who were now getting frightened, into her apartment. An elderly man was sitting at the table with a piece of toast in his hand, and looking bewildered by everything that was taking place.

Noreen stepped back into the apartment. "Jerry," she said, her voice cracking. "Jerry, are you all right?"

She walked around him, not wanting to wade through the garbage and vomit, and knelt by his head. He was breathing, but barely. Noreen stepped to the window and, reaching into her purse, brought out her cell phone and dialed 911.

"Emergency Dispatch," the operator said. "How can I help you?"

"My husband is unconscious." Noreen said. "Please send an ambulance. I'm not sure about the exact address... it's not my place."

"That's okay, honey, we have the address right in front of us." The woman had a southern accent. "Any idea why he's unconscious?" she asked.

"No, I'm not sure," Noreen said. *I could say he's drunk out of his mind,* she thought, but she didn't. She checked his breathing once more and it was ragged, but regular. Noreen started to cry as she knelt beside him, running her hand through his greasy hair. *Why Jerry? Why do you have all of these demons chasing you?* She thought of another day fifteen years ago when they had been in school together. He was the football player and she was the smiling, doting cheerleader. They had been so good together and then, after they got married, his drinking got worse and everything just mushroomed. He had gotten violent with her when he was drunk and she was afraid of him. Then, when he was sober, he was good old Jerry again. *Why, God, did it have to end this way?* she thought.

I better get back to the boys. She wiped her eyes on her sleeve and walked out, leaving the door partly open. Outside, she could hear the sirens approaching and the fire rigs pull up. She would have to find someone to watch the boys, and then she would go to the hospital to check on him. Somehow, she felt responsible. He had no one else.

CHAPTER EIGHT

DAVID PULLED THE CORD TO the electric pump that emptied his barrel, out of his portable generator and started winding things up. Another section of a sprinkler system had been filled with his precious, volatile fluid. Another whole building was simply a waiting bomb. He had installed an igniter on the second floor in a large office area that held lots of furniture and combustibles below it. He rolled the empty barrels out to his truck, the barrels clanging on the cold concrete deck of the loading area. At the lip of the dock, he stood them up and pushed them into the back of his truck.

A man on a forklift, while enjoying a smoke break, hunched over the steering wheel of his idling machine, wistfully watched him. "All done?" he asked David.

"I think so," David answered. "At least, I'm all done for now. You guys open for business already?"

"We open next week," he said. "I'm just trying to get the inventory in place. We moved from a smaller place in South Chicago. This place is awesome."

He didn't answer the man, but got in his truck and drove off. His diabolical plan was nearly done. Now all he had to worry about was an accidental fire in one of the buildings, and some nosy fire inspector finding the cause—although that was highly unlikely. He was going to call it a day and go home to rest. His legs had stiffened up again and he could only move his foot from the brake to the accelerator by lifting his leg with his hand. Each wave of pain brought back more hatred for Mike Flanagan, from the Minneapolis Fire Department. Maybe, after he torched Chicago, he would go back there and finish the job he had started. After all, it had been ten years. Flanagan thought he was dead and must have forgotten about him by now.

When Jerry woke up, he was in the hospital. He didn't know where, but he did know why. His mouth tasted like vomit and cigarettes and his head felt like it was going to explode. His hands were shaking as if he was in the throes of a bad shivering bout, although he wasn't cold. His stomach heaved and he wretched a yellowish, greenish mess onto the bedclothes. A nurse, who had heard him, came running with a pan, but it was too late. She looked with disgust at the mess in the bed and asked him if he could get up and sit in a chair.

Jerry nodded and slid out of the bed on his shaky legs. "Why am I here? Who put me in here?"

The nurse, who had balled up the bedclothes, said, "I'll send in my supervisor to talk to you." She reached over, and taking the phone, called a two-digit number. "Can I get Dr. Ron down here?" she asked. She took the soiled bedding and left the room.

Dr. Ron Sardinski came into the room with a chart. He sat on the edge of the bed with his arms folded, looking at Jerry. He flipped through a couple of pages and said, "You had a blood alcohol of .35 when they brought you in this morning. That's lethal in most people."

"Who sent me here?" Jerry croaked.

He went back to the first page of the chart. "Says here, Noreen Martin. Friend or relative?" he asked.

"My ex-wife," Jerry said, running his hands through his greasy hair. Then, reaching for the wastebasket, once more had a bout of the dry heaves.

"You need to go into treatment, my friend, or next time you might not be so lucky to have someone find you." The doctor was looking at him sternly but, before Jerry could answer, Noreen walked in. She sat in a chair beside him and reached for his hand.

"I'm going to let you two talk," the doctor said, and he got up and left.

"Why did you do this?" Jerry asked Noreen.

Noreen looked at him quizzically, as if she couldn't believe what Jerry had done.

"Look, Jerry, when I found you, you were close to death. You were lying in a puddle of puke, barely breathing." The tears were falling now and she wiped her eyes with the back of her hands. "I hate the way you act," she said loudly. "If it weren't for our sons I would leave you alone with your booze and your selfish thoughts, but they need a father, Jerry. If you give a tinker's damn about these boys, you will go into treatment and get cured or, so help me God, Jerry, I am going to move far far away and you will never see your sons or me again."

Jerry looked at her out of his bloodshot eyes. Maybe it was time to bite the bullet. Noreen would do what she threatened to do and then what would he have left?

He took her hands in his. "Help me, babe," he said.

It was all set. Jerry would go into treatment for sixty days at Hillcrest Rehabilitation Center in East Chicago. Tomorrow, he would meet with his boss and Belinda here at the hospital. He would be taken over to Hillcrest that afternoon. He would be confined to the hospital for those sixty days, but he would be able to go outside in a small courtyard and sneak a smoke. He had none of his own, but he thought that those who went out there with the same idea would be willing to share with him.

Would he be demoted? Maybe lose his job? The thought went through his mind all day. Noreen had arranged for the treatment, but she would not see him off or come to see him for a while. If—and that was a big if—he showed progress and a sincere effort to quit, then she would bring the boys to see him.

Belinda was at work in the office when Norm Shuster, the head of the inspectors, stopped by to see her. He was a big man of about fifty, with wavy sandy hair, dark blue eyes and a habit of getting too close to people—close enough that his rank breath often made you uncomfortable. Today, he sat across the desk from her and fidgeted with his cap while he talked. His hands were scarred from some long-forgotten fire injury many years ago. They looked red and had skin peeling from his thumbs and fingers. When he was nervous he would pick at the dead skin, as he was doing right now.

"You know about Jerry?" he asked her.

"I heard bits and pieces," she answered. Noreen had called her yesterday.

"Well, the long and short of it is he has been committed to treatment for alcoholism. He will be gone at least sixty days. When he returns he will be working under you, and will not be your supervisor. Does this make you uneasy?"

"I don't know," she said. "Jerry has so much knowledge, and that sixth sense that allows him to find clues that most of us miss." She was drumming a pencil up and down on the desktop as she talked, but she noticed that Norm was watching her and stopped.

"I think you guys will work it out even if you do switch places," he said. "This doesn't make Jerry any less of an inspector; he just needs to earn his stripes back. In the meantime, if you need help with anything don't be afraid to ask. I'm not going to assign anyone else over to this office because I have no one." Norm stood up and offered his hand across the desk. "I've got to run," he said. "Stay in touch and be at St. Luke's tomorrow morning at nine. We'll meet with Jerry before he goes away. He needs to hear the changes from me but I want you there." He smiled, put his hat back on, and was gone.

She looked down at the reports she was working on. They were lab tests from the fatal fire in the apartment building by the lake. Nothing conclusive had been found for an accelerant, but they would send them into the State Crime Bureau for further tests. She remembered a conversation she had had with that fire inspector from Minneapolis at the convention. In it, she remembered him talking about a psychotic arsonist that had used something that never showed up in tests. She also remembered him saying the man had burned to death with one of his own devices. Opening her center desk drawer, she took out a small booklet that she kept notes and business cards in. It was the second card from the top of the pile. **Mike Flanagan, Minneapolis Fire Investigation**. She stuck the card back on top of the pile and closed the booklet.

Belinda had laid awake half of the night worrying about how Jerry was going to take his demotion, but now, as she walked up the steps to the hospital doors, she felt more at ease. Maybe all of the fretting about it had put her mind at ease a little. She stopped at the main desk and asked for Jerry's room. *I might as well take my time,* she thought. *It's only a quarter to nine.*

She had been at St. Luke's before so she knew the building well. Jerry's room was just down the hall a ways. *Oh, the heck with it, let's go talk,* she thought.

Jerry was lying on the bed, dressed and dozing, with his hand clasped over his chest. For a few seconds he seemed to not notice his company but then awoke, looking startled.

"Hi, kid," he said, smiling. "I screwed up bad." He looked like he was close to tears.

She sat down on the edge of the bed but he sat up and swung his legs over the side so they were sitting side by side. "What brings you down here?" he asked.

"Norm Shuster wanted me to be here. I guess I'm going to be in charge while you're gone."

"You heard about where I'm going?" he smiled weakly.

"I think it's for the best, Jerry. We all want you well and we all want you back."

"Is Shuster coming down here?" he asked.

Belinda looked at her watch. "He should be here any minute," she said.

"Look, kid, before he gets here I want to share something with you. Yesterday—no, I guess it was the day before yesterday, I went back over to that apartment building. I want you to go back there and take a screwdriver with you. In the kitchen, where the fire started, there is a pipe or hose clamp on the sprinkler pipe. I see no reason for it and Knowlton needs to explain what that clamp was holding there."

"You think it had something to do with the fire?" she asked.

"I'm not sure, but right now we have nothing so we need to look at everything."

Just then, Norm Shuster walked in. He wore a tan trench coat and kept his big hands in the coat pockets as he stood beside the bed. "Belinda tell you what's happening?" he asked Jerry.

"No, I didn't say anything," she replied.

Jerry looked confused, but listened carefully, as his boss told him the same thing he had told Belinda yesterday at the office.

"Jerry, I know it seems harsh," Norm said, "but it's the way it has to be for you to keep your job."

Jerry nodded his head and bit his lip. He wouldn't look up at Norm.

Just then, two orderlies showed up in the doorway. "Time to go, Jerry," one of them said.

Belinda took his hand. "I'll be in touch, Jerry," she said. "I can't wait until you're back."

Jerry got up and walked out of the room with the two men. He stopped in the doorway long enough to look back and wink at Belinda, even though his face was filled with sadness. Then he was gone.

It seemed awkward with Jerry gone, and the two of them just standing there. She really could think of nothing to say to the big boss so, she just smiled and said, "I'd better get to work."

CHAPTER NINE

BELINDA DIDN'T GO BACK OUT to the burned apartment building that day after she left the hospital. However, the following morning she went there right from home. The owner was anxious to get the building back, and get repairs made, so he could be back in business. In fact, the building was being turned back over to him the next day. Already, a couple of big dumpsters had been dropped off, and they sat right in the middle of the parking lot.

The day had turned bitterly cold, and the wind coming in from the north off the big lake only made it seem twice as bad. She shivered and pulled her coat tightly around her as she negotiated the slippery steps. She had her flashlight and a screwdriver—just like Jerry had asked her to bring with her.

The inside of the first floor unit was as dark as a tomb. Workman had screwed plywood over the broken-out windows. Her light played across the ceiling, looking for the sprinkler pipe. The building creaked and, for a moment, she turned around and shined the light back out the door she had come in. Satisfied that she was alone, she found the pipe again and then the clamp Jerry had told her about. It was odd. The clamp was one of those adjustable clamps that were often used on hoses, but it had no practical purpose here.

It was too high for her to reach to take it off so she had to go scrounging for something to stand on. This unit was empty of everything. In the kitchen, across the hall, she found a wooden chair and dragged it back over to the spot.

The screw on the clamp was very tight, and she had to use both hands. She fell off the chair once but, getting back up, she finally broke it loose. Before she took it off, she examined it once more. There appeared to be a piece of some kind of copper wire sticking out from under the clamp. Carefully, she loosened it more until she was able to grab the wire with her fingernails and slide it out from under the clamp. It was only about half an inch long, but it must have been connected to something. She finished loosening the clamp until it broke apart, and then she slipped it into a baggie with the piece of wire. Directly over this spot was a hole in the flooring and she could see into the unit above. *How did the fire up here burn upwards with a sprinkler head a foot away, throwing water at it?*

Belinda got down off the chair and knelt in the spot directly under the area where the clamp had been. She swept her hand over the charred boards but only came up with ashes. The floor was clean. There had been some kind of vinyl floor covering there but it had been ripped out and thrown outside, most likely in overhaul. Anything on top of it most certainly went with it. She sat down on the chair she had been standing on, looking at the clamp and the wire through the transparent baggie. Maybe it was nothing, and maybe there was an easy explanation for it. She would have to call Knowlton's. She put the chair back where she had gotten it, knowing full well it was going in the dumpster, anyway. She stepped outside and locked the padlock on the door. She had better get into the office.

Noreen was at work at the hospital where she worked in the pediatric ward, as a newborn nurse. The babies brought so much joy into her life. Sometimes, she wondered what was ahead for them when a single mom would come to pick them up. Life was hard enough for two parents but, in the rough distinct she lived in, two parents seemed to be the exception and not the rule.

She was tired today, and she sat feeding a baby girl who was sucking noisily on a bottle. Normally, she would hold the infant when she fed it, but this one was a preemie. She had so many tubes hooked to her that Noreen didn't want to disturb all of that. Instead, she just rested her hand on the baby's tummy as the baby looked up at her with her big blue eyes. She was working so hard to get nourishment. Sleep had not come easy last night. She had tossed and turned thinking about Jerry. She still loved the fool; there was no argument about that, but at what price? That argument had played out over and over in her head. The boys needed a father, and yes, she needed a husband, but Jerry had failed at both. She could only hope that he would get cured and come home a better man.

"Noreen," One of the other nurses was standing just inside the nursery door holding a phone out for her.

"Who is it?" she asked.

The nurse shrugged her shoulders. Noreen took the bottle, which was now empty, from the sleeping infant. "Can you burp her?" she asked.

"This is Noreen," she answered the phone.

"Noreen, Belinda—Jerry's partner. Can I ask you a question?"

"Yes, what is it?"

"Well, I had a question about something that Jerry was working on and I called over to the treatment center, but they said only family could talk with him. I was wondering if you were going to visit him?"

"Maybe this weekend," she said. "What do you want to ask him?"

Belinda looked at her calendar. It was Tuesday and this weekend was too far away. "You know what—I might be able to get some help from headquarters. Do you know when he will be able to have visitors?"

"I don't," she said. "But I'll find out for you. Let's have coffee someday next week. I'm working nights so all of my days are free with the boys in school."

"Sounds good," Belinda said. "I'll call you."

She cradled the phone and looked at the piece of wire again. She couldn't ask any of those other jocks in Inspection for help. Jerry had been her only help in this job. She had no credibility with any of the rest of them. Maybe she should just call Knowlton's and ask. Maybe, even if she wasn't one of the boys, it was time she grew a set of her own!

David wasn't home but he got the message when he returned. "This is Belinda Clayton, with the Chicago Fire Inspection Department. Please call me as soon as possible. I have some questions I need answers to and you seem to be the right man to answer them."

David thought for a moment. *Had she found something or were these just some run-of-the-mill questions about sprinkler systems?* He had to be careful here, but he had to call her or he would appear to be more suspicious. It was probably nothing.

Belinda was just going out the door when the phone rang. It had been a long day and she wanted to get home to Samantha. But, at the last moment she said, "What the hell," and went back to her desk and picked up the receiver.

"Investigation and Inspection," she answered.

David cleared his throat. "I was asked to call Belinda because she had a question. This is Knowlton Sprinklers calling."

"Yes, yes," She answered. "This is she. Thank you for calling back. I wanted to ask about a fire we had in an apartment building a few days back. We went out to the scene to do some routine investigation. While we were looking at the sprinkler system we found this clamp on the pipe, close to where the fire started, and wondered if you could tell us what that clamp was used for?"

"What kind of clamp?" David asked.

"Like a radiator hose clamp. You know, the kind that comes apart and has a wheel inside that rolls on a little rack to tighten up the clamp."

"Oh, those clamps." David was buying time, trying to come up with some kind of an explanation. I guess if I saw it, and where it was, I could tell you, but I'm a little confused right now. It could be a lot of things."

"Could you meet me out there tomorrow?" she asked. "You know the building I am talking about?"

"Not sure that I do, but I can meet you. Shoot me the address."

She gave him the address and told him to meet her there at ten a.m. She looked at her watch. If the traffic wasn't too bad she would be home by six. It was time to think about her daughter and not some burned-out building.

For David, it wasn't a red flag, but it was troubling. Things had gone fairly well until now, but the day of infamy was still almost ten or eleven months away. This should have been the year but he wasn't ready and all he could hope for was that none of these buildings had an accidental fire before next October eighth. He wished that he could have done it this year but he was at the mercy of the market. He had to sell people on the concept of putting oil into their sprinkler systems and that had proved to be a daunting task. So many of them thought that the oil would plug up intricate flow gauges or valves and were reluctant to try it. His new installs were much easier; he had just done it, anyway.

There was also the matter of location. He needed buildings all over the city and not just in one location. When the day came to bring this to a city-wide inferno, he needed to have as much confusion as possible. If the fires were too close and they couldn't control them, they would just let an area burn and surround it to protect the rest of the city.

David laid back on his bed, deep in thought. *What was he going to say to her tomorrow?* He knew just what she was talking about when she spoke of the clamp on the pipe. *What would be a decent explanation? She had probably found a piece of copper wire under the clamp.* That had been the wire that went to the battery and, in the tests he had run, it had always been the only thing that would survive the fire and heat. It was under the clamp and the water in the pipe would not allow either the clamp or the wire to melt and burn in the intense heat.

He had thought about using string or tape to hold the igniter up there but in tests, it had burned away before the head was activated. The whole thing just fell onto the ceiling tiles or the floor.

Sampson had jumped up on the bed and was purring loudly while walking softly around his head. David grabbed the big cat and held him on his chest, stroking his back, while he was deep in thought. Suddenly, he sat up and threw the cat on the floor. The cat meowed loudly and scrambled under the bed.

Slipping on his shoes, he went out to his truck and opened up a side compartment. There in a bag were some red tags that had copper wire through the grommet in them. They said, in bold black letters, **Leaky Pipe.** These tags were tied next to a head that needed repairs, or a leaky pipe or coupling when they did the tests on a new system. Sometimes, a pinhole in a pipe could be temporarily repaired with a hose clamp and a rubber patch. He would lie and say the rubber patch had burned up in the fire along with the tag. Just the wire survived. The only way she could prove him wrong was if she charged the system and found out there was no leak, but that was unlikely.

Belinda was never so happy to get home to Samantha. Working without Jerry was not only hard, it was scary, and she was so afraid she would make a wrong move. Yet, she was too proud to call the boss and ask for help. She had to prove all of the hecklers wrong. Those overly proud idiots that only believed that you would never understand this business if you hadn't paid your dues on the lines and ladders.

But, for tonight, all those thoughts about fire and arson and sprinklers were the farthest thing from her mind. Tonight, she belonged to Samantha, and they were going to have a special night. No fire department, no mother, no Jerry Martin, just her and her child.

The alarm startled her, and Belinda sat up quickly, holding the blankets to her chest. What day was it? It was Friday, and it was payday, and she had better get to work.

Samantha was wide-awake, just looking at the beads that were strung across her crib. Her tiny, chubby hands reached for them, but then she saw her mother and smiled so wide it brought a giggle from Belinda's throat. She quickly took off the baby's nightclothes and wet diaper. Then she shed her own clothes and they got in the shower together. The warm water felt so good. She washed Samantha first and laid her, wrapped in a towel, on the rug outside the door and finished washing herself. Slipping on her robe, she dressed the baby and herself, then sat on the edge of the bed and nursed her. She was going to have to give up on the nursing and rely more on formula; she wasn't around enough and her milk was leaving her, anyway. She put Sam in her highchair and, warming up some cereal, fed her while she had her coffee.

The drive into work was the same hassle every day—a monotonous parade of honking horns and shouting people, all trying to get one car length ahead of the other. The sun was warm coming through the windshield. An old song by Percy Faith and his Orchestra called, "A Summer Place" calmed her down. Maybe someday she would find her prince charming and she would spend her summers carefree with all of her children. *She could dream, couldn't she?*

Just then, a gravel truck behind her laid on his air horn. She thought of an old joke called, "What is a split second? It's the time from when the light turns green till the guy behind you honks his horn." For some reason, it lacked humor this morning.

CHAPTER TEN

David wasn't as much nervous as he was mad, that he had to meet with this so-called puss fire inspector and explain why there was a clamp left on a pipe. *Why couldn't he just tell her over the phone what the damn clamp was doing? They always had to make a big thing out of everything. He ought to show her. He should meet her there and tie her to that sprinkler riser pipe in the hallway. He could rip off her clothes and, if she wanted to make a big thing out of this, he could show her a big thing. He would make her cry and beg for her life. She would wish she* had *never heard of David Bennett.*

The thought of doing this pleased him, and he smiled in a sadistic way. Then, he knew that would cause problems that would only bring more people and ruin what he had planned for, for so long. *No, he had to be diplomatic and convincing, and treat her with respect as much as he hated her guts. He hated her just like he hated Mike Flanagan, back in Minneapolis, from so many years ago. He wouldn't make the same mistakes he had made with Flanagan this time, though. Flanagan had survived, this bitch wasn't going to, but today would not be the day.*

When she arrived at the office, there was a note about a fire in a house up on Shorewood Drive that needed looking into. The note was from Carl Clemmons, the Captain on Engine Sixteen. He was one of the men who had treated her decently. It wasn't far from where she was going to meet Bennett, and she could catch it on the way back. At least something was going her way. She cleared up a few messages and then made a phone call to her mother. She needed to tell her that Samantha had a slight fever this morning, so she should check her temp a couple of times today to see if it was going down. She also told her she would be late getting home tonight so not to expect her before six.

"Donna, I'm going over Northeast for a few hours," she told the receptionist on the way out of the office. Donna smiled and waved goodbye because she was talking on the phone. *Talking to her boyfriend,* Belinda mused.

With her coat collar pulled up, anticipating the frigid air, she stepped out the door. It was not a nice day in Chicago. Mid-twenties and a ten-mile-an-hour wind, as always, that persistent wind, especially annoying in the winter. The old Inspection car growled a few times when she turned the key but it started with a clatter in the engine. She let it warm up for a while as she scraped some ice off the windshield with her ID card. Then, once back inside the car, she took the frontage road out to the freeway; it was about a half-hour drive. The car stunk like cigarette smoke and, as cold as it was, she cracked the rear windows open to let in some fresh air. For a moment, the smell angered her, but then her thoughts turned to pity for Jerry and his addictions. She wished he were back. Just then, a beer can rolled out from under the seat, and she burst into laughter. *If she found a used condom in here, she was getting out.*

Bennett's truck was in the drive when she got there. His window was half down and he was enjoying a cigarette. *My God, does everyone have to smoke?* she thought. There was another truck there also, and she could hear workmen inside the building. *Good! There was safety in numbers and this Bennett character gave her the creeps.*

"Hi, David," Belinda said as she met him in front of his truck. "It's the first unit on the left," she said "right inside the door."

David smiled but said nothing. *I know which one it is. I was there, baby.* He had a gray jacket on with **Knowlton Sprinklers** written across the back. It was dirty and tattered and one of the pockets was ripped and hanging open.

For David it was a chance to view the scene of the crime—something he was rarely able to do. He had a flashlight in his hand and the bag full of red tags that he was going to place the blame on, on the wire she had found.

Just inside the door, while there was still sufficient light, Belinda reached into her coat pocket and pulled out the plastic bag with the clamp and the wire she had taken down. "This is what I was talking about when I called you," she said.

David turned the clamp over in his hand. "Yep, we use a lot of these. It was probably covering a pinhole leak."

"You fix leaks with these?" Belinda asked. Her face screwed up into a frown.

"Yes," David said. "Sometimes when we charge up the system there will be a pinhole leak. It's a big job to take the pipe apart and put a new one in, so we put a piece of rubber over the leak, and hold it in place with the clamp. It happens quite often, believe it or not. Especially with all the pipe we put up. Then, we tag it with one of these tags so we can check it more closely in our annual inspections." David took a tag out of the bag and handed it to her. He was so close he could smell the fragrance of her shampoo in her hair. *What the hell was a woman like this doing in a job like this?* The desire to grab her was strong, but the noise and chattering from the workmen upstairs was stronger. *There would be another time, another place.*

"Do you just leave them like that?" she asked.

"Mostly. Sometimes we do send a crew out to repair them, if they still leak, but that's not very often. It looks like the sheetrock boys closed this ceiling off before we could get to it. It's not a big thing, they rarely leak, even if they aren't fixed."

Belinda turned the tag over in her hand and studied it. The wire was identical.

"I never found any rubber under the clamp," she said.

"It probably burned in the fire. There are very few places that sprinkler heads don't reach once they are activated but, right above them like this one was, is one of those areas." David seemed very business-like and not defensive at all.

"Can you explain why it was so hot in this area?" Belinda asked. "Look at that hole burned into the floor above."

David ran the beam of his flashlight back and forth. "Looks electrical to me," he said. "Lots of wires in this area. But then, I'm just a sprinkler man and not a fire investigator. What do I know?" There was a flash behind him and David turned to see where it came from just as another flash went off.

"Sorry," Belinda said, "I just wanted to get a picture of that burnt spot."

David scowled at her but quickly recovered.

She thought about what he had said. Then, putting the clamp back into her pocket, she turned to David and offered her hand. "I'm sorry I made you run way out here," she said. "Thanks, you've been a great help."

"No problem," David said. "I'll probably be back out here to put the sprinkler system back in order once the repairs are done, anyway. All right if I look around?"

"Help yourself," she smiled. "I'm out of here."

What he had said did make sense and, somehow, she felt foolish for even asking him the question, but Jerry had always told her that sometimes, the most foolish question turns out to be the right one. *Leave no stone unturned,* she thought. She backed carefully out into the street and headed for Shorewood Drive, which was about a mile away.

David waited until she was out of sight and then walked out to his truck. He had no intention of ever coming back to this building and, lucky for her, those workmen were here because he knew now—risky or not—he would have raped and killed her. He was super-excited just thinking about it. He had to get home.

The house Captain Clemmons wanted her to look at was a stately old mansion, right across the drive from the lake. Dark smudges of smoke and ash covered most of the windows but the building seemed, otherwise, structurally fine. On the front door was the usual posting from the Fire Department that said the building was uninhabitable. The key had been sent over to the office yesterday and Belinda tried it in the brass deadbolt. It clicked and the door opened. Inside, the smell of smoke was still so strong it took her breath away. She had to overcome that as she had a job to do. Somewhere, a motor was running, and she realized the heat was still on and the furnace was working. She threaded her way through mounds of refuse and furniture piled high with magazines and books. *Whoever had lived here was quite the pack rat,* she thought. *However, none of this was burned. There was only smoke and heat damage.*

She tried a light switch and the overhead chandelier came on, but the smoke encrusted bulbs gave off a yellowish glow. She went through a small hallway. Now she was in the kitchen, but sill no sign of char and then, there it was to her left. A room that was once a library, or a study, gutted from flames. Books had fallen or had been pulled from the shelves by the firemen and they lay in soggy piles on the floor. In one corner was the remnant of a bed—under a boarded-up window. Her flashlight played over the annealed bedsprings and twisted metal. This was where it all started.

She had no information on the fire, but that was only because she hadn't taken the time to read the report, and to go talk to the Engine Company that had responded first. The meeting with David Bennett had gotten her all rattled. *Here I go again, putting the cart in front of the horse,* she thought. *Jerry would have done it right, but he's not here. I need to stop and think right now. What am I looking for here?*

She dug out her phone and called her office. "Donna, see if there is a report filed on a fire on Shorewood Drive. 6700 is the house number. I believe Engine Sixteen handled the call."

She reached down and picked up a soggy book off the floor. *Great Expectations* by Charles Dickens. She opened it up to the front. *This is a rare first edition. These books must be worth a fortune,* she thought.

"Belinda." Donna was back on the line after several minutes. "This call was two days ago and the owner was dead on arrival. Engine Sixteen was the first responding unit. Captain Clemmons, who wrote the report, just seems to be asking for our office to confirm his suspicions of careless smoking."

"Where was the body taken?" Belinda asked.

"County Medical Examiner, it says here." said Donna.

"Thanks, Donna I'll be back in an hour or so."

She went back to the bed. On the floor, upside-down next to the bed, was an ashtray, also an empty cocktail glass. There was no doubt the bed was the source of the fire. She went back out into the kitchen, and on the counter there was an empty bottle of Beef Eaters Gin. She would call the coroner this afternoon but it looked to her like Clemmons was right. She wanted to explore the rest of the big house but the smoky smell was making her sick. She went outside and sat in the car for a moment to gather her thoughts. Finally, she went back, locked the door and drove slowly away.

David was going straight home. He was troubled about the intrusion into his life by this fire inspector, but he was more troubled because she was a woman. *He would have had no trouble getting rid of her,* he thought. *I got rid of my mother and a few other women back in Minneapolis.* Even the thought of this got him excited and he had an immediate reaction. He would take care of that when he got home.

It was Saturday and Noreen had the afternoon off. She took the boys and headed over to Hillcrest to see Jerry. It had been almost a week since they took him away. She was curious as to how he was getting along, and the boys had been asking to see him. She missed the old fool, but yet, the hurt was still there. She had to be careful.

Jerry was sitting in a chair, looking out the window, when Noreen got there. He smiled and got up and greeted the boys first. "Hey, thanks for coming. If I had known you were coming, I would have dressed up." He tugged at the old robe he was wearing over pajama bottoms and a tee shirt, to emphasize what he had said.

Noreen laughed. "You could be wearing a three-piece suit, Jerry, and you would still look rumpled. But that's the way I always remember you, anyway. How's it going?"

Ryan, the youngest, had crawled up in his father's lap; Todd stood beside him looking bored.

"Why don't you boys go down the hall to the vending machines and get yourself some chips and soda," Noreen said. "Daddy and I need to talk." She gave both of the boys a handful of quarters from the bottom of her purse.

"It's hard, Noreen, but it's not the lack of beer and cigarettes that's killing me, it's the loneliness."

"Jerry, you drove everyone away from you, what did you expect?"

He didn't answer her at first. "Look, Noreen, what I'm getting right now I deserve and I have no excuses. I have resolved to get well and then go out and win back your respect and my friends and fellow workers respect. Chastising me more doesn't help."

"I wasn't chastising you, Jerry; I was simply stating the facts."

They both dropped the subject.

"Have you heard from Belinda?" he asked her.

"No, should I?" Noreen asked. "Why are you worried about her?"

Jerry sensed some animosity here, or was it petty jealousy? She had often brought up the fact that Belinda was single and pretty, and he was lonely and available, and that could only spell trouble. Jerry had brought up the fact he was nearly old enough to be her father, but it didn't seem to make any difference. "We were working on a couple of strange fires when this all happened. I know she can't call me here and

I just thought she might have had some questions that she would run through you to me."

"Do you want me to call her?"

He shrugged his shoulders. "If you don't mind," he said. "She can be shy and I just want to help her all that I can, despite the circumstances."

"Is there no one else available to help her?" The boys were back and fighting over some candy. "Behave yourselves," Noreen scolded.

"There are lots of people who could help her, but I don't think she would ask."

"I'll call her tonight and ask her to call you if she can. Is there anything I can get you, except beer and cigarettes, that would make you more comfortable?"

Jerry wanted to say, "some respect," but he didn't. He would have to earn that. "Maybe a couple of magazines would be nice. Not much to do around here. Just something you might have around the house. Don't go buy anything."

"Boys, we're going; say goodbye to your dad." Noreen was standing up now and buttoning her coat. The boys gave Jerry a hug and kiss. Jerry looked like he was on the verge of tears.

Noreen walked over to him and bending over kissed him on the forehead. "Hang in there, Jerry," she said. He reached up, touched her cheek, and smiled weakly.

"We'll see you in a couple of days," she said. Then they were gone. He listened to their footsteps echoing off the hard hallway floor and then, slowly fading away to nothing. He ran his fingers over his lips. He needed a cigarette so bad, but he needed Noreen and the boys back in his life even more.

CHAPTER ELEVEN

DAVID HAD HIS MAP OF the city out again, spread on the kitchen tabletop with all of his potential targets vividly marked. He had only enough petrocyclomate left to do maybe two more buildings. He was looking for the best spots to place them. *If he was successful, all of these buildings would burn and fall like a row of dominoes.* He had to put in quite a few more ignition devices yet, so that would be his main focus for now. He had several boxes full of them that he had made up.

A lot of the buildings didn't have suspended ceilings and David realized that anything he put up on them could be seen. He had worked diligently to make his ignition devices appear to be a simple monitoring device that, he explained to the building maintenance people, was needed to monitor the air that might get into the lines and cause pressure problems. So far, no one had questioned him about it but he still tried to hide the devices as good as he could, using air ducts and speaker systems to his advantage.

It bothered him a lot that he couldn't be more active in his fire making right now. Lying on his bed, with his arms buried beneath the pillow under his head, his thoughts went back to Minneapolis and another day gone by. *He had had so much fun back then, and half the fun was just watching the Minneapolis Fire Department trying to catch him. That is, until that day in the parking ramp.* He looked down at his scarred-up legs and torso. It looked like he had alligator skin. *Oh, if only he could have gotten Flanagan in that elevator with him, instead of that wino! Maybe when he was done here in Chicago, he would go back there and even the score. In fact, that was going to be the plan.*

When Belinda got back to the office she called the Cook County Coroner's office, and asked for the autopsy report on the victim in the house fire up in Shorewood. A young intern read the report to her. The victim, Gertrude Stemmer, had died of smoke asphyxiation. There was no other trauma to the body that would lead one to think that her death was anything but accidental, and the coroner had ruled it as such. She filed the report and checked her messages. There was a phone call from Jerry's wife, Noreen, that said, "Call me." The rest could wait until Monday. In fact, she would wait and call Noreen when she got home; but for now, it was time to call it a day. It had been a full day, and as bad as it had started out, it had ended well. The wire and clamp issue had bothered her a lot, but her mind was at ease with the subject right now. When she went to see Jerry, she would fill him in on things, but she was sure he would concur. Hell, he might just be proud of her for a change. As for the cause of the apartment fire and the Atlas fire, well, they may never know the answer. They had a file cabinet full of cases like that.

It was Sunday afternoon when Belinda called Noreen back. She had almost forgotten about her message on Friday.

"Noreen, hi! It's Belinda Clayton. I had a message to call you, and then one thing led to another and here it is Sunday afternoon already, and I'm just catching up. What can I do for you? By the way, how's Jerry doing?"

"He's fine—I think. You know Jerry, he can't be tied down for long, but he is now—until after the first of the year."

"I hope they do him some good," Belinda said.

"I hope so, too. His boys need him in their life. He wanted me to ask you if there was anything you needed from him while he was gone."

"I think I have it all handled here. There are some things I would like to talk to him about, but it can wait until I can visit him."

"Yes, right now," Noreen said, "he probably should stick to getting his head screwed on right. I think he can have visitors after next week, but I have to check on that for you. How's the baby?"

"Growing like a weed. I just wish I didn't have to leave her so often."

"That's hard," Noreen said. "I was lucky when the boys were that small because Jerry's job was enough to keep us going so I didn't have to work."

"That would be nice," Belinda answered, "but I don't see any help on the horizon like that for me." She wanted to get off that subject. "I'll keep in touch and if anything comes up that Jerry can help me with, I'll call. Otherwise, it can wait."

"Thanks for calling," Noreen said, and hung up the phone. She tapped her nose with her forefinger as she thought, *maybe she was out of line thinking that Belinda and Jerry had anything but a business relationship going on. Maybe there was hope for her and him somewhere down the road.*

It was going to be Thanksgiving next week so Belinda had made plans to go to her sister's to celebrate the holiday. Noreen had called and told her Jerry could have visitors after the weekend. Belinda had said, maybe, if she could get her sister or mother to watch Samantha some day next week, she would go to the hospital to see him.

The following week at work, Belinda was kept quite busy. There had been two fires in their district over the weekend that needed looking into. One of them was arson—to have a fire sale in a dying business— she was sure of that. The other seemed to just be revenge in a family feud. It wasn't her job to find the motives; it was just her job to find the cause.

Wednesday morning, after a staff meeting, she checked her messages and there was one from Jerry. At first, she seemed almost afraid to call him; she had no idea what kind of Jerry she would be talking to. *Was he angry about what they had done to him, or was he repentant, and willing to try and turn his life around?*

She picked the phone up and dialed three digits and then set it down. *What was she going to say to him if he asked about work? Maybe she should get her thoughts in order before she called. Oh, to hell with it,* she thought, *it was time to grow a set and just call him. What was she so afraid of?*

Jerry did not have a direct phone at the hospital, but the nurse said that she would tell him Belinda called and he would probably call right back. "He's bored out of his skull," she explained. The call back from Jerry came just a few minutes later.

"Hey, kid. How are you?" he asked.

"I'm fine, Jerry. I think the bigger question is—how are you?" Belinda shifted uneasy in her chair. "We're all pulling for you to get well and get back to work."

Jerry chuckled. "Thanks, kid. I think my biggest problems are behind me. At least I hope so. Right now they're saying maybe just a few more weeks and they'll let me out, but that's not the reason I called you. I know I should keep my mind on my problems and not work problems, but I couldn't help wondering what you came up with, with that hose clamp on that pipe in the fire out by the lake. Did they give you a reason for that, and was it theirs?"

"I did talk with the guy from the sprinkler company. He said it was just to hold a tag and a rubber patch up there. They said there was a pinhole in the pipe. They apparently never came back to fix it and it was covered over with sheet rock."

Jerry was quiet for a moment. "Was the guy from Knowlton's?" he asked.

"Yes," Belinda answered. "He wasn't overly explanatory but I thought he was sincere."

"What's happening out there right now?" Jerry asked. "Did you check to see if there was a hole in the pipe?"

"Where? At the fire scene? They're tearing the building apart as we speak." She ignored the question about checking for a hole. "I had to release it, Jerry. We had it long enough. Don't you think you should try and get well, and quit worrying about work?"

Jerry ignored her question. "It doesn't add up to me, Belinda. There was some kind of accelerant used in that building, and there was no fire load in that empty apartment. Whatever was used was not poured on the floor. It came through the air. Belinda, you need to look into this Knowlton guy. Go look at some of his other jobs. I've never heard of, or seen, sprinkler pipes fixed with a hose clamp and rubber patch. There had to be something in that sprinkler system that added to the fire, and not put it out. It's too damn late now to look into that one, but we can look at other Knowlton jobs."

"So let's say, Jerry, there was gasoline or something in the sprinkler pipes. What started the fire that activated the sprinklers?" Belinda seemed to be defensive now and she had to change the subject as he was making her angry now. *Why was he always second-guessing her?*

Jerry didn't answer her question, but just sat staring at his lap and shaking his head.

"Do you need anything, Jerry? Cigarettes or maybe something to read?"

"No, thanks. I just need you to follow up on what we have talked about."

"I'll call again, Jerry. You just take care of yourself." Belinda hung up the phone before he could say anything more. She had two more calls to return.

Jerry was upset and walked down the hallway away from the phone, angry and feeling helpless. He wasn't mad at Belinda, but mad at himself for screwing this whole thing up. *God, a beer would taste good right now.*

A seed had been planted in Belinda's mind but right now her stubborn streak was not going to recognize it. *Why the hell did Jerry have to see everybody as some kind of nut, born to burn the world down,* she wondered. *Isn't it possible for a pipe to have a pinhole in it? Maybe she would call some other sprinkler company besides Knowlton's and ask them how they handle it when that happens.*

She grabbed the yellow pages and started looking for sprinkler companies.

Belinda talked to two other companies, and both of them said they had never heard of pinholes in pipes and, if they did have one, they would weld it up or replace the pipe. Maybe Jerry was right about this. Tomorrow she was going to go out to some other Knowlton jobs and do some snooping around.

CHAPTER TWELVE

DAVID HAD HAD A RESTLESS few days even though he was convinced he had won over that goofy city inspector. In hindsight, he wished he had never burned that apartment building. It had been an ego booster, but it had also raised a lot of questions in the fire department that they didn't seem to want to let loose of. He had almost ten months until he unleashed this firestorm on the Windy City. Maybe it was time to get rid of the sprinkler company and just lay low for a while. Maybe he would talk to a couple of his competitors and see what they would offer to buy him out, but first, he had to get the rest of those ignition sources planted.

He looked at his map again. There were eleven places he needed to visit and wire up with his fire starters, and then he would be ready. He would try to do one a day until he was done. David picked up the phone and called a company that sold used auto parts. He had installed their sprinklers over a year ago and it was time for a checkup.

"Casey's South Side Auto Parts," the lady answered.

"Hi, I'm calling from Knowlton Sprinklers," David said, "and I see by my records you are due for an inspection. They're supposed to be once a year and it has been over a year. I was wondering if I could stop by tomorrow and look things over—there is no charge for this."

"Beats me," the lady said. "Casey isn't here right now, but if it's free I'm sure he won't mind. Sure, come on over."

Belinda parked her car and walked up the long winding walk to the Chicago Museum of Natural History. Her records indicated that it had a sprinkler system installed and Knowlton Sprinklers had installed it two years ago. This building and Casey's Auto Parts were only about a block apart so she thought, if she had time, she would catch them both today. If she didn't find anything, then she was going to tell Jerry that she believed Knowlton's story and that's all there was to it.

The entrance building to the museum was an old brownstone

building that belonged in a museum by itself, by nature of its age. There was a more modern one-story glass and aluminum building, built off to one side of it, which was a city block in size. The two buildings looked out of place next to each other, both built in a far different era.

Inside the new building were artifacts and memorabilia from over two hundred years of Chicago history. They had been organized in displays, set in some kind of chronological order that virtually took you through the history of the great city, going from the old to the new.

Belinda was to meet Grace Collins, the curator who had offered to take her through the buildings. When Grace had asked her over the phone what she was looking for, Belinda said she wasn't sure, but she would know it if she saw it.

The steps up to the massive doors of the museum showed the wear of millions of feet over the years. Belinda thought how nice it would be just to come and visit a place like this someday, when she had time to enjoy it for what it was intended. She loved the Chicago area and it would be nice to get in touch with her roots.

The old part of the museum was mostly administration offices but arrows on the floor pointed you to the actual museum. Signs indicated that all people had to be accompanied by a guide, and the fee schedule and times was posted right underneath it. Another sign pointed the way to the Curator's Office, so that's where Belinda headed.

Grace Collins had a sophisticated, matronly look about her that smacked of knowledge and experience. She grabbed a ring of keys off her desk and the two women, after exchanging pleasantries, headed down the long hall to the museum.

Every spare inch of the museum was used for some kind of display or other, but the thing that garnered the most interest from Belinda as they entered the room, was the large mural painted on a long wall that depicted the Great Chicago Fire. She stood in awe of it for some time, looking at all of the intricate paintings that had gone into this huge depiction of that holocaust of 1871.

"How awful that must have been," she said. 'I certainly hope we never live to see anything like that."

Grace smiled, and said."Let's hope not. Now, what can I show you?"

"Well, what I would like to do is inspect some of the piping on your sprinkler system. I am looking for some clamps that we believe were supposed to be used, and believe me they are not going to be easy to find with all of the pipe in this huge building, but maybe you could just let me browse around for a while. I hate to waste your time if you have other things to do."

"Sure, that's not a problem. If you need ladders or some help, just come back and get me and I can get one of the maintenance people to help you out."

Belinda had her Mag light flashlight, and with the building lights nearly all turned off, she walked the aisles of the museum, following each pipe with her beam of light, looking for any of the elusive clamps. *This is crazy,* she thought, *but I'm not going to be happy until I know there are no more of those clamps. Besides, it's the only way to shut Jerry up once and for all.*

It was slow, painstaking work following the pipes wherever they went. Her neck was getting sore from looking up, and she took a few minutes to stop and rest while she massaged her neck and turned her head from side to side, trying to get the kinks out. She was amazed at the vastness of the museum and the collection of artifacts. There were thousands of items, and from time to time, she caught herself looking at the displays instead of what she came there to inspect. Then, looking at her watch, she saw that time was running short. She hadn't thought it would take this much time. She had a meeting at eleven she had to be at. Maybe the auto parts store was going to have to wait for another day. It looked like two more aisles and she would be done.

In the next to the last aisle there was an old milk delivery truck that had been restored. The truck looked to be from the turn of the century, probably the early twenties. A sign, which had been attached to the sprinkler pipe overhead, hung down with a brief history of the truck and the company name written on it. Belinda, distracted again, slowly read the sign, caught up in the history. Then, her flashlight reflected off of something next to the chain that the sign hung from. It was a hose clamp on the pipe next to the chain.

She walked around to the backside of the truck to get a look from the other side of the pipe. There was more. There was a small black box on top of the pipe and, on one end of it, appeared to be some kind of a glass vessel.

She hurried back to the office and asked Grace Collins if she could get a maintenance person to help her for a second.

"Not a problem," Grace said. "Where do you want him?"

"By the old milk truck," she said. "We'll need a stepladder—and thanks." Belinda hurried back to wait for the man and the ladder.

At the auto parts building, David was just getting done with installing his latest fire starter. He had one in the museum and one in a paper company just two blocks away so now he would be done with this end of town. He had three stops already set up for tomorrow. It took about two hours at each site.

David was in a lot of pain today; last night one of the scar tissue patches on his thigh had broken open and it was weeping out some kind of bloody fluid. It was if his body had given up on healing itself. His condition seemed to be deteriorating, not getting better. True, it had been a long ten years of physical pain and suffering, but the real pain wasn't physical, it came from the anger he couldn't get rid of and his hate for the man who did this to him, Mike Flanagan. *There would be one more CHAPTER in Flanagan's story,* he vowed, *but not until Chicago burned.*

He could feel the bandages he had put on were already saturated. Some kind of fluid was running down his leg and had come though his pants in one area. Just bending his leg brought a scream to his lips, and he grimaced as he climbed down the ladder. As soon as this was done, and all of the igniters were in place, he was going to lay low for awhile. He would put the company up for sale, but he couldn't relinquish control before the 8th of October. Someone new might find out his secret.

The young man held the ladder while Belinda climbed up and examined this apparatus she had found attached to the pipe. She approached it tentatively, as if it might blow up in her face at any moment but, at last, she was at eye level with it. It was a small black box, which had some kind of a glass test tube fastened to one end of it. There were two wires that ran from the box, into the top of the tube.

The tube was filled with some kind of clear liquid. She jiggled the tube and the liquid sloshed inside of it. On the other end of the box was a stiff copper wire like a grounding cable, about two feet long, that was also fastened to the box. It appeared to do nothing more than go under the pipe clamp, and hold the whole thing to the pipe. She wondered why it was so long, as most of it just hung out the other side of the clamp, seemingly doing nothing. There didn't appear to be any other connections to the building, or the sprinkler system.

Belinda wiped her sweating hands on her pants, and looked down at the young man holding the ladder, while she tried to think what her next move should be. The young maintenance man just smiled weakly at her and said, "What are you looking at?"

"I'm not sure," she said. "Do you have a screwdriver?"

"Philips or straight?"

"What do you mean?" she asked.

"What kind of head is on the screw—Philips or slotted?"

"It has a slot in it," she answered.

He reached into his tool belt and retrieved a long screwdriver with a yellow handle and, climbing up a couple of steps, handed it to Belinda. Before loosening the clamp, she had another thought. *That guy from Knowlton's had told her the clamp was used to hold a rubber piece in place to plug a leak. Was this holding back a leak, and if it was, what was all this other stuff for?*

For a second, she studied the whole thing again, but then she thought. *This isn't any leak clamp; this is some kind of device that doesn't belong here. I might not be that experienced with this crap but I'm not that naïve.*

Slowly she loosened the clamp, waiting for any sign of water, but none was forthcoming, so she turned the screw until the clamp separated. Being careful to not drop either the screwdriver or the device, she lifted it and it all came off the pipe cleanly. There was no hole in the pipe, and it was then she noticed the proximity to the sprinkler head, only inches away. The same place the one in the apartment building that had burned had been.

"Coming down," she said to the maintenance man.

She didn't want to alarm the man as to what she had, so she held it close to her shirt and covered it with a silk scarf she had worn around her neck. "Thanks, buddy," she said.

"Not a problem. All done?" He didn't seem to have much interest in what she had.

"Yes, and thanks again. Would you have a small cardboard box I could use?"

"I'm sure I can find something. Can I have my screwdriver back?"

Belinda laughed, pulled it out of her back pocket where she had stuck it, and handed it to him. This whole process had taken way too much time and she was going to have to hurry to her meeting. With the device safely packed into a box, she went out to her car and taking off, turned left towards downtown. Had she turned right, she would have seen the Knowlton Sprinkler truck.

Jerry was frustrated about the slow pace that it was taking to get the cure, as they liked to call it. His days were spent more in daydreams than in any kind of constructive thinking. Noreen and the boys came every other day or so, and that was the only bright spot in his life right now. Last night when they had left, he cried when he realized how much he had failed them.

Work was his other regret. He had been on to something, which he had so rudely interrupted by his drinking binge. Jerry had thought long and hard about it—the fire in the apartment and at Atlas. They had to have been set and fed by an accelerant; he had known that from the start. The sixty-four-thousand-dollar question had been "how?"

He needed to call Belinda today and ask her if she found anything new. He didn't have much hope that she had paid any attention to him the other day. She seemed frustrated with him when she left. *Face it,* he thought, *he was just a washed-up alcoholic who didn't have much influence with anyone anymore.*

CHAPTER THIRTEEN

THE DEVICE FROM THE MUSEUM, still in the cardboard box Belinda had put it in, lay on a table in her office. Belinda looked at her watch. It was past quitting time and she needed to pick up Samantha and get home. The daycare wasn't too happy with her when she was late. The damn meeting had dragged on for four hours, and it was a time when she wanted to be working on this.

Her first thought was to call the bomb squad and have them look at her prize, but now that was going to have to wait until tomorrow. In retrospect, now that she had time to think about it, she probably should have had them remove it from the building, but she hadn't thought about booby traps or anything like that until she had already acted. *Oh well, it wasn't going anywhere and by the looks of the dust on it, it had been there for some time.* What intrigued her the most, right now, was the fluid in the beaker. It was as clear as water, and when she tried to smell around the two tiny holes where the wires went in, she could detect no odor. *After all,* she thought, *she was a chemical engineer, was she not?* There didn't seem to be any kind of sealant around the wires, but the holes in the glass were almost the exact size of the wires going in and they gripped the wires tight. She could see scratches on the wires where they had been forced through the holes. The fluid was about three quarters of the way up in the tube, and the wires hovered just over it, but not in it. They were twisted together in an effort to form a dead short. *This was a bomb of sorts, but what activated it?* The thought sent a chill up her spine. *What if it went off here in the office,* she wondered. *What if it had gone off in the car or in her hands? The secret must be in that little black box.*

She wasn't going to touch that black box. The bomb squad could look at it in the morning; she had to get going home. Maybe if she had time tonight, she would call Jerry and talk it over with him. She put a manila file on top of the box and wrote, **'Do not move'** in large black letters. She didn't need the cleaning staff fooling around with it.

90

Matt Wetzel had been on the bomb squad for over twelve years. He had handled everything—from nitroglycerin to radioactive waste. He saw each bomb as a unique challenge with its dirty, dark secrets. Most bombs were made to inflict damage on something, or someone, but every so often they would find one that had a booby trap meant to take out anyone who tinkered with it.

Right now, he hovered over the box in Belinda's office while she stood across the room, watching him intently.

"I can't believe you moved something like this," he said. "I also can't believe you brought it here to your office, and let it sit here on this table all night." He chastised her.

Belinda didn't offer any defense. *Last night when she was home thinking about it, she knew she hadn't done the right thing. Right now, she would just take her lumps, but she wanted that beaker of fluid and they could have the rest. She needed to find out what that clear liquid was.*

Matt bit his lip as he thought about his next move. "I want to move this to a safer location before I dig into it," he said.

"Matt, I want that tube of fluid so I can take it to our lab." She had walked part of the way across the room and now stood just a few feet from him. She couldn't help thinking, *what made anyone take on a job like his?*

Matt looked back into the box again. The tube appeared to be fastened to the little black box by some kind of epoxy. The wires were clearly meant to short out and cause a spark that would ignite the fluid. The electrical charge had to be in the box. The cover to the box appeared to just snap on. The thing that was puzzling was the long, stiff wire that ran out of the other end of the box for about two feet.

He motioned for her to come over by him. "This wire here—was it pointing up in the air, or how was it positioned on the pipe, before you took it down?"

"It was just running parallel with the pipe," she said. "The clamp that was holding the whole thing up there was over it."

"Where's the clamp?" he asked.

She went over to her desk and retrieved the now-open clamp and handed it to him.

Matt looked the clamp over. It appeared to be nothing more than the same kind of clamp that held a radiator hose on a car, or any hose, for that matter. "You can keep the clamp for now," he said. "I'm going to take this back to our garage and disarm it. I have to believe this long wire is some kind of an antenna, but I won't know that until I get inside of the black box." Matt reached down and tugged at the wires going into the beaker, but they seemed tight in their holes.

"I'll call you as soon as we know something," he said. "I'm sorry if I seemed condescending about you moving it. Sometimes we get caught up in our job. It just might turn out to be nothing or, best case, even part of the sprinkler system. He held out this hand and Belinda took it, noting the gold band on his finger.

Well, I know two things, she thought. *He's married and left-handed.*

Matt had been her first item of the day and it was time to get back to work. She checked her messages. There was one from Jerry and one from her boss. She called her boss first, but Norm wasn't in, so she left a message for him to call her back. *I bet I'm getting hell for something,* she thought, as she dialed Jerry.

One again, she got the nurses' desk. *They screened all of his calls,* she thought. She identified herself and asked to be connected to Jerry's room. He now had a phone for outgoing calls only.

"Hi, kid!" It was Jerry, and he sounded chipper for a change. "Thanks for calling back."

"No problem, Jerry. I do have some news you might be glad to hear, although I think I screwed up again."

"What's that?" he said.

"Well, I did go check up on some of Knowlton's sprinklers like you asked—at least one of them—and I did find something suspicious."

"What was that?"

"Some kind of a device that was fastened to the sprinkler pipe with a clamp, just like you found at the apartment building."

"Describe it to me."

She went into a lengthy description of the device; how she had taken it down and brought it back to her office, and how stupid that had been. She also told him that it was positioned next to the sprinkler head, just like the one on the apartment building, and it was not a leak patch, that she could tell.

"I knew it," he said. "Belinda, you need to do two things. Get that tube full of liquid and find out what it is. Then we need to find out if there is more than water in those sprinkler pipes. That device is only the fuse, Belinda. It was meant to create enough heat to trip that sprinkler head next to it. Son-of-a-bitch, it makes me so god-dammed mad that I am stuck here in this rat hole. You're onto something big, honey. I just know it!"

The word "honey," caught her off-guard for a moment. "I'll keep you in the loop, Jerry," she said softly. "Just take care of yourself and get well quick."

The light on her phone was blinking, indicating she had an incoming call.

"Belinda, it's Matt. I took that thing apart, and it is a fuse of sorts, but I'm not sure if it could do much damage by itself. I couldn't detect any odor from that liquid; it could be water for all I know, but I'll send it over to you. I put it in a smaller bottle with a cap. "

"What powered it?" she asked.

"A battery," Matt answered. "It was set up similar to a garage door opener. That long wire we talked about was an antenna and, when it got the signal, it closed two contacts that sent power through those two wires. The fluid in the tube must be volatile, but we'll leave that up to you to check out. You're the chemist. I'm still not sure, if it did fire off, how so little fluid could do much damage."

"Thanks, Matt," she said. It was time to get her boss in this discovery. She called Norm Shuster again, and this time he was there.

Shuster didn't seem to be that impressed with what she had found. Interested—yes, but seriously interested—no. "Let's find out what that fluid is in that tube," he said, "before we go off half-cocked on this thing. As for the sprinkler pipes themselves, it doesn't seem realistic to me that they could be full of something that would burn. There is a mile of pipe in that building and it would take a tanker full of something to fill them. Let's hold off on that for the time being. We might run a background check on Knowlton Sprinklers, but hell, they have been around longer than all of us. Anyway, good work on finding it. How's your partner doing?"

"I just talked to Jerry this morning," she said. "He's doing good."

"Well, thanks for the call, and keep me in the loop." he said.

She set the phone down and, just then, there was a knock on her door. It was her secretary with a small bottle. "A messenger from the police brought this over," she said.

The lab was in a separate building, and Belinda had been there many times. Hell, she had started out working in this lab. There would not be any of the techs on duty examining this case, though. This one was hers and hers alone. The chemical composition of the fluid was hard to pinpoint and, after several hours, she hadn't made any progress. However, she had found out two things. It was highly volatile—one drop almost burning through the spoon she had held it in, and getting the metal so hot she dropped in on the bench top. Also, it didn't mix with water; no matter how hard you tried, it floated to the top.

It was time to call it a day. She took her jar, and leaving the lab, returned to her office. She would work on it more on Monday.

As Belinda sat in traffic, making her way home, she was preoccupied with the job at hand, and frustrated that she hadn't found out what it was. *Maybe she would have to turn to some independent lab for help,* she thought, *but who?*

Then she had a crazy thought. She remembered a fire inspector from Minneapolis that she had talked to, over a glass of beer, at a conference a while back. *What was his name and what had they been talking about?* She had his card at the office, and now she remembered what they had been talking about. *A flammable liquid that burned hotter than anything he had ever seen.* It was time to put it away for the weekend.

CHAPTER FOURTEEN

IT WAS JUST A LITTLE over a week before Christmas and Mike Flanagan walked down Nicollet Avenue in Minneapolis, looking in the store windows of Dayton's Department store. He still had some shopping to do for his wife and he was looking for ideas. Cindy, Mickey, and Cara—the kids—were easy to buy for. Laura, his wife, did most of the shopping anyway, but what could he get for Laura that would show how much he cared for her? It was a hard question and his eyes scanned the windows, looking for a hint.

Cindy was seventeen and a carbon copy of her mother with her long blond hair and fair skin. She loved her family and was a straight-A student in the private school she went to. Both Mike and Laura were extremely proud of their daughter. Cindy was also a gifted musician and they both had dreams of sending her to Julliard some day. In fact, she had a recital coming up that could go a long way towards getting a scholarship. It was somewhat of a competitive recital between her and another girl from St. Paul, and people from Julliard would be there.

Mickey, on the other hand, was a little bit of a rebel with a somewhat rebellious attitude. He liked to push his mother's buttons, but Laura didn't let it rattle her, chalking it up to just being a budding, confused teenager. Mike had pushed him into sports and, for the most part, he showed a lot of promise in football. He couldn't wait until next year when he could play in Jr. High School. It gave him an outlet to let off some of his constant energy.

Cara had just turned ten, and Mike and Laura had kept her a baby in some respects. Laura found out after Cara's birth that she couldn't have any more children, so maybe that had something to do with it.

Laura was as beautiful as the first day Mike had seen her, back in that summer of 1959 when he first came to the city from the country up north. Their love had never faltered in the years they had been married, and Mike still worshiped her and the life they had made together.

He glanced at his watch and noted he was late to work again and he had better hurry. Granted, he was the boss of Inspection at Minneapolis Fire, but that didn't give him any special privileges. He would just have to finish shopping another time. He quickened his pace and pulled his collar up. The cold winter winds seemed to whistle through the streets, between the big buildings, as if they were squeezed into being something more ferocious than they would normally be. He turned right off Nicollet onto Fifth Street, and headed for the City Hall building where his office was.

Mike's office was in a corner of the third floor, along with Building Inspection and the office of the Fire Chief. He and his three inspectors worked from there, solving arsons and investigating fires. They were also kept busy enforcing fire codes in the city.

He missed the days he rode the rigs and fought the fires he now investigated. He missed the camaraderie, he missed the excitement, and he missed the thrill of living life on the edge, but he had made a promise to Laura that he would never go back to it, and he intended to keep it.

He would be thirty-five in a few more weeks. Not too old to be a fire fighter by any means, but too young to be heading up his own department. He had been made a hero ten years ago when he had brought David Bennett down, in a fiery end, in the parking ramp across the street. It had all mushroomed for him from there. Today, he was well-known and respected in the circles of fire investigators all over the country.

Belinda picked up the phone, and dialed the number for Flanagan's office in Minneapolis. She had thought about it more than once last evening. The conversation they had had in that hotel bar that night was etched into her mind because he had talked about a fluid that had burned so hot it etched metal. It was a fluid that had no usable purpose right now, and how some mad college student at the University of Minnesota had invented it. *Was it possible that someone had resurrected the formula?*

She had thought about calling Jerry and asking his opinion, but for now she didn't think that was a good idea. Jerry seemed a little unstable right now. She had given some thought to asking her boss if he thought she should do it but, the last time she had talked to him, he gave her the impression she was bothering him. He just wanted results and he didn't care how she got them. *Maybe it was time she made some decisions, good or bad, for herself. It sure didn't hurt to ask. As much as she hated the cliché, it was time to grow a pair.*

The phone rang twice before it was picked up and a soft female voice said, "Fire Investigation and Inspections."

"I...I wondered if I could talk with Mike Flanagan?" she said.

"Well, he's not here at the moment, but we are expecting him soon. Whom shall I say called? I'll have him return your call as soon as...oh, never mind, here he is now. Can you hold for a minute?"

"Yes," Belinda answered.

"Mike, line one," she said, as he passed her desk and grabbed the handful of messages she handed him.

"Who is it," he asked.

"I'm not sure," she said, "do you want me to ask?"

"No, just give me a minute to get my coat off," he answered, appearing to be mildly upset.

Mike hung up his coat and grabbed a cup of coffee. Whoever it was could just wait a second. Finally, he sat down at his desk, picked up his phone and pushed the flashing button.

"Flanagan," he said. He was thumbing through his messages as he listened for a reply.

"Mr. Flanagan, this is Belinda Clayton from Chicago Fire Inspection. I met you at a conference last fall here in Chicago. Do you remember me?"

Mike had set the messages down and was now paying attention to the caller. "Were you with Jerry Martin?" he asked.

Great, she thought, *He remembers Martin, but not me. Some impression I made on him.* "I was with Jerry, yes."

"Yes. Yes, I do remember you now," he lied. "How are things in Chicago, and how's Jerry?"

"Well, Jerry has been sick, but he's getting better. Right now, I'm trying to hold down the fort myself."

You're the only inspector in Chicago?" he asked.

"No. There are lots of them but I'm the only one in my district. I wondered if you could help me with a problem."

"I'll try," he said. "But if I have to come to Chicago, you'll have to buy me a beer."

Belinda laughed. *Damn, maybe he did remember her.* "Here's my problem," she said, choosing not to comment on the beer. "Last week I found an incendiary device in a museum. It contained some clear fluid that we haven't been able to identify. My first thought was to send it out to an independent lab for analyses. Then, I remembered you talking about a similar fluid that some crazy guy had used in your city some years ago. This sounded remarkably alike, so I thought I would pass this by you and see what you think."

Mike had picked up a pen and was making notes now as she talked. "Alike how?" he asked.

"Well, this stuff burns hotter than anything I've ever seen and I am a chemist. Just a couple of drops burned almost through a metal spoon. It has no odor and it has one of the lowest flashpoints I have ever experienced."

"What was it contained in," Mike asked, "and how much of it was there?"

"It was in a glass beaker, connected to a battery with some contacts and wires that ran from the device into the beaker. It looks like they were meant to short out and cause a fire. The whole thing was rather airtight, so I'm not sure how it would burn without air. Also, I should tell you, we think this kind of a device was used in a fire we had this fall—that caused a death and a lot of damage. I only have a few ounces of the liquid."

"Sound intriguing," Mike said, 'but how can I help you?"

"Well, if I send you a sample of this fluid, could you check and see if it is the same stuff you ran up against?"

"Yes, I could do that," he said, "but as far as I know, this stuff was never made again after our incident—but yes, I'm interested in doing that."

"How are you going to send it?" he asked.

"Well, I thought that I would just put some in a jar and mail it to you."

"What do you have it in now?" he asked.

"A bottle." Belinda said, as she reached across her desk to retrieve the stuff. "Just a glass bottle with a plastic cap and–oh, my goodness, it looks like this stuff is eating the cap right off the bottle!"

"Just hang on to it," Mike said. "Get a different cap on the bottle and don't let it slosh on the cap. I'm coming to Chicago to get it, and talk with you more."

"Wow, I didn't expect that, but that would be nice. I'll buy you that beer."

Mike laughed. "See you tomorrow," he said. "What's your address and phone number?"

Laura was sitting at the kitchen table, sorting through Christmas cards, when Mike got home from work that night. She smiled as he came in the door, and pointed to a chair. "Sit down, babes. I want to talk to you before you get involved in something else."

He bent over and kissed her gently and then sat down. She was still the most beautiful woman he had ever known. Even though many years had passed between them, she seemed ageless. Her hair still glowed naturally, like strands of gold; her skin was still as soft and firm as their teenage daughter, Cindy's; and her smile still never failed to warm Mike's heart.

"I was looking at our calendar," she said, "and outside of Cindy's recital on Wednesday, we don't have anything else pressing. This is the last week before Christmas. It's next Tuesday already, Mike; can you believe that? It's just a week from tomorrow and I'm not done shopping."

"How would you like to go to Chicago tomorrow?" Mike said. "You could finish your shopping there, and you and I could spend the night at some fancy hotel." He reached across the table and squeezed her hand. "I already talked to my sister. She said she would come stay with the kids, and they love it when Liz comes."

It had caught Laura entirely by surprise. "What brought this on?" she said.

"I have to go for business, but it's just to meet an inspector and get some evidence. We'd have most of the day to ourselves, and we could fly back on Wednesday, and be home for Cindy's recital."

Laura grinned at him, "You just want to get laid, don't you. You guys are all the same," she giggled. "Every time you go to some hotel or motel, you think you're back on your honeymoon."

Mike laughed and went around the table, hugging her from behind, his hands finding her breasts. "I am on my honeymoon, sweetheart. It's never ended—but if you want to throw in a roll in the hay as part of the deal—well, it doesn't get any better than that!"

"I better pack," she said, "and you better order another airline ticket."

"I already did."

CHAPTER FIFTEEN

DAVID HAD REASON TO CELEBRATE. Tomorrow he would put the last of his ignition devices in place. It would be a long wait until October and "the big show" as he liked to call it, but that was alright. It would give him time to sell the sprinkler business and let things cool down. *Maybe he would go back to Minneapolis for a while and just play around. After all, he did have one barrel of fluid left, and he owed Flanagan some big-time trouble.*

There was always the outside chance that an accidental fire in one of the buildings could set things off, but that was remote. Petrocyclomate was only in one zone in each building. Some of these buildings had as many as fifty zones in them. No one had questioned him when he explained about installing extra monitoring equipment so he believed he was above suspicion. Right now he was on a roll.

David lay naked on the bed, dabbing ointment into his weeping sores. Each time he touched them, he would think of Flanagan, through the searing pain. Maybe he could dream up some diabolical deed, when he was back in Minneapolis, to let Flanagan know the hell he had been through. He tried to energize his flaccid penis and masturbate, but it no longer responded like it used to. Age and injury had taken their toll. *Just another victim,* David thought. He pulled up the sheet, disgusted at looking at his body.

Today was a big day for Jerry. Today, he would meet with his counselors and his doctor to go over his progress, and maybe—just maybe, he would find out more about his release date. He had been a model patient, doing everything they asked of him. He was also more confident than he had ever been that his drinking days were behind him. He had one goal right now, and that was to get out of here and be the best dad he could be. Maybe, if things went right, he would get another shot at being a decent husband, too. Noreen had even hinted that that could happen if he proved himself. She still loved the old fool and she wanted them to be a family again. Right now though, his thoughts were on work and Belinda. She hadn't called him back after she had found that device. *What was she doing about it? This was serious business and Jerry wasn't sure it was perceived as such by his fellow workers. Belinda was too naïve, too easily swayed, and she was being put in a hard spot right now. He needed to get back to work and help her out.*

The plane bounced once, and then settled smoothly onto the runway at O'Hare, in Chicago. The steady drone of the jet engines they had become accustomed to was now cut by two-thirds. Mike looked out the window as they taxied to the concourse. He had been to Chicago many times over the years but never tired of the big city. Laura was busy putting away all of her needlepoint she had worked on, on the trip down. She was excited about going shopping in Chicago, getting away from her daily grind, and spending a day and night with the man who had made her so happy for over ten years.

"I'll get us a taxi," he told Laura. "We have one small piece of business to take care of and then the rest of the day is yours." They held hands like a couple of high school lovers, as they walked through the concourse, to the front doors of the terminal.

Mike handed the driver the address he had written down yesterday, when Belinda called back. In his attaché case, he had an empty small glass jar with a glass cap that screwed onto it. He wasn't taking any chances with this stuff, although most likely it was not the same substance. He had been told, by the University of Minnesota where David Bennet had developed it, that it was never going to be made again. *David Bennett was dead—why would anyone else have the recipe?*

"Look at the houses," Laura said, as they drove by row on row of mansions. "Can you imagine what life was like when they were built?"

"You mean when Bugsy Segal and Al Capone were running Chicago?" Mike asked.

"No, silly. When the roaring twenties was in its heyday and this city was so alive."

Mike wanted to say something, but he smiled and patted Laura's knee. His hand lingered there for a minute, fingering her thigh, but she made no attempt to move it. Instead, she looked in the mirror to see where the driver's eyes were. She loved it when he touched her like that. There had been little time for that in their lives lately. The car pulled into a circular driveway and stopped. The sign said, **Offices of the Chicago Fire Department–District One.**

The meter said $8.18. Mike gave the driver a ten spot and said, "We won't be long but I'm going to pay you now, in case you have to leave. Otherwise, you might wait for us." The driver just gave them a confused look, but nodded his head.

Inside, the Directory on the wall read: **Office of Investigation— Third floor.** They waited for the elevator, still standing side-by-side and hand-in-hand. Mike smiled tenderly at Laura and squeezed her hand. Laura was in awe of the big city; she couldn't wait to get this over with and get on with the day. Mike's business was boring to her.

Belinda wasn't sure what time Flanagan was coming, so she had planned to spend her entire day staying in the office. She did have a lot of paperwork to catch up on. She had thought long and hard last night about what she was doing, involving a fire inspector from another city in this investigation. *Jerry would have a shit-fit if he knew what I was doing,* she thought. *Maybe I am being hasty—there were other ways to find out what this stuff was. But Flanagan had been interested in this from the start, and if he wanted to come here and help her, then what was it hurting? My God, the guy was a legend in fire inspection circles!*

Belinda recognized Mike, through her office window, when he entered the outer office. She had only seen him that one time, but she hadn't forgotten him. But, who was the woman with him? *My God, she looks like Princess Grace,* she thought.

"Mr. Flanagan, thank you for coming." Belinda had met him the minute they entered the door to her office.

Mike smiled and extended his hand. "Mr. Flanagan was my father," he said. "Mike would be more appropriate. Belinda, this is my wife, Laura. We decided to make it a little vacation for both of us."

"Laura, I'm so glad to meet you," she said.

Laura gave her a puzzled smile and said, "Wow, forgive me if I'm somewhat in awe of you—I'm not used to women doing this job. Most of the associates that Mike introduces me to are men."

Belinda laughed. "Yes, that's the pioneer in me," she said.

She had gone behind her desk, and came back with a jar about the size of a baby food jar. "This is the stuff, Mike," she said.

He held it up to the light and gazed at it, then took the cover off and smelled it. It had very little odor, but then, he had never really smelled the real stuff. It was always burned up along with a lot of other things when he had smelled it in the past. "I have a safer bottle I want to put it in," he said. "If the airlines knew about this, they wouldn't want me on their plane, but I couldn't risk having you put it in the mail."

Mike got the little bottle out of his attaché case and transferred the product, except for a few drops, and screwed the glass lid on. "I would like to test what's left in here. Is there an empty lot we could go to?"

"Like a parking lot?" Belinda asked.

"Yes. I'm sure there isn't enough in here to do anything spectacular, but I know how it should act and I need to make sure."

"Let's go to the Fire Training Center," she said. "It's just a mile or so away."

It had turned bitterly cold outside, but it was warm in Belinda's car as they drove down to the training center. Laura sat in the back, while Mike sat up front with Belinda. "So, how's my old friend, Jerry Martin?" Mike asked. "Gosh, it's been a while since I last saw him. In fact, I guess it was the same time that I met you."

Laura sat, deep in thought. *What made a pretty young woman like this get into this business when there were so many good jobs out there?*

"Jerry is doing great," Belinda said. "He had some medical problems, and he has been out for a while, but we're expecting him back soon. I do miss him—the whole department misses him."

"How did you get started in the Fire Department?" Laura interrupted.

"Well, I was a chemical engineering student, who was supposed to be working in their laboratory," she said, talking over her shoulder while she drove. "One thing led to another and here I am."

"Do you like it?" Laura asked.

"I do like it. The hard part is getting accepted in a man's world," she answered. Then, looking at Mike, wished she hadn't said it.

Mike smiled at her. "I know what you're talking about," he said, "and I'm a man."

Mike suggested that Laura that stay in the car, which she was only too happy to do. It was cold out there.

Mike and Belinda went into the first floor of a concrete building that reeked of smoke. The cement walls were black with soot and the light, on the only light bulb shining, tried to get out through the tar and soot on it. "This will do," Mike said. He poured the few remaining drops of liquid on a steel table that was in the room. "You might want to stand back," he said, as he lit a stick match and took a couple of steps back. Just to be safe, Belinda stood behind him.

She watched over his shoulder while he threw the match on the table. There was a blue white flash and it was over. No smoke—no sound.

Mike approached the table and looked down where the few drops of fluid had been. The fire had etched the tabletop and he ran his fingers over it.

"Wow!" Belinda said. They were now standing side-by-side at the table. "All that from those few drops." She remembered the one drop she had burned in the spoon in the lab.

"Yes, imagine what a gallon could do." Mike said. "If it's not the same thing I'm thinking about, it's very close. Professor Rasheed at the University of Minnesota will be able to tell us. I'll get back to you as soon as I know."

"Hey, I was wondering if you could drop Laura and me off at our hotel. It's just down on West Randolph."

Belinda let out a low whistle. "Hotel on Randolph Street. Wow— I'm impressed!"

Mike laughed, "I hope for the price of it, Laura is impressed," he said. *He hoped the cab driver he had told to wait, hadn't waited for them.*

After dropping Mike and Laura off, Belinda drove slowly back to the office, deep in thought. *If this was the same stuff Mike had seen in Minneapolis, where had it come from? Why was it attached to, of all places, a sprinkler pipe and what would be the motive for burning down a public building like the museum? Were there more of these devices out there? So many questions and so few answers.*

The traffic was barely moving and she draped her arm over the steering wheel, waiting impatiently for the light to change. She was thinking about Flanagan right now. *Why did he have such an interest in this case? To pack his bags and come here just to help her out was one thing; yes, he had brought his wife and maybe they were making some kind of a holiday out of it, but at the same time, he seemed deeply interested—too deeply interested.*

For the rest of the day, Mike and Laura walked the streets of downtown Chicago, taking in the sights and shopping. It was a lot like Minneapolis, but on a far bigger scale, with totally different stores. By five, they were exhausted, and they made their way back to their hotel. They still held hands as they walked, burdened down with packages. Life for them had been just one great adventure after another. From the humble beginnings, when they had fallen in love in that house on Dumont back in Minneapolis, and then parted—to the day they found each other again, they wanted nothing more than to be sure they would never be parted again.

"Let's just have supper in our room," Laura said. "I'm too tired to get dressed up to go out."

"You're the boss, babe," Mike said. Actually, he was happy with the suggestion.

They ordered up a seafood platter and a bottle of wine. They left the drapes open so they could enjoy the ambiance of the city lights. They laughed and giggled and fed each other shrimp, sitting on the bed in their underwear, giddy from the wine. At last, they lay back in each other's arms and slowly, the underwear was peeled away. As they had done so many times before, they explored once more the dark recesses of each other's bodies and minds until, at last, the time was so right and Mike slowly and tenderly made love once more to this beautiful woman he adored so much. Afterward, they lay still in each other's arms, looking at the lights and listening to the bustle of the city below them—content in their thoughts. Laura's were about her family and Christmas. Mike's were about the contents of a small glass jar hidden away in his attaché case.

CHAPTER SIXTEEN

MIKE LOCKED THE JAR UP in a fireproof safe over the holidays. He had wanted to get it analyzed the day he returned to Minneapolis but Rasheed had gone back to the Middle East for the holidays to be with his family. There were very few Christians in his country and it was time for him to be together with his family. As for Mike, he wanted nobody but Rasheed to test it. He had to be sure.

The Christmas holiday has a way of making all of its participants put things off until after the festivities, and it was no different for Mike, or for Belinda, even though five hundred miles of land between the two great cities separated them.

For Mike, it was three days off and time with his family; a time to be thankful for all that they had. They had a quiet Christmas Eve with the kids and then, on Christmas Day, with a fresh coating of snow on the ground, they went cross-country skiing in Theodore Wirth Park in North Minneapolis. Mike always remembered the days he and Laura had spent there before they were married. Back in those carefree, youthful days when the world could do no wrong and every day was just another adventure. Then he thought of the time when he had lost Laura, and the years he had searched for her, and how it had all come back together that day at that laboratory where she worked. Life had been so good for him since then.

She turned and smiled at him as they followed the kids through the park, on their skies. "I love you," she smiled. He sped up and tackled her and they both went down in a cloud of snow. He pinned her down and kissed her—a long, lingering kiss, interrupted by Cindy's voice saying, "Oh, please. Get a room, you two!"

They got up, giggling, and brushing themselves off. Mike threw a snowball at Cindy and she shrieked and took off after her brother and sister. *When I grow up*, she thought. *I want to be just like my parents.*

For Belinda, the holiday was a time with her baby and her mother. Maybe she still had the problems of work in the back of her mind but at the moment, it just didn't seem that important. After all, it was Christmas. The two women took baby Sam and went on a holiday to Southern Illinois for a couple of days. They rented a room at a bed and breakfast and just enjoyed being together at this time. But always, in Belinda's mind, was the missing part of the puzzle that would complete her life, a man who would love both her and Sam.

Two men did not enjoy the Christmas Holiday, however. They were Jerry Martin and David Bennett.

Jerry had been told that his recovery was progressing well, but he would not be released until late January at the earliest. On Christmas Eve, Noreen and the boys came and had supper with him. Jerry had no money and no opportunity to buy gifts so, in some ways, the holiday only served to sadden him more. He remembered some fun Christmases he, Noreen, and the boys had had. That was before things had gone to hell in a hand basket.

Noreen smiled at him and held his hand while the boys watched the little black and white television in his room. They walked down the hallway, to a quiet corner that had a couple of over-stuffed chairs, and sat down.

"I hope we can make the best of this, Jerry. I have given it a lot of thought, and I want us to try and be a family again. When you get out, I want you to come home again to your family. Let's try it for a year and then, if everything works well, let's get married again. I do love you, you old lunk, and I haven't been able to find any younger guys." She laughed at her attempt at humor and Jerry laughed with her.

He got out of his chair and knelt beside hers and took her chin in his hand. He kissed her softly, his tears spilling over and running down his cheeks. "Thank you," he said. "It's the best Christmas present I could wish for. I won't disappoint you or the boys."

She looked back at him and then, running her hands through his hair said, "We both made mistakes, Jerry. You had problems, but I gave up on you way too early. I want you back in my life. In our lives," she corrected herself. Then they put their heads together and held each other, and they both cried.

David Bennett didn't believe in God or any higher deity. His only

God was the fire he loved to make. Christmas was to him a time when a group of self-absorbing people, who called themselves Christians, celebrated their mysterious God because they needed a reason to party. They nauseated him with their behavior. Maybe when the city burned this October, they would have a chance to call on their God and see if he could save them. For now, he was content to wait until the day came, and then he would be the Supreme Being who would control their destiny.

He would bring the one remaining barrel of petrocyclomate back to the house, and clean out the warehouse, later. He was dissolving the business altogether. He had enough money to last him until the time came for the big fire. He would sell the warehouse building, his trucks and remaining pipe and fittings. That would bring him some added income. He had contracts with the businesses until the end of the year and he would honor them from his home. It would be minimal maintenance at most. There wasn't a lot to go wrong with a sprinkler system.

There were only two glitches he could imagine interrupting his diabolical deed. One meant one of the buildings having an accidental fire, but it would have to happen in the one zone he had chosen to use, and that was highly unlikely.

The other concern was those nosey fire inspectors from the Chicago fire. He hoped that what had happened over on the East Side, with that apartment fire, was now a dead issue. It had appeared that way the day he met with that puss inspector about the clamp on the pipe. The thought of her questioning him brought a new round of anger, and he punched another hole in the sheetrock wall he was standing next to. Calming down a little, he thought, *Anyway, the building was now torn down and being rebuilt and it was too late for them to probe into it any further.* He had been by there yesterday to see what the progress was. At one point, he had wanted to put the sprinkler system in the new building but backed off on the idea, and didn't bid on the job. *What good would it do? The building was way outside of the area that he wanted to burn. He didn't need, or want, the business or the exposure, and it was time to fade into the shadows—at least until October.*

Delmont Rasheed was back in his classroom writing out formulas on a white board that Tuesday morning after Christmas when Mike Flanagan stopped by. It had been warm and comforting to see his family in Syria; warm weather and, yes, a warm reception from a large, extended family. He was a hero to all of them for going to America and making something of himself. It was their dream also, but not a realistic one anymore. Delmont had distinguished himself among his peers and his family was very proud of him.

"Professor Rasheed," Mike said as he crossed the room with his hand extended. "I hope I'm not interrupting anything."

"No, No!" he said. "Come in, come in. Class doesn't start for half an hour. I haven't seen you for some time, my friend. How have you been?"

"Good," Mike said. "And yourself?"

"Well, I just got back from Syria, where I went for the holidays. It's always good to see family you don't get to see very often. How was your holiday?"

"I had a wonderful Christmas," Mike said.

The pleasantries out of the way, Rasheed's gaze went to the bottle Mike was cradling in his hands. "What do we have here?" he said.

"Well, I'm not sure, but I was hoping you could tell me. Do you remember the arsonist we had back in sixty-five that was using some kind of volatile fluid that was developed by accident, right here in your labs?"

"I do," he said. "Not sure if it was an accident, but go on."

"Well, I think this fluid is being made again and I just wanted you to analyze it and see if you concur."

"You mean someone is starting fires with it again?" Rasheed had a puzzled look on his face.

"Well, maybe," Mike said. "At least they're trying."

Rasheed had gone to a file cabinet and was pouring over some old notes. At last, he stopped and took a few sheets of paper out.

Mike stood waiting for him, the bottle still in his hands.

"Ah yes," he said. "Petrocyclomate. Very nasty stuff indeed, Inspector," and pointing to the bottle, "you think that is the same thing?"

"Not sure," Mike said, holding the bottle out to him. "But I would like to find out."

Rasheed took the bottle from him and uncapped it. Cautiously, he smelled it, and then put the cap back on. "It will take me a few days," he said. "I do know this about the product; it has been refined and made by a company in Texas. I think they were going to use it in some kind of incendiary bombs during the Vietnam War; but it was too unstable, so they scrapped that idea. I also know they experimented with leaving out one key ingredient, and then it had about the same explosive potential as alcohol. Not sure if they ever found an application for it, however. My student who created this, wasn't he killed in a fire in Minneapolis?"

"Yes." Mike said. "I was there the day he died. I don't think he has any way of being connected to this, but that's not saying someone else couldn't, right?"

"Right you are, inspector. Let me look into it and I'll get back to you."

Mike gave Rasheed his card and they shook hands. "Good to see you again," Rasheed said.

"The same to you," Mike said.

Outside, in the bright sunlit but cold, crisp air, a whole flood of memories washed over him regarding David Bennett. *He never wanted to see someone like that again,* he mused. *Now it was time to get to work.*

With the turning of the New Year, everyone went back to their nine-to-five jobs, and the days slipped quickly by. Belinda was busy working on a new inspection process that had been initiated last year, but was just going into law now. It involved much more paperwork than they had before, and more inspections of businesses to update preplan books. It had been found that a lot of businesses had been sold, and turned into something more than what the Fire Department was aware of. As an example, a building that was a floral store was now found to be a battery outlet. Firemen needed to know, before they got there, what was in a burning building. The responsibility to provide that information fell on the Inspection Department. So, in the process of preplanning, arson investigating took a back seat. She was interested in the results of Flanagan's tests on the liquid, but had no way of knowing how long they would take, so she didn't press.

Flanagan, back in Minneapolis, was still waiting on results of the tests from Rasheed. He hadn't forgotten about them but right now, he too was very busy, and the results, when they did come in, lay on Rasheed's desk for about ten days.

Finally, on Monday, January 19th, Mike called Professor Rasheed.

"Professor, I was wondering if you ever got back any results on that liquid you sent in for me for testing. This is Mike Flanagan, from Minneapolis Fire."

"Mike. I must apologize, my friend. I got caught up in a new semester here and, yes, I did get those results several days ago and I have been meaning to call you. I am so very sorry."

"No—no, that's okay. I should have called sooner but I got waylaid here, too."

"Well, in answer to your question," the professor said. "Yes, it is the same stuff. I did some other digging around for you, and I found out that the refinery that manufactured it didn't make it complete. They left out a key ingredient—the very ingredient that makes it so volatile. It had to have been added later, by whoever bought the product."

"Were you able to find out who that was?" Mike asked.

"Yes, I did find that out. It was sold to another refinery here in the Twin Cities. What they did with it, they aren't saying to me, but I have a phone number for you. Maybe they will talk to you."

"Ready to write it down." Mike said.

The refinery was in the Twin Cities area, but it wasn't in the city of Minneapolis. Mike was going to go out there, anyway, and see what they would tell him, even though he had little jurisdiction outside of the city. He had thought about calling them and saving the trip out there, but it was his past experience that saying, "no" over the phone, was much easier for people than a face-to-face. Mike didn't have much of a case to be made for them to give him personal information but if worse came to worse, he might be able to get the local authorities involved. He just hoped it wouldn't come to that.

The weather had turned bad in Minneapolis and snow had been falling heavily for several hours. It was just another typical Minnesota winter and the weather could blow up bad, or be a winter wonderland. It just depended on the day and your attitude. Today, his car seemed to slide all over the road and he was having second thoughts about the decision he had made to drive way out to this refinery. An hour later, he pulled in and parked in the visitor's lot.

He stood in the lot and looked at all of the gleaming towers, and miles and miles of pipe that snaked around the refinery. Off to his left, one impressive tower had a flame coming out of the top and going about a hundred feet up in the air. Although it was a ways off, the flame could be heard like a jet engine in the cold winter air. There was a putrid petro chemical smell in the air, also. A lot, across from the lot he was parked in, had quite a few tanker trucks sitting quietly, in the process of being loaded.

Inside the building, however, it was just another office building and another environment. Mike stopped at the receptionist desk and introduced himself. "Hi, I have an appointment to talk with Blake Turner. I'm Mike Flanagan, with the Minneapolis Fire Department."

She smiled and said. "I'll page Blake for you, if you want to have a seat."

The visitor's area was decorated with the logos of many oil companies and some pictures from days gone by in the petroleum industry. Mike was standing and looking at a picture of an old oil well installation with a wooden derrick, somewhere in Pennsylvania, when he heard footsteps behind him and turned to meet an elderly gentleman dressed in a three-piece suit. "Hi, I'm Blake Turner. How can I help you?"

Blake Turner was much older than he had sounded on the phone, but he had a firm handshake and a jovial attitude.

"Anyone out traveling around on a day like this must have some serious business," he chuckled. "How can I help you?"

"Well, we're trying to track down a chemical shipment that came to this refinery about ten years ago from Beaumont, Texas. It was two hundred barrels of something called petrocyclomate. Does that ring a bell?"

"No, but let's walk over to recordkeeping and maybe they can ring that bell for us," he said.

Mike and Blake stood and made small talk about the weather and the economy, while a young woman looked up the information on a microfilm machine.

Finally, looking confused, she said, "The only thing I have from Beaumont for that year is not called petrocyclomate, but there was about two hundred barrels of it."

"What was it called," Blake asked, putting his hand on her

shoulder—which she didn't seem to be real comfortable with, turning and looking briefly at him. She pointed to the screen with her index finger and Blake wrote it down on a scrap of paper.

"Thanks, Ruby," he said.

They walked out into the hallway and Blake turned and faced Mike, more serious now than he had been. "What is it you need to know about this shipment?" he asked.

"Was it petrocyclomate?" Mike asked.

"Almost, I think. I might have to do some research on what petrocyclomate really is. I'm not real familiar with that product, but I do remember hearing about it. It might take me a day or two, if that's all right."

Mike shrugged his shoulders. "No big hurry," he said. "Can you call me when you find out?"

"Sure, I'll call you someday this week. I might have to call Beaumont and getting to the right people down there isn't always easy."

They shook hands and said their goodbyes. Mike pulled up his collar and stepped back outside. It was time to call it a day. He wasn't sure why he was doing all of this for a woman called Belinda, five hundred miles away, but then, on second thought, *it wasn't about her, it was about petrocyclomate and some very bad memories of a man called David Bennett.*

CHAPTER SEVENTEEN

IT WAS WEDNESDAY AFTERNOON WHEN Mike heard back from Blake and the refinery. "I'm not sure if this is going to be much help for you, Inspector, but here is what I was able to find out. The two hundred barrels of chemical that came here to our refinery was not petrocyclomate, but it easily could have been made into it. Basically, it wasn't much more volatile than wood alcohol in the form we got it. We were supposed to destroy it if we couldn't use it for other things, but then we got an inquiry on it and, in November of that year, we were able to sell it to a firm in Chicago."

"That year was what year?" Mike asked.

"1965," Blake answered.

After David Bennett's death, Mike thought. "What was the name of the firm in Chicago that bought the stuff?"

Mike heard papers being shuffled during a brief pause, "Knowlton Sprinkler Company." Blake answered.

"Any contact person?" Mike asked.

"The name we have is David Boston."

It was as if he had been hit in the head with a nerf ball. The name instantly got his attention but the impact wasn't great enough to make the connection. *David Boston—where had he heard that name before?* "Thanks, Blake," Mike said. "You've been a great help."

"You're welcome," he said. "There is one other thing that may or may not be any help to you. The buyer asked that the barrels used for shipping be acid barrels. They certainly weren't necessary for the product."

"What are acid barrels?" Mike asked.

"They're glass-lined barrels. They're often used for corrosive products that eat through metal or plastic. Very expensive packaging," he added.

Mike thanked Blake. He couldn't get off the phone fast enough to get to his files. He'd just remembered who David Boston was—or, at least, who he used to be.

Belinda sat wide-eyed, listening to Mike Flanagan. Jerry was right, there was more to this than met the eye and she couldn't wait to go see him tonight. He was in his last week of treatment and it sure would be good to have him back. Maybe, with Jerry gone, she should have involved some other people from their department in this investigation. She really had no expertise in what she was doing right now but it had been thrust on her, and it wasn't what she had been hired to do for this department. She was a chemical engineer—not a fire inspector—and not one who was interested in putting up with all of the harassment and crap she had gotten out in the field from this male-dominated department.

"So you think that this has some connection to Knowlton Sprinklers?" she asked.

"I'm not sure," Mike answered. "But why else would they buy up a product like that?" Mike had another reason for being concerned about this whole thing, but right now he was still trying to sort that out. *He had been there when they buried David Bennett, alias David Boston, so how could*—he didn't want to even think about it.

"Look, tell Jerry to call me when he gets back and let's talk about this."

"I will," she said, "and thanks for the information."

Jerry was in the homestretch now, and he was doing everything he could to shave even one day off of his incarceration. *He had to admit, for the first time in a long time, his mind was fresh and clear. Not that he didn't still crave a good beer—that urge would always be with him—but he had his head screwed on right now and his priorities were back where they belonged, with family and his job.* He had told the staff about him and Noreen getting back together again. They could see in his face the happiness it was already bringing him when Noreen and the boys visited. A member of the staff had even offered him a conjugal visit with Noreen, if she approved, but he turned it down. *Not that he didn't want her again in that way, he did. He just wanted her in their bed again and that could wait six more days.*

He had also talked with Holbrook, his supervisor at work, and they were anxiously awaiting his return. Belinda was coming to see him this afternoon, and he was hoping she could bring him up-to-snuff on what had been going on in the investigation.

It was a little after three when Belinda walked down the hall to Jerry's room. He was sitting on the bed reading the paper when she knocked lightly and came in, handing him some new magazines. "Hi, buddy," she said.

Jerry jumped down from the bed and said, "Let's go down to the cafeteria and get some coffee." With coffee in hand, they found a couple of chairs off in the corner, where they could talk without being overheard.

"We're really looking forward to getting you back," she said.

"I'm looking forward to being back. Not sure if you knew it, but Noreen and I are going to try and make a go of it again."

"I'm so happy for you, Jerry," she said, squeezing his hand. "To be family again."

"Yes," he said. "A chance to be family again. So what's been going on at work I should know about?"

"Well," she wasn't sure where to begin, but it was now or never. "You remember that device I found at the museum, strapped to the sprinkler pipe?"

"I do," he said, talking a swig of coffee and looking at her over the top of the cup. "Yeah, what came of that?"

"Well, I wasn't able to identify what was in that glass tube, but it bore a striking resemblance to something that Minneapolis Inspector talked about when you and I saw him at the seminar last fall."

"You mean Flanagan?"

"Yes. So I called him to talk about it and it just so happened that he and his wife were coming to Chicago for a couple of days, so he stopped by. Well, long story short, we went to the training center and did a test on some of it. Mind you, Jerry, just a few drops. I have never seen anything explode like that stuff did."

"So he thought it was the same stuff?"

"Well, better than that. He took it back to the University of Minnesota where it was developed and had them analyze it."

Jerry had set his coffee down and was now listening intently. Belinda was waiting for him to come unglued like he usually did when she did something wrong, but instead, he seemed to be all ears. Maybe she had done the right thing in his eyes, for once.

"So what was the verdict?'

"It was the same stuff, Jerry, and we found something else out, also. Two hundred barrels of it was sold to Knowlton Sprinkler Company here in Chicago."

Jerry stood up and clapped his hands. "I knew it," he said. "Something stinks with that company, Belinda, and we need to get to the bottom of it. When I get back on Monday we're going to get that guy you talked to about that clamp back in here. That bastard!" he said disgustedly, pounding one hand into the other. "You need to call him," he said, "but don't alarm him or he won't show up. Make up some other excuse."

"Like what?" she asked.

"Use your imagination. Tell him we have some new rules and regulations. Anything so we can corner him. We can't have him arrested for anything yet; we don't have enough evidence. It's a shot in the dark, I know, but I have a hunch it might work."

"Look, not a word about this to anyone. This could be big stuff, my little friend. Two hundred barrels of it! Holy shit, what did he have planned?"

"Jerry, there was less than six ounces of it in that glass tube."

Jerry had walked over and now, squatting in front of her as she was still sitting in the chair, he put his hands on her knees. He had never looked more serious. "That glass tube was meant to start a fire, Belinda. It was meant to light off something bigger." He had lowered his voice, and now he looked around to make sure no one was within earshot. "I'm betting there is more close by. When was the last time you talked to Flanagan?"

"Yesterday," she said.

"Any chance you could get him back here? I'd like to talk some more about this with him. The guy's good with this stuff, Belinda. He's like a legend in the industry."

"I'll call him in the morning," she said. "What's today...Tuesday? When do you want him here?"

"Next Monday, if he can be."

Jerry stood up and took her hand as she also stood. "How's Sam?" he asked.

"Getting big," she smiled.

"Thanks for coming and thanks for doing such a good job while I was gone."

They dropped their hands and Jerry walked her to the front door. "See you Monday," he said.

She was going straight home from the hospital, but for some reason, the drive tonight was shorter and happier. She had been afraid Jerry would be mad at her for involving some other agency, but apparently, she had made the right decision.

Mike Flanagan had the whole David Bennett file spread out on his desk. He was confused and perplexed right now. David Bennett was dead, right? He thought about having the body exhumed, just to make sure, but that took a court order and he had no grounds for that. That would have to come from the Chicago department—if it was going to come at all. He read the coroner's report in front of him again, from way back in 1965, but nowhere in it had they been able to establish that it had been David Bennett for sure. It was just a bunch of circumstantial evidence. There had been very little left of the body after the fire, and after ten years, there would be a lot less left of it—he was sure of that.

The fires had stopped after that day he supposedly died, and that seemed to be the best piece of evidence they had that David Bennett was dead. If he wasn't dead, he wasn't working anymore, that was for sure, at least not in Minneapolis. He thought back to that day in the parking ramp when he had been chasing Bennett. *How could he have possibly escaped him? It was impossible. He had seen him going in that elevator through the half-closed door. Mike remembered it like it was yesterday. He remembered throwing that switch and stopping the elevator. He remembered the elevator repairman shouting at him, then showing him his badge to calm him down, and then the subsequent explosion and fire. What could he be missing? This was going to drive him wacky, even though it wasn't his problem.*

On Wednesday morning, Belinda made the call to Mike Flanagan. Mike had just gotten in to work after a long night at an apartment fire in the uptown area on the South side. It had looked like a fire that had been started by the absentee owner for insurance purposes. The building was mostly empty, and the fire was suspicious. There was a lot of this going on with the economy the way it was right now. He was still getting off his coveralls when the receptionist hailed him from the other room, and told him he had a call from Chicago Fire.

"This is Flanagan," he said.

"Hi. This is Belinda Clayton. How are things with you today?"

"Good—I think. What can I do for you?"

"Well, I had a conversation with Jerry Martin yesterday. He's coming back to work next Monday, and he is very concerned about the fluid I gave you, and the person who is using it. Mike, he wanted me to ask you if you could come to Chicago someday next week to bang heads with us on this?"

Mike was flipping through the calendar on his desk as he listened to Belinda. *Yes, he was more than interested in going to Chicago. He almost felt as if he had a vested interest in the case. It was almost naïve to think that no one else could come up with this formula, but his gut told him that wasn't the case here. His gut had been wrong before, but not often.*

"So what day would be best for you?" Mike said.

"Jerry would like to tackle it first thing Monday morning, if you could?"

"Okay, Monday morning it is. At your office?" he asked.

"If that works for you." Belinda could not believe it had been this easy. She couldn't wait to call Jerry—maybe she would stop by and see him in person after work tonight.

"Thanks for getting him to come up here," Jerry said, "and thanks for stopping by. I wish you and I could handle this ourselves, kid, but I know this guy can help us and I want to wrap this case up as soon as possible. Did I tell you I'm getting out of here a couple of days early?"

"No," Belinda said. "Did you twist some arms?"

Jerry laughed. "No, but I'm glad it happened. I've learned my lesson and it will help to have some time with my family before I come to work. Noreen and I have a lot of healing to do."

"I'm happy for you, Jerry. I wish I had a man to even argue with."

"You will, kid. You will. You're too hot a commodity to last for long on the open market."

"Gee—Thanks, Jerry. I never thought of myself as a commodity, but I think I'm honored—maybe."

Jerry laughed and patted her on the back. Suddenly his mood sobered. "As long as we have Flanagan coming Monday, let's get that guy from Knowlton's in here on Monday, too. Think that's possible?"

David sat staring at the phone, mad and deep in thought. He had no desire to meet with her again. *Hadn't he answered all of her stupid questions the day they met at the apartment building? He had the option of just ignoring her now but that would draw attention to him and he didn't need that. At least right now, he didn't.* Her phone call had caught him completely off-guard. He hated meeting with these people, and especially on their turf. *Well, this would be the last time,* he thought. *After this, they would have to find him. If she wasn't alone, when he got there Monday morning, he would just leave and they would never see him again.*

Belinda hadn't mentioned anything about the device they had removed, or the clamps. She had taken Jerry's suggestion and told him they were trying to update their records and they were calling in all of their sprinkler installers to go over some new rules and regulations.

David didn't take the bait whole-heartedly though, explaining that he was getting out of the business and it was up for sale.

"You will need to do this before you can sell the business," She said. "It's that, or the new owner will never get licensed by the city." She hoped he didn't have any other questions. *She was getting in way too deep and she had never been a good liar,* she thought.

.

CHAPTER EIGHTEEN

FLANAGAN HAD GOTTEN UP IN the middle of the night to head for the airport. He peeked in on the kids, like he used to when they were babies. Cindy's light was still on and she was sleeping with an open book on her chest. Mike carefully took the book and put it on her nightstand. He clicked off the lamp, but not before he kissed his fingers and touched her forehead. *My God, she was beautiful, just like her mother,* he thought. Carefully, he closed her door.

He didn't go in the other children's rooms. They were just lumps under covers in their beds.

He grabbed his attaché case and his overcoat and then, setting them on the kitchen table, he walked back to the bedroom and bending over, kissed Laura softly.

"Have a good flight, sweetheart," she said.

"Love you," he replied, and kissed her once more. *I'd better hurry—my plane is leaving in an hour,* he thought, as he looked at his watch.

The drive to the airport was uneventful, but each corner, each neighborhood, took him past memories of fires and emergencies that had happened in this city he loved so much. There had been a time when David Bennett had threatened this town so many times and now there was a new David Bennett in another city. If he could help stop him—well, he felt he just had to.

Jerry rolled over and looked at the clock. Noreen was sleeping soundly yet, so he slipped quietly out of bed. They had made love last night into the wee hours of the morning. Trying to catch up for all of the times they had missed, yes, but more so, trying to renew their love for each other. *I learned my lesson,* Jerry thought. *I had the world by the short hairs and I let it all slip away. It won't happen again.*

Softly, he padded to the bathroom and the shower. Today was his first day back to work and he wanted to emerge as a new Jerry, at work, as well as at home. They didn't live far from the elevated trains and he felt the rumble of the passing train long before he heard it. Thousands of workers, heading downtown to bring the city back to life after the weekend. Today, he would join them, and it felt so good.

The water was hot in the shower, and his eyes were closed tightly as he let the hot stream pound onto his head, trying to erase the sleep that still lingered. For a brief second, he felt a wave of cold again. He opened his eyes to see why, and Noreen stepped out of the mist and into the shower with him, wrapping her arms around him. "No sense wasting water," she said.

Jerry was almost giddy. He never dreamed that, the day they committed him, people would hang with him the way they had; his boss, and Belinda, for sure, but most of all, his wife and family. Last night, watching television with his sons, knowing he didn't have to get up and go home, or they didn't have to leave—well, he couldn't put it in words how good it felt. Noreen had clung to him last night after they finished their lovemaking. It was as if she never wanted him to leave her again; as if she couldn't get close enough. He had made a terrible mistake, letting his drinking come between them. For a long time he had blamed her for the divorce, but really, it was a no-brainer. He had left her no choice. "Did the boys see me the day you found me in the apartment?" he had asked her in the hospital.

She shook her head. "They would never have been able to forget that day, Jerry. Now you must let me forget it." She had said. "Let's not talk about that issue again."

He looked around him on the train. *Had anyone seen him wipe the tears from his eyes? Well, too bad if they did—they were good tears.* The train stopped at his station. He would have a city car to take home tonight.

Belinda had a skip in her step this morning, also. Jerry was back and now she didn't have to make those kinds of decisions any longer. She would be the best attagirl he ever had working for him, she just didn't want the lead.

His flight had been uneventful, and Mike stared out the window at the Chicago skyline. *A city this big never sleeps,* he thought. *It just relaxes enough to get ready for another day. Like a napping dog, one eye still half-open.* He gave the cabbie a twenty and stepped out on the sidewalk in front of the Fire Department offices. It would be great to see Jerry again. It had been a long time, and over the years they had shared so many thoughts and theories, almost always from afar. But they always made an attempt to get together face-to-face at conferences and seminars to just socialize for awhile. Business was business, but you had to take time to talk about life now and then. He looked at his watch; it was five to nine.

David almost blew the whole thing off. He could feel the pressure tightening around him even though he had no facts to support that. But he was suspicious; he didn't trust any of these people. He had spent way too much time and money perfecting this plan and he wasn't going to have it come apart at the seams. At the last minute he relented, and said to himself, *No, he had to follow through. Fear could make you paranoid sometimes, and he would be cautiously watching their every move and word, but for now, this had to be part of the plan. Not one he had intended, but part of it just the same. For him not to cooperate right now—well, that would be suspicious.*

He parked his truck in a ramp about a block away and sat for a few minutes with the engine idling. It was almost nine and he didn't want to seem overeager. He wanted to go into their office, answer their questions, listen to what they had to say and then be out of there. His gray pickup was just another truck now, as he had removed the decals and taken the pipe racks and tool boxes out of the back of it. He smoked a cigarette as he tried to anticipate what was going to be happening today. Then he flipped it out the window and exited, walking towards the Fire Department offices.

Mike saw Belinda first; coming down the hall with a cup of coffee in one hand and a stack of papers under her other arm. Her face lit up as she saw him. "Well, hi, stranger," she said to Mike as he walked towards her. She tried to extend her hand with the papers in it, but some of them slid out from under her arm and fell to the floor. Mike rushed to help her pick them up.

"Sorry about that," Mike said.

"No, no, it's not your fault. Jerry is going to be so happy to see you and I am so happy to see you, too. Poor guy has been here for an hour, raring to go like a kindergartner on the first day of school."

"Well, I'm also curious as to what you have going on here," Mike replied. "The guy that we had using this stuff was just a total nut case. Let's hope we don't have something similar here…" Mike's voice trailed off and his face bore an expression of astonishment. He was looking over Belinda's right shoulder at a man limping up the hallway towards them.

Belinda noticed Mike's expression and frozen gaze, and turned to see what he was looking at. It was at that moment that David recognized Mike. For a second he froze and then, realizing that this had to be a trap, he turned and took off back around the corner, the way he had come from.

Mike didn't react at first; he couldn't believe he had seen whom he had seen. Stuffing the papers he had in his hands back in Belinda's arm, and leaving his attaché case, he took off in the direction that David had gone. David knew he would be followed and, crippled as he was, he would be no match in a foot race. He ducked into the first office door he could find. Luck was with him as the office was empty. The door had a window in it and he saw Flanagan go by and disappear down the stairs to the outside.

Mike took the stair steps two-at-a-time, nearly knocking over a package man that was coming in. "Did you see someone leaving in a hurry?" he asked him, visibly shaken.

"No, you seem to be the only one in a hurry, buddy. Slow down before you hurt someone."

Outside on the sidewalk, he glanced both ways, but no one of interest was there. Belinda appeared beside him, looking very puzzled at what had happened, still clutching all of her papers and his attaché case.

"What did you see?" she asked.

"A ghost from the past," Mike answered.

David had left the office he was hiding in just after Belinda walked by. He then walked down the hall the opposite way until he came to the Fire Inspection Offices. He nodded and said, "Good morning," to

Jerry, who was just coming out to check on Belinda, who was overdue. David went to the right, past the office and towards a set of doors marked Exit.

Outside, David had no idea where he was at the moment, but he knew he was in an alley. He followed the alley to the next street and he was back in familiar territory. The ramp, with his truck, was just at the end of the block. He walked briskly, but not so fast as to draw attention, knowing with his funny limp he stuck out like a sore thumb. He, too, was visibly shaken. Shaken, because the man he hated the most had seemed to appear out of nowhere. It had been ten years but he would remember that face for the rest of his life. He had recognized him immediately, and he had also seen the Minneapolis Emblem on the pocket of his blazer. Right now, he needed to get out of the area and home, where he could think. *But wait—would home be safe? They could connect the dots now that he had been identified. His name wasn't in the phone book, but Knowlton Sprinklers was. They must have found one of his devices, but how did that bring Flanagan to the scene? He had to get home and clear out as fast as he could.*

"I think it's time you get the police involved," Mike was saying to Jerry and Belinda. "There is no telling what this guy might do."

"I thought he was dead." Jerry remarked, with a questioning look on his face.

"I thought so, too," Mike answered.

"Are you sure that it was..."

"Yes," Mike answered. "I could never forget that face."

Belinda had been quiet the whole time. "It was the man from Knowlton Sprinklers, who met with me," she said.

Jerry lifted the phone and asked for the police operator. "Can I get an all-points out right away?" he asked. "Belinda, do you have his address?"

"The name is David Bennett," he added.

"No, but I have his phone number," Belinda said, "No, wait." She ran to her desk and rummaged through a side drawer and came out with a business card. "This is the card he gave me when he met with me."

The card said, **Knowlton Sprinklers, New Construction and Maintenance of Fire Sprinkler Systems**. It listed an address in South Chicago of 7649 Charlton Road.

Jerry relayed the information to the operator and heard her put it out over the air. "If they catch him, what do you want him charged with?" she asked dryly.

Jerry looked at Mike, who had been listening. "Suspicion of arson," Mike said.

"Did you copy that?" asked Jerry.

"Gotcha. I'll call you if they find him."

CHAPTER NINETEEN

DAVID CAREENED INTO HIS DRIVEWAY, his tires squealing and scratching for traction, and came to an abrupt and grimy stop at the back door. There wasn't much in the house he needed before he left, but there was one blue barrel in the warehouse that he had to get out of there.

He tried to think. *First things first. He would load the barrel into the back of the truck. It would be sitting in a special padded harness and clamping system he had devised to keep the glass liners from breaking when he hauled them. He had transported all of them this way without a problem, but right now he was guessing the cops were on the way to his house, so he had to take care of business here first and fast.*

He grabbed some clothing and some papers he wanted to keep. At the last second before he left, he looked at his beloved cat, Sampson, sitting on the end of his bed. He wouldn't be able to care for him where he was going. He picked the cat up and stroked his fur; Sampson purred and then screeched as David snapped the cat's neck. He laid his lifeless body on the bed and then, going out to the porch, got a small can of gas and poured the contents over the bed. Looking at the room one last time with its maps on the wall, and boxes of porn and newspaper clippings sitting everywhere, David walked out, flipping a burning disposable lighter into the room just before closing the door. It lit with a loud whoosh, which shook the small house.

The truck engine roared once more and he was gone, out of the driveway and heading for the warehouse, a short distance away. His mind was racing. *He had gone into this survivor mode before back in Minneapolis and had lived, and he would succeed this time, too,* he thought. *He just had to be cautious, but time was short and of the essence. They would come to the house first to catch him, but then it wouldn't take long for them to come to the warehouse.*

The barrel of petrocyclomate sat in the far corner of the tin building—like a lonely sentinel amongst the racks of pipe and boxes of hardware. He backed the truck up to it and then, using an overhead chain hoist, he cautiously lifted it into the vehicle box. Clamped securely in place in its harness, he slowly backed outside and then parked outside of the small office. He fished under the seat of the truck and came out with a rubber ball, about the size of a soccer ball, and a long syringe. Not since his days back in Minneapolis had he done this. It brought back good memories.

David crawled into the back of the truck and, opening the cap on the end of the barrel, he withdrew some of the clear fluid. He repeated the process several times, injecting the fluid into the ball through the rubber grommet meant to fill it with air, until it was about half-full. Then, carefully, he took it in and placed it on his desk. He fished through a file cabinet and came out with a small candle in a saucer. *How many times had he sat at this desk in the dark and watched that flickering flame. It was such a tiny flame but it had much potential with just a little help,* he mused.

He lit the candle and set it about a foot away from the ball. When the fluid ate its way through the ball it would meet the burning candle and then—well, it would be so beautiful and, if he was lucky, maybe some cops would be in the building when it went off.

Back in the truck, he slowly drove out of the driveway and headed south. He had no idea where he was going, but right now he had to get out of the Chicago area.

Mike, Belinda and Jerry raced along the expressway, weaving in and out of traffic, the siren on the old car blaring, heading for Bennett's house. The police should be there any second and they could only hope—so was Bennett. Mike had gotten over his initial shock of seeing the man he had feared more than any person on earth seemingly resurrected, but he still couldn't believe it was true.

His thoughts went back to that day, some ten years ago, when Bennett had dashed through those elevator doors. Mike had relived that moment in his mind a thousand times. *He could still smell the acidic stench of the body in the burnt-out elevator car. He had seen him going in, and how he ever escaped was still a mystery. But the puzzle was starting to come together now that he thought about it. There had been a time just a few weeks ago when he thought, theoretically, it could have happened that Bennett survived. It just seemed so far-fetched, but now when he thought about it, there had been no way to positively identify the charred remains.* He had tried, with the little circumstantial evidence left, but that was all they had back then. Now, he understood why the courts didn't have much faith in it in other cases.

Jerry slid the car sideways for a second as a motorcycle had stopped suddenly in front of them, but he quickly regained control and went to the left into a clear lane. Mike took a deep breath and pulled his hands away from the dash where he had braced himself. He looked up in the rearview mirror; Belinda was nowhere to be seen as she had hit the floor, fearing the impact.

Just then, the radio crackled and the dispatcher came on. "The police are on the scene there, Inspector, but it looks like he torched the house and left. I've called the closest station to put it out but the officer says it's really cooking."

They were still a few minutes off but they could see the smoke cloud off to the east. "Did he work out of his home?" Mike asked.

Jerry shook his head. "No, I don't think so," he said. "He lived in a residential area. Belinda, do you have the address for the business?" he asked, over his shoulder, to his partner in the back seat.

"His business address that I have is the home address, she replied, but let me call the office and have them look up Knowlton's warehouse." She was dialing the cell phone and talking at the same time. "Now that I'm done wetting myself from this guy's reckless driving." She punched Jerry in the shoulder and he faked a painful look through his laughter.

"Hey, you're still in one piece," he said, smiling.

Belinda was talking with the office now. "Thanks, Darcy," she said, as she wrote on the back of Bennett's business card. It was the only thing she had to write on.

The house was just a smoldering ruin when they pulled up on the scene. A red Chicago fire engine sat at the curb and several lines from the truck snaked up to, and around, the house. Most of the fire had been knocked down in just a few minutes. The Captain walked down the driveway and met Jerry, who had walked towards him. They obviously knew each other by the way they were laughing and talking. Mike and Belinda stayed back by the car, parked across the street.

As Jerry and the Captain talked, another fire rig pulled up and several men jumped off and walked over to the Captain. Jerry waved goodbye and walked back to the car.

"He says it was set." Jerry said to Belinda and Mike. They could smell the gasoline when they had pulled up."

"Gasoline? That's a new twist for him." Mike said. "He must be out of his real stuff."

"Real stuff?" Jerry asked.

"Yeah, petrocyclomate. The stuff Belinda found in the device on the sprinkler pipes. When he was in Minneapolis that's all he used. It's wicked shit, people!" Mike kicked at the dirt with his toe and shook his head. *He still couldn't believe this was happening.*

"Let's get over to the warehouse," Jerry said, looking at the address Belinda had written down on the back of the card. "It's not that far away. There's nothing we can do here, anyway, until the place cools down."

David drove quickly but warily. The truck, with the signage removed, blended in well with the traffic but he still knew it was just a matter of time before his license plate got broadcast. Then, there would be no safe hiding place. He had covered the barrel in the back with a tarp, that had some bungee cords wrapped around it, that did little to hide the fact it was a barrel underneath. He was heading south out of Chicago but had no idea where.

David was sweating profusely and appeared to be very agitated. He had worked so hard to get all of his ducks in a row. Now it was all falling down around him, and the only thing he could think was that his nemesis, Mike Flanagan, had come back to ruin everything. It would have been the fire of the century and a fitting reenactment of the Great Chicago Fire.

David angrily reflected on how he had botched the whole thing, some ten years earlier, when he didn't make sure that Flanagan went to a fiery death back in Minneapolis. Right now, he didn't know how, or when, or where, but this time Flanagan was going to go down, even if it meant taking him with him. Right at this moment, he had a barrel to stash, and then he was going to quickly go back to Chicago and have some fun.

When they reached the warehouse, it was deserted. Just a lot of pipes and fittings scattered around and empty barrels stacked in the corner. The big, overhead door was open, and the small door that led into the office was also ajar. The three of them turned their attention to the empty barrels first, ignoring the empty office.

"I bet if you check these barrels you will find that they held petrocyclomate," Mike said. "The sixty-four-thousand-dollar-question is, where did it all go?"

Mike scratched his head, deep in thought. "Jerry, you don't think he might have put this stuff in the sprinkler pipes of buildings, do you?"

"Jeeze, Mike, that would take a lot more of it than these barrels would ever hold. In fact, some of his accounts are big enough to accommodate all of this in one building."

"Have you checked any of the sites beyond taking down the ignition devices? How many of them are still out there?"

"Most of the sites he serviced haven't been checked." Jerry answered.

"Let's get back to the office and get a list," Mike said to Belinda. "We need to work fast. We can investigate these sites when we get time."

Jerry closed the building up and put a restricted access tag on the door that said, **'Crime scene—stay out by order of the Chicago Fire Department.'**

As he closed the office door, he noticed the soccer ball on the desk and turned to ask Mike, "Did this guy have kids?"

"Not that I'm aware of," Mike said. "Why?"

"Well, there was a soccer ball right in the middle of his desk. It just looked out of place and…" Just then, there was a flash of light, and then an explosion. Belinda, Mike and Jerry all turned their heads as shards of corrugated metal flew in their direction, and then the whole place was involved in fire.

"That, Jerry, is what petrocyclomate can do." Mike said. "Better call the rigs over here and let's get going. This place is toast, anyway."

On the way back to the office, Belinda called and asked the girls to make up a list of all of Knowlton's accounts. There were over a hundred of them.

CHAPTER TWENTY

RIGHT NOW, DAVID'S PLAN WAS to go back to Chicago and go on a burning spree. He wasn't sure what they knew, or how many buildings they had found his devices in and disabled, but he intended to drive by each one of them and find out. They couldn't have found them all that was for sure.

Fires were always so much prettier at night, so he would take care of his chores, get something to eat, then wait for dark and go back. Maybe the dates for the huge fire he had planned would be wrong and that pained him, but the end result could still be achieved if he hurried.

He had settled down a little and appeared to be thinking more rationally. He stunk, a result of his fear that had induced sweating, and his oozing sores he hadn't been able to attend to. The disgusted look he had gotten from a woman, at the place he had stopped for gas, was a good indicator of how bad it was. He vowed to cause trouble for her when he came back to get gas in his barrel. He was tired of being treated like some kind of a freak.

"There is no way we can get to all of these people and check out all of their buildings in any kind of a quick timeframe," Jerry said. "I say we call these people and have their sprinkler systems turned off by their maintenance staff for now. We will call in some extra help and we can get them all checked out within a day or two."

"Sounds like a plan to me," Mike said. "Speaking of checking out, I have to be back in Minneapolis tomorrow, but I would like to go with you today for a couple of buildings, if that's alright?"

"Let's go," Jerry said. With the list of businesses in hand, they were out the door.

Belinda decided that she would stay back and make sure all of the people were called and told to shut down their sprinkler systems. It wasn't an easy job because many managers were reluctant to shut down their systems and, in a few cases, they couldn't even be reached. It became evident that the girls in the office could handle the chore, so she went down to the lab to do some testing. It was quiet in the lab today, so she put on some soft music and strapped on her rubber apron.

The small glass bottle—with the petrocyclomate in it—sat in front of her on the black slate countertop. She was looking for a way to break this fluid down so she would know the chemical composition of it. She could just call the refinery that produced it, but there appeared to be something else in it—some kind of soluble oil. The problem was the oil had blended so well with the fluid that there didn't appear to be any way to get a pure sample. Sometimes, when fluids were spun in a centrifuge, they would separate if they were different densities and that was what she was going to try and do. She washed out a clean beaker to put in the machine, and then cussed herself out because she forgot to dry it and now there was water in the sample.

The phone in the lab rang, interrupting her. She went over and picked it up. It was her mother, asking her to come over to the house tonight for supper. She had someone she wanted her to meet.

"Mom, look, it's going to be a long night here at work but I'm glad you called. I need you to go get Samantha from daycare at five. I'll be there when I can get away so don't set me up with anyone tonight, okay? In fact, Mom, quit trying to find a husband for me. I have to go."

When she got back to the bench she picked the beaker up. She would have to discard this sample but, right now, didn't know where to put it. That's when she noticed the water layer on the bottom of the beaker. This stuff didn't mix with water, and now she knew where the petrocyclomate was being stored. She ran for the phone and called Jerry's cell.

It was headline news in the evening papers that afternoon. The media had monitored the call for the police, and now they were demanding answers. Was there a serial arsonist loose in Chicago?

David had driven as far as the small town of Bassett's Beach, fifty miles south of Chicago. It was a bedroom community, where the well-healed lived around a picturesque lake. The streets were wide and lined with small shops and boutiques. Most of the people drove fancy cars and were dressed to the hilt. He knew he looked out of place but he wouldn't be here long.

He had something to eat at a fast food joint and then drove slowly around the hamlet, looking for a storage place to rent a locker. Right outside of town, he found a place that had storage lockers and trucks for rent. He pulled in and stopped; getting out of the car, he walked through a door that said, **Office**.

A bespectacled, miniature old man peered at him, through trifocals that were as thick as magnifying glasses, from behind a short plywood counter. Behind him on the wall, a large board held rows of keys and, somewhere behind a curtain, he could hear a woman's voice—seemingly in a phone conversation. He could smell something cooking.

"I need a storage unit," David said.

"How long do you want the unit for," the old man asked, "because I can't rent for less than six months. Just too damn much paperwork, otherwise. Makes Ma mad," he chuckled, "and when Ma ain't happy, well, nobody's happy." He chuckled again.

"Six months is fine," David answered. He had no intention on being there six days, but right now, he didn't want to raise suspicions.

The old man slid a piece of paper across the counter. "Here's the lease form. Fill in the first page and sign it—I will need three months in advance." He loosened his lower denture plate with his tongue, and moved it around in his mouth before settling it back into place, and smiling widely.

"You from around these parts?" he asked.

"No," David said, and didn't elaborate. *He knows damn well I'm not from here*, he thought.

He finished the form and paid the rent. The old man gave him a padlock key and told him it was number 43. "Way in the back on the other side," he said. "14 x 24 she is. Should hold a lot of crap for you." He chuckled and moved his teeth again.

"Before I go," David said, I might leave my pickup here in the unit because I'm having some problems with it, so could I also rent a truck from you?"

"Yep, the more the merrier," the old man chuckled, and popped his teeth out of place once more.

In just a few minutes, David was on his way back to Chicago with only a garage door opener on the seat beside him. He drove carefully, but determined. He was a man on a mission and nothing was going to get in the way this time—not Mike Flanagan, not anybody.

The owner of the rental place went back into his living quarters where his wife sat, at an old Chrome Kraft kitchen table, with a cup of coffee in her hand. "Good customer?" she asked.

"Not sure," the old man said. "He was the smelliest man I've met in a long time. Man stunk like a damn corpse."

They went to the museum first because that's where Belinda had found the first device.

"We're from the Fire Department," Jerry said to the manager.

"Yes, they just called and asked us to shut down our sprinkler system. What was that all about?"

"I'll let you know in a few minutes. Where is your riser room?"

A maintenance man appeared on the scene, and said, "Follow me, gentlemen."

Once inside the riser room, they noticed that the long screw on the main valve was in, and the valve was closed. There was a bleed-off port, so they opened it and drew out some water into a paper cup. Mike smelled it, holding it close under his nose. "Smells like water to me," he said.

Jerry also smelled it. "Mike, do you suppose…"

His phone rang, interrupting him. It was Belinda.

"Jerry, I just ran some tests on that fluid in those devices we found. It doesn't mix with water, Jerry. It's in the pipe ahead of the water!"

Jerry was quiet for a second while he digested what she had told him.

"It's in the pipes ahead of the water," he told Mike.

"Thanks, doll," he said to Belinda. "I think you might have just cracked this case."

The two men ran back to the receptionist desk. "Get that maintenance guy back again, please," he said, "and hurry!"

"Were you here the day the inspector removed a device from one of your sprinkler pipes?" Jerry asked.

"I helped her," the young man said.

"Take us to the site."

A few minutes later, with ladders in place, Mike and Jerry used a pipe wrench to loosen the sprinkler head that had been located next to the now-removed device.

"Just loosen it enough to make it leak," Mike said to Jerry. "Otherwise, we're going to have a flood and you don't want a lot of that stuff out in the open. He held a five-gallon plastic pail while Jerry turned the head loose. They drained out about a pint of fluid, and then Jerry re-tightened the head. Setting the bucket on the floor, they both smelled its contents while the maintenance man, looking perplexed, looked on.

"It's not water," Mike said. "Let's take it outside to the parking lot."

They poured about two ounces of it in the gravel. Mike lit a balled-up roll of paper on fire and threw it at the fluid—it went off like a napalm bomb.

"Holy shit!" Jerry exclaimed.

"He's trying to burn your town down," Mike said. "We need a lot of help to find those devices that are out there. With the risers shut down they won't be big fires, but there will be fires just the same. We have to make sure everyone complied with the shutdown order. I don't think it will be long before he is back. He's been discovered now and I'm sure, if this is the David Bennett I knew, he's pissed. You'd better get some help and fast."

"Help—like whom, Mike?"

"Call out the troops." Mike said. "You have a big department."

CHAPTER TWENTY-ONE

JERRY AND MIKE WERE IN the car heading back to the office, and Jerry was talking on the radio with his boss, Norm Shuster. He hadn't kept Shuster in the loop as much as he should have with this incident as it unfolded, so he had a lot of explaining to do in a hurry.

"Norm, basically, this guy has turned one hundred and eighty one buildings into potential fire bombs and, right now, we need to get to these buildings before he does, to disarm them."

"How does he set them on fire?" Norm asked.

"Remotely, with some kind of hand-held device. It could be as simple as a garage door opener—we don't know. We were on his trail yesterday but he gave us the slip. Right now, we have no idea where he is. We have an APB out on his vehicle, but I'm sure he knows it and has probably changed vehicles by now."

"So you want me to do what?"

"Call out the stations, have them go to these locations and make sure their sprinkler systems are turned off."

"Turn off the protection? How can that be right? Are you nuts?"

"No, Norm, I'm not nuts. The protection is where the accelerant is being stored."

There was a low whistle on the other end of the phone. "Okay, but if one of these buildings burns down because we shut off their fire protection, your ass will be in a lot of trouble. Send the list to Dispatch and I'll call the Chief's office."

David was almost back in the city limits in his orange and white rental truck, the map of his intended targets was on the seat beside him. He knew each building intimately, but he didn't want to forget and miss one. He was starting to sweat profusely again, and wished for some water as he was dehydrating. When you don't have most of your skin, that's how your body reacts—it leaks like a sieve. He wheeled into a service station and, walking more stiff-legged than usual, went straight to the coolers and brought a six-pack of spring water to the front counter. There was a long line at the checkout, but he went around all of them, and threw a ten-dollar bill at the cashier, saying, "Keep the change, I'm in a hurry," and was out the door.

A large black man yelled, "Hey, asshole, wait your turn!" But David was long gone, outside in the truck and speeding away.

"Wow," the clerk said. "Some jerk, huh?"

"What a smelly dink that guy was!" the black man said. "I'd rather touch a skunk than him. Probably a good thing he left, for more than one reason. I'd kick his ass, man." He took a boxing stance and threw a fake punch, to the amusement of everybody.

"I'm not complaining," the young cashier said. "He left me a five-dollar tip."

At Channel Seven Television downtown, young Curt Clausen jumped in a company van with his cameraman. He had been told to get over to Fire Department Headquarters and find out what was going on. He could use a big story. The people at headquarters were less than happy with him right now, and had told him he was on thin ice. "I get no decent leads," he told his boss.

"You have to have a nose for the news, son. It's not going to jump out and bite you in the ass. If you can't find a story, make a story, but make it believable," he had been told.

Right now, all he knew was every fire station in Chicago had been put on high alert. It was his job to find out why and he would not be the only one asking questions. The van pulled up to Fire Department Headquarters and Curt, with his cameraman following, ran up the stairs and into the building. They ran down the same hallway David Bennett had run out of a few hours ago, heading for Jerry Martin's office. That's the name Curt had been given as the man to talk with.

"Jerry's not in right now," the receptionist said.

"Can you tell me where I can find him?" Curt asked.

"Just then, Belinda walked out into the office and heard Jerry's name being mentioned.

"Can I help you with something?" she interrupted. "I'm Jerry's partner."

Curt couldn't believe his eyes. He had been on several fire scenes and always he had to deal with some grizzled old chief, who didn't have the time of day for him. Now this beautiful young woman was asking if she could help him, and she was even smiling at him.

No one was more secretive about what was going on than these people. He had to be careful.

Curt felt himself blushing, but pushed his doubt about his good fortune aside long enough to ask, "Maybe you could answer a few questions for me—I'm from Channel Seven KLOX." Belinda pushed the swinging gate open, and walked out. "Let's step out in the hall," she said.

The list of addresses of buildings with Knowlton sprinkler systems in them had been faxed to Central Dispatch. Fire stations throughout the city were being filled in on which addresses to respond to. In some districts, it involved more than one address. There were very few districts without at least one building, and those who didn't have one were being asked to come out of their district and assist other stations.

The fire fighters had been told only to make sure the sprinkler systems had been shut down, and to stay on the scene of these buildings unless they were called to other emergencies. If one of these buildings burned from an accidental fire after the fire department shut down their fire protection, the city would be in big trouble. The fire fighters had no idea what was wrong or what they were looking for—there was not enough time to go into detail yet. They were to treat it like a bomb scare for now.

The list of buildings serviced by Knowlton's totaled three hundred and fifty six. Of this number, one hundred and eighty-one had been set up to burn by David Bennett, but there was no way to know which ones they were.

"Look, there's not a lot I can tell you right now because we're kind of in the dark ourselves. Jerry is headed back this way and he might be able to shed more light on things than I can." Belinda was leaning against the hall wall with a roll of papers in her hand as she talked. It was the list she had compiled and sent to Dispatch.

"Can you tell me if, in fact, there is an incident going on?" Curt asked.

Belinda was choosing her words carefully. She had always been told to cooperate with the media, but to stay close-mouthed unless she had been given the go-ahead to talk about a subject, by higher-ups.

"Look—Curt, was it?"

"Yes, Curt Clausen. KLOX."

"Curt, I'd like to tell you more but I just don't know anything else. Can you give me your card, and if the story breaks I'll call you. Right now, it might be nothing."

"You'll call me? You're not just saying that."

"I'll call you, Curt, I promise." She smiled and touched his arm.

Curt gave her his business card and said, "Thanks. You've been super."

The office door opened and the receptionist stuck her head out. "Belinda, I have about ten calls for you."

"Darcy, before I talk to anyone, will you get Jerry on the radio?"

She watched Curt and his cameraman walking away down the hall. *He sure seemed like a nice young man*, she thought, *and he didn't have a wedding ring on.*

"Jerry," she said, "when are you coming in? The media is going nuts, and I have no idea what to tell them."

"Bullshit them for now, kid. Hey, go get that device you found in the museum and take a Polaroid picture of it, scan it, and get that out to Dispatch so the guys can start searching these buildings. If we can disable these devises that will stop a lot of trouble. Mike and I are going to stay out here for now. We have a few things to look at back at Bennett's house and warehouse."

They pulled into Bennett's driveway just as Jerry hung up the radio microphone. There was just a lone squad car there for security, as all of the fire trucks had left the scene. The whole yard was surrounded by yellow police tape. A few wisps of smoke still came from the burnt-out house, and several kids were riding their bicycles back and forth, through the puddles in the street. All of the other spectators had left.

Both men put on coveralls and walked through the house, checking the floor with each step they took. Most of the furniture and things had been reduced to rubble, but in David's bedroom they found several thing of interest. In a pile of documents that had not burned all the way through, they found directions for making incendiary devices. They found the burnt body of an animal—most likely, judging by the size of it, a cat. On the kitchen table, they found two more of the devices, like the ones that Belinda had found strapped to the sprinkler pipe in the museum.

"Let's get to the warehouse," Mike said. "We can come back here later."

The scene at the warehouse was not as charred because the Fire Department had been close by when it started. For the most part, the building was still standing, except for the office off to the side that had collapsed in the explosion, when Mike and Jerry had been there. Mike walked through the piles of pipes and fittings. There, in the back of the building, was what he was looking for; a small mountain of empty, partially melted, plastic barrels. Mike unscrewed the cap on the closest barrel and stuck his finger inside, feeling of the top of the barrel. "Glass," he said to Jerry. "Now it's making sense," he said.

David was parked in his rental truck, in a church parking lot, while he went over his maps and charts. He had gone through this so many times in his dreams and fantasies, but always it was the anniversary of the Great Chicago Fire, and the city would burn once more. He knew now he was busted, and he knew they would be disabling the system he had worked so hard to put in place. He had to work fast to salvage what he could and tonight would be the night. He just had to get them going in the right order.

His plan right now was to overwhelm the Fire Department. They were a huge, well-oiled machine, but he would pick at their heels like a pack of wolves at a desperate, injured moose and eventually, they would crumble. He put the truck in gear. He had his plan and there was no time to waste.

His first target would be the huge Wafer Cracker Company in South Chicago, on Delmont Boulevard. The sprawling plant sat on over sixteen acres, a hodge-podge of turn-of-the-century buildings, connected to each other. Tonight it was brightly lit and, by the scope of the cars in the lot, fully occupied with workers. He had two devices in the building—one on each end.

David drove into the lot, slowed and came to a stop. There, in front of the building, sat an engine from the Fire Department. There appeared to be just one man, sitting inside the idling truck, behind the steering wheel. *Why were they here?*

For a second he was unsure of what to do, and then he remembered the other device on the other end of the complex and he drove past the fire truck, and threaded his way through the parking lots until he came to Building F. David checked his charts once more. Yes, this was the area. He reached down for the garage door opener and pressed the button.

Inside the building there was a muffled explosion that could not be heard outside. Workers scrambled to get out of the way, not believing their eyes and ears as to what was going on over their heads.

Outside the building warning bells started ringing, signaling that the fire alarms had been triggered, followed by a mass exodus of people coming out of the exits. David slipped the truck in gear and headed back to the other end of the complex where the fire truck had been parked. He got there just in time to see four fire fighters run out of the building, and jump on the truck. The big engine headed to the back of the complex where he had come from. He reached down and triggered the second device. Then he saw the clouds of billowing smoke and flames in the back, where he had come from, just as the windows upstairs in Building A blew out, and scores of workers exited the building.

At Headquarters and Dispatch, a frantic call came in from Engine Sixty-eight. "Send help immediately! There has been an explosion in Building F at the Cracker Company." This was followed by, "Holy shit—now the other end is on fire!"

David was on his way to the museum, a few blocks away.

CHAPTER TWENTY-TWO

THE FIRE AT THE CRACKER Company had escalated to four alarms by the time David reached the museum. Both of the devices had acted just like he had planned. The fires had quickly over- whelmed the sprinkler systems and now were burning freely throughout the complex. Worried supervisors were trying to count heads and account for all of their people. Several were missing. The police had shut off all of the roads into the area so responding fire units could get into the fire. This one fire was going to tie up a good deal of manpower and equipment. Several of the buildings—that fire units had been sent to as a precaution— were abandoned as they were reassigned to the fire scene. The war had started.

Mike, Jerry and Belinda were back at the office, listening to the radio. Was this an accidental fire or was this the work of David Bennett? Whatever, they had to make sure those sprinkler systems had been shut down. The word from the scene of the Cracker Company was that they had not yet shut down the system when the fire had started and that the sprinkler system did, indeed, seem to have fed the fire.

Outside the museum, David parked where he was sure his sending unit would be able to reach the antenna of the device in the building. He had so many stops to make but he just couldn't resist waiting and watching. The devices exploding themselves were too small to be seen outside the buildings but, when the sprinkler systems were tripped, the results were quite obvious and so stimulating to him, he had to be there. At the Cracker Company, the explosion had gone right out through the roof, and he was so sexually excited that he had almost had an orgasm. It was far better than anything he had ever enjoyed in Minneapolis so many years ago, and right now, it was made even more exciting by the presence of Mike Flanagan. David had no idea why he was back in the picture but, when this night was over, Flanagan would wish he had stayed home. This was his entire fault.

He was at the museum now and he pushed the button on the garage door opener, and then waited patiently, with his eyes glued to that part of the building where the fire would start. This building would be a special fire and one he had dreamed many times of burning down, if only because of the large mural of the Great Chicago Fire that hung inside. *Oh, how he wished he could be sitting on a chair inside, watching the flames devour it*, he thought. He drummed his fingers impatiently on the top of the steering wheel. He should have seen something by now.

David moved the truck closer to the building, and pushed the button again, but still no luck and now his excitement was being replaced with anger. *Had his system failed him, or had the fire department found it?*

He threw the truck in gear and, with tires squealing, David left the lot in a cloud of dust. He could wait no longer. He was on his way to the next building on the list, six blocks away.

Of the next twenty buildings, only two burned, and David was livid. At some of them, fire rigs were already present.

Back at the Fire Department Headquarters, Jerry, Mike, and Belinda were glued to the Dispatch radio transmissions. Right now, there were five buildings burning on the South Side of Chicago and the manpower was being taxed like never before. All off-duty fire fighters were being called in, and suburban departments were being sent into the city to cover vacant stations. So far the fires were in a small area and the rest of the department, from the north and east, was being moved around to make sure there was coverage. The situation was serious but not grave. The Chicago Fire Department was a huge, well-oiled machine. Then, all hell broke loose on the North Side.

David had done most of his business on the South Side of the city over the years, but he did have three businesses that he had inherited from Knowlton on the Northeast side of town and one of them was huge. It was an old railroad depot and roundhouse that dated back to the day of the steam engines. It had been refurbished into a huge fun park. With failure after failure at getting buildings to burn, he had become increasingly angry and out of control. He sat, parked in a neighborhood parking lot, brooding and smoking cigarettes.

World War 11 had been won because of brilliant leadership and not who had the best offense or defense, he thought. *He would outmaneuver them.*

Currently, they had saturated the South Side with men and equipment. It was time to attack their unprotected flank.

It took only twenty minutes to get over to the fun park. The city was under siege, but still asleep, in the early morning hours. Most residents had no idea what was going on around them. This was another place where he'd set up two devices, and filled two zones with petrocyclomate. When he got there, the place was empty. The giant parking lot had a padlocked gate across the entrance. He could walk in but, right now, his legs hurt so bad he might not make it. For a minute he sat, fuming and fighting the urge to scream out from his frustrations and pain. Then he dropped the truck in gear and blew through the gate—the shattered lock and chain landing on the hood of his rented vehicle. The front bumper, with the license plate still on it, tore off and skidded across the lot but David was oblivious to it. He drove straight for the building—spittle flying from the corner of his mouth. He squealed to a stop and pushed his garage door opener. It only took a few minutes and the fireball that erupted could be seen from a mile away. The building was burning on both ends.

Mike and Jerry were at the Cracker Factory when the call came in for the theme park on the other side of the city. Jerry called back to the office and asked the receptionist to tell Belinda to get over to the theme park, and see if this fire was related or not. After all, fires did happen from other reasons than David Bennett. A quick check of his list indicated that the theme park building was not on the list of buildings Knowlton had serviced. Another company had done the original installation, and David had taken over the account after he bought the sprinkler company from Knowlton's, unbeknownst to the Fire Department.

It was two-thirty in the morning and it had been a long night for everyone. Belinda was at the office, her head down, sleeping at her desk. Curt Clausen, from KLOX, was on his way back to her office. Something big was coming off in Chicago and he was going to try and get some more answers. He just hoped someone was still there.

Downtown, the Chief of the department was meeting with his

assistants to discuss the gravity of the situation. So many fires were burning that the department was stretched to its limit, and many of the calls they normally answered every day, were going unanswered. Only the fact that this was happening in the middle of the night had kept the casualty list down from what it could have been, but hospitals were getting numerous casualties, anyway. Help was pouring in from suburban departments, but lack of pre-existing agreements and union rules were getting in the way.

As grave as the situation was, David was fast running out of buildings that would burn, and was so far out of control, he was no longer thinking with any degree of rationality. *Flanagan was the reason,* he fumed. *He had come here and ruined everything. He had trashed all of his plans and dreams of burning the city once more. There was only one thing he could do and that was, go back to Minneapolis and make him pay for this, but first, he needed to go back and get his truck and his barrel. As far as he was concerned, this night was over. Maybe Chicago would live on, and maybe there was little he could do in Minneapolis, but Mike Flanagan was going to pay for this with his life.*

Curt wasn't sure, at this late hour, if anyone would be at the office. If they were, would they even talk to him? There was a story here, no doubt, and right now every reporter in the city of Chicago was digging for the facts for the morning paper. They all knew that someone, somehow, had hatched a mad plan to burn the city down, but *who*, was the sixty-four-thousand-dollar question, and the first one to find that out would be famous—but the fire department wasn't talking.

He met Belinda in the hallway, coming out of the office. The last time he had seen her, she had looked impeccable but, right now, the weariness that had accumulated over the course of the long day showed on her face. She looked up at the last moment before he spoke, and then stopped.

Curt shifted nervously with his pad and pencil in hand. "Belinda, look—I know you're busy and I'm the last person you want to talk to but can you help me out at all? Just a general outline of what is going on or…"

"Curt, come with me. We can talk on the way." This young reporter intrigued her and she knew if she said the wrong thing, she would be in a lot of trouble. But, it was late and she was lonely and, suddenly, he was here and she wanted the company in this crazy, mixed-up night.

Belinda's car sat way in the back of the lot and, for some reason, it looked off-kilter; like one side was higher than the other. A quick look showed her the flat tire.

"Shit," she said. "Why does this kind of crap always happen to me?"

"Where do you want to go?" Curt asked.

"Northeast, to a fire over at the old railroad complex—the Big Sky Theme Park—do you know where that is?"

"It's on fire?" Curt asked.

"Yes, and I have to get there."

"Let's take my car," he suggested. "It's parked right out front."

They didn't have an emergency vehicle like Belinda would have had, with lights and siren, but Curt drove like it had one, anyway. It was about six miles to the fire scene. Belinda's knuckles were white, from hanging onto the dashboard, and they hardly exchanged two words on the way over. At last, they turned the corner and the huge round building lay out in front of them. The roof had collapsed, and pockets of fire were still showing in the blackened structure, but the Fire Department seemed to have it under control. Belinda showed her credentials to the police officer at the gate, then they drove up to an area where it seemed safe to park, and she and Curt got out.

There was little she could do until she got into the ruins but, right now, she was looking for the first-in units to talk to. "Stay here," she told Curt. "I'll be back in a few minutes."

"Gotcha," Curt said, and gave her a wink. She was cute in her own way, but he knew that business came first. After he got his story, maybe he could get to know her better. Maybe he would walk back to the gate where they drove in and talk to the cop—anything to get a story.

The air was heavy with smoke, and the wind seemed to be blowing it his way. Curt walked to his left to get out of the smoke cloud, coughing into his hanky. *How the hell did these guys work in this crap all of their lives?* he thought. His eyes were watering so bad he could hardly see, and then he tripped over something and went sprawling, face-down, in the parking lot. It was the front bumper to a truck or car. The bumper was heavy but he turned it over. The license plate, still attached to it, would provide a clue of where it came from. The cop, who had seen him fall, had gotten out of his squad car where he had been sitting—staying out of the smoke—and was now walking towards him.

"You alright, fellow?" he asked.

"Yeah, I'm fine. I tripped over this bumper that was lying here. Who the hell loses their bumper and then just drives away?" The minute he said it, he knew the significance of it, and so did the cop, who copied the numbers off of it and ran back to his car and his radio.

The broken chains and the bent gate, it all fit together in the cop's mind. The bumper belonged to the person who had done this.

By the time Belinda got back to the car, the police officer had the information. The license plate belonged to a truck from a rental place in Bassett Beach.

"Can you send someone to check on that?" she asked the cop.

"Already did, honey," he answered, smiling at her.

Belinda grimaced, but said nothing. *It never stops*, she thought. She called Jerry and told him what she had found out. "The fire was most likely set," she said. "There had been some kind of an explosion, and this building hadn't shut down their sprinkler system. Jerry, we found the front bumper and license plate from some rental truck from a place out in Bassett Beach. It looks like they used the truck to blast through the gates and chain."

"Police checking on that?" he asked.

"Yes," she said. "Jerry, I have a reporter from a television station with me. What can I tell him?"

"Tell him what you know, but don't speculate. The whole town knows what's going on right now, anyway."

"They don't know why," she answered.

"Use your best judgment," he said.

CHAPTER TWENTY-THREE

By four thirty a.m., things had quieted down. There had been no more suspicious fires for two hours, and the biggest ones were all under control. Jerry and Mike had gone back to the office, and Belinda and Curt were at an all-night diner, having coffee and talking shop.

The Chief of the department had called off the help from the suburbs, and most of the fire rigs were going back to their respected stations. It looked like the battle was over, for the time being, anyway.

When the squad from Bassett Beach reached the rental place and managed to wake the disgruntled owner, the officer had been told by the old man, and his equally angry wife, "Yes, a man had rented the truck and a storage unit yesterday, and no, they could not look in the storage unit without a search warrant." The officer radioed what had happened back to his office. He really didn't care if he ever saw what was in the storage locker. It was the end of his shift and he wanted to go home.

Mike was on his way back to the hotel. His flight for Minneapolis left in an hour and he still had to grab his clothes and check out. He was tired and confused. His mind had thought back over Bennett's evil plan. Had it gone off the way David had planned it, they would have had an uncontrollable inferno in the City of Chicago. He still could not believe that this evil man had somehow reappeared, as if he had been reincarnated. But, as much as he didn't want to believe his eyes, the proof was in last night's fires.

Only Belinda's last-minute discovery, about petrocyclomate and water not mixing, had saved the city. The answer, as illusive as it had seemed, had been right there in front of them all the time. Right now, he just wanted to get home to Laura and the kids, and he hoped that Chicago would take care of David Bennett once and for all, but something told him he had not seen the last of Bennett.

David had seen the squad at the rental place and parked a block away behind a dumpster, and walked slowly between two buildings to watch. From there, he could also see the storage unit his truck was in. He needed his truck back but he was just going to have to wait. He also knew the Chicago Fire Department was actively looking for him, and it was just a matter of time before they would be here, too. If that cop got in the storage unit, David knew he might have to do something drastic. There were lights on in the office and he could see the officer and the old man talking animatedly, the old man's arms thrashing in the air. Then he saw the officer turn and leave. Slowly, the squad pulled out onto the boulevard that went around the lake, and disappeared from sight.

His anger had subsided somewhat but maybe it was just because he was exhausted, and so filled with pain he couldn't think straight. He leaned against the building, trying to stay in the shadows. In a few minutes, he was going to have to do something because he was ready to pass out. His shoes were wet from the drainage from his sores that had run down his legs and been absorbed by his socks. As use to his own stink as he had become, now it was grossing him out too.

The light went back out in the office and David limped across the street. He had his access card, but the old man had forgotten to close the gate into the complex so he walked in and, staying in the shadows, went down to the storage unit and unlocked the door. He started the truck up and let it idle a moment. Then he slipped it in gear and slowly drove out.

The old man had not gone back to bed, however. He was too angry at his sleep being interrupted. Right now, he was standing in his bathroom taking a leak and, through the little bathroom window, watched David go to the storage unit.

The old man ran out into the driveway with his flashlight in hand, shouting, his pants still unzipped and his white underwear sticking out of his fly. He aimed the beam of light for the center of David's windshield, shouting for him to stop, while holding his hands up in the air.

David gunned the accelerator, and the truck surged forward. The old man's lithe body was no match for the tons of steel and glass. He was catapulted over the truck, coming down in the road behind him, as David sped off and the old woman watched, petrified, from the office window. His body quivered in the dust and rocks for a minute and then fell silent. David's taillights vanished in the inky darkness of the early morning. The old man's head, hitting the windshield, had left some mess on the glass and David turned on the washers. The wipers ran back and forth, creating a gory mess of blood, hair and washer fluid.

He drove west, away from the metropolitan area. He would need to sleep soon, so he watched for a park or some place he could park his truck and remain inconspicuous. In the small town of Glenview, about ninety miles away from Bassett's Beach, he found an old run-down motel. It consisted of several cabins set in a circle like old west settlers with their Conestoga wagons. The first one was marked **Office,** and a red neon vacancy sign that flickered on and off was lit. David pulled up to it and stopped. He was exhausted and could go no farther.

"You have your days and nights mixed up," the obese young woman said, laughing, and shoved a form across the counter for David to sign. David said nothing, but scribbled a name no one could read.

"That will be thirty dollars," she said, and slid him a key, attached to a wooden token with a number seven on it.

David gave her two crumpled twenty's from his pocket. "I like to travel at night," he said. "Less traffic."

She straightened the bills, but didn't pick them up. Reaching into a drawer she came out with two fives and slid them over to him. "Check-out time is usually noon, but I guess for you, it will be midnight. Usually the only daytime business we get is when some kid wants to poke his girlfriend." She laughed again, and her smile showed several brown teeth.

She watched David go back out to his truck and, as he drove away to the cabin, she jotted down his license number. She picked up one of the twenty-dollar bills, and smelled it, because it felt damp.

Must have pissed his pants, she thought. *His money is damp.* She set the bill back down and smelled of her fingers. *My God, what is that stink? It isn't piss.* She slid the bills in the drawer and turned on the black and white television across the room. *Jeeze, that guy stunk up the whole office. If business wasn't so bad, I would have sent him packing. I'll have to burn the sheets when he checks out.* She turned her attention back to the television.

A blonde reporter on television, in a red blazer and black slacks, was talking in front of a red Chicago Fire Truck. "It seems like the worst might be over for now," she said. "It was a long night for Chicago fire fighters and, behind me, you are looking at the ruins of the Wafer Cracker Company." She gestured with her hand, to the smoking ruins behind her. "Several people are still missing," she went on, "and many more are being treated in area hospitals. The fire chief said, through his office, that there were a total of sixty fires last night, and a dozen buildings were destroyed. All of the fires seemed to be related and were set on purpose, but at the present time, he cannot tell us how. This is Jill Claxton—Channel Seven News, in Chicago."

Back at the cabins, the fat girl shut off the television, shaking her head. *They have some weird damn people in Chicago,* she thought. *I better get to washing laundry. Man, that guy was so weird this morning. He walked like a duck. Maybe he shit his pants, too.* She laughed again.

David stood, naked, in front of the sink in the bathroom of the small cabin, dabbing at his weeping sores. He had been so dehydrated from his loss of fluids that he had drunk two quarts of water, and he'd been hurting so bad, he had taken three morphine pills out of his dwindling supply. Now, he had to sleep, because he couldn't think straight anymore. He lay down on top of the bed covers, his mind spinning back to that hot summer night in Minneapolis so many years ago—when he had lit up the night sky, at the Sheridan Apartments, on East Eighteenth Street. It had been one of his first big fires, and one of his better fires. A subtle smile came over his thin lips. It felt so good to reflect on those days when he had so much fun. His hand went to his groin, but there was no response from his body, and he slipped off into a deep sleep.

Jerry had called Noreen, but she already knew what had happened last night. "I'm going to sleep here tonight, babe," he said. "I guess it's almost daytime, isn't it? I have a meeting with Norm and the Chief at nine a.m., but I would like to try and catch a few hours."

Noreen rolled over and looked at the clock on the nightstand. The red letters read 5:14. "Be careful, sweetheart," she said. Then, as an afterthought, she said, "What happened, Jerry? It was all over the news."

"I'll fill you in when I get home, honey. I wish it was now." He hung the receiver up.

Noreen held her receiver to her breast, until the screeching noise started, and then she hung it up and got up from the bed. Pulling her top off, and stepping out of her underwear, she headed for the shower. She would never be able to get back to sleep now.

Jerry had given Belinda the rest of the day off to go get some sleep. The crews from the fire department were out combing the Knowlton Sprinkler buildings that hadn't burned, for any more ignition devices. Bennett had triggered over a hundred of them in his mad dash around the city. In most cases, they started small fires that were handled right away, or burned themselves out. But, of the ten buildings where the sprinkler systems had not been shut down, all of them suffered extensive damage, and six of them were total losses. He shuddered to think what would have happened had they not shut down the sprinkler systems.

The death toll was going to be over twenty, most of them at the Cracker Factory. The monetary damages were in the hundreds of millions.

The next step would be to drain all of the systems, but the pipes with petrocyclomate had to be drained first, and the fiery fluid captured. They would worry about what to do with it when the time came. Ironically, some of the glass-lined barrels that were being used to store it were from David's old warehouse. All of the work was being handled by private contractors and hazardous material teams.

As for the police investigation, it had been ramped up considerably now that they knew who they were looking for. But, how much information do you release to the public in times like this? It has long been one of the biggest debates in criminology. When are you helping yourself get information from the public, and when are you telling the perpetrator what you are doing and where you are looking for them, and how do you reassure the public they aren't next. Pictures of David Bennett appeared on the news and in papers. KLOX broke the story with a rookie reporter, Curt Clausen, who seemed to know as much as the police did. There were on-air interviews with the Fire Chief and Norm Shuster, the Head of Investigation. The police weren't sure if this open-minded investigation was going to help them catch David Bennett, or chase him to another city, but they couldn't risk having him on the loose much longer.

The morning after the fires, the rental truck was found by the Basset City Police, who were out investigating the running over of the old man at the rental place; the old man who, by the way, was miraculously still alive and talking to Chicago Police Department detectives, his body in a full body cast. He had suffered over twenty broken bones, and a skull fracture, and he was pissed. "You tell that smelly son-of-a-bitch that, when I get out of here, he will be one lucky asshole if I don't get my hands on him." Then he moaned loudly and yelled, "Get a nurse in here, I think I just crapped in the bed."

The truck was full of evidence, and it was towed back to Chicago to be reunited with the front bumper that was in the Chicago police garage. Most of the lab people, who were processing the vehicle, could not believe that there wasn't a cadaver in there someplace because it stunk so bad. What was in there that was helpful was a map of all of the buildings that David had wired up. Not that they didn't know about most of them, but it corroborated their evidence, and that made for good courtroom success stories. Another critical piece of evidence was the detonator device that lay on the floor amongst a dozen empty water bottles.

CHAPTER TWENTY-FOUR

BY EIGHT O'CLOCK THAT EVENING, David was up and sitting on the edge of the bed. His weeping sores had left a slimy mess on the bedspread, but his clothes that he had rinsed out in the bathroom seemed almost dry, so he got dressed. There had been a time when he would bandage his sores, but he no longer cared, and there were just too many places to cover now, anyway. *To hell with them all if they don't like the way I smell,* he thought. For many years after Minneapolis, the sores would partially heal over, but lately, they seemed to just get worse and worse, and bigger and bigger. It took a lot of water to keep him hydrated and now, for the first time in two days, he was hungry. *Maybe he would find a fast food place where he could go through a drive-through. It was almost five hundred miles to Minneapolis and he would need his energy when he got there.*

Later that day, Belinda, now rested, sat on the stoop outside of her apartment house and watched the traffic going by. She was holding Samantha, who was playing with a stuffed Beanie Baby elephant.

Life looked a lot brighter for her right now. She was finally getting some recognition from her fellow workers at the fire department. She had saved many people from a lot of grief and the papers were giving her a lot of credit. But the thing that pleased her most today was that she had a date this Saturday night with Curt Clausen. It wasn't a thank-you gesture by him for her help in breaking the story that had made him a newsroom sensation, it was a genuine date between two people whose hearts had been attracted to each other, and she was so excited.

Back in the apartment she dialed the phone. She couldn't wait to tell her mother.

By noon of the following day, the city was declared secure by the fire department. All of the buildings that were involved had had their sprinkler systems purged of the fiery liquid, refilled with clean water and turned back on. Traffic was back to normal and the city went on with living its frantic life once more.

In Minneapolis, Mike Flanagan was back at work. He hadn't told anyone but his wife, Laura, about his experiences in Chicago yet. There was a department meeting today and maybe, if there was time, he would bring it up.

TIME TO GET EVEN AT LAST

David was now in southern Wisconsin, making his way through the hilly countryside. He had made the decision to stay off the freeways and major highways. The police would be looking for his vehicle and, by now, would have a good description of it and of him. He also had to slow things down for his own sake. His body and mind had been pushed to their limits and he was feeling very taxed.

There was some snow on the roadways, but warming weather had melted most of the snow and they weren't in bad shape. His biggest problem, was finding roadways that were smooth enough to not break the glass liner his precious cargo was resting in. He knew if it leaked it would quickly eat through the plastic skin of the barrel, and it had the potential to make him, and the truck, into one gigantic firebomb.

The trip to Minneapolis would take at least two days, maybe three, but he wasn't in any hurry. He was resolute in his quest to get rid of Mike Flanagan but, at the same time, still cautiously aware that Flanagan probably knew that and wouldn't be letting his guard down. After all, he had screwed up badly the last time they had squared off—some ten years ago back in Minneapolis—because he hadn't been cautious enough. He would not make the same mistake twice. He looked at his watch; it was three-thirty and would be getting dark soon.

It had been three days now since that fiery night in Chicago. *Had Flanagan gone back to Minneapolis by now? Were the police aware of where he was at, and did they anticipate where he was going? Maybe he should stop for a while, before he got out of range of the Chicago News networks, and see if they were talking about him. After all, all he had was the radio in the truck for information and, although there had been a lot of talk about the fires, there had been little information about whom they suspected. For a while, he thought maybe Flanagan hadn't recognized him that morning. There had been no mention of his name on the news, and if they were looking specifically for him and knew it was him, why not? He stood out like a sore thumb—he knew it and so did they. But no! The look in his eyes that morning had said it all and it was wishful thinking to even go down that road. He had recognized Flanagan right away, but then, Flanagan wasn't supposed to be dead.* David slapped himself across the side of the head. He was thinking in circles and getting paranoid about this. It was time to stop and give it a rest.

Belinda's date with Curt had gone well. In fact, better than she had hoped. For so many years she had learned to tolerate the media at work, even though they always seemed to be in the way. They were always demanding more than they should have. The animosity that had built up bordered on suspicion of each other that knew no bounds. They, too, seemed to not take her seriously, like many of the men in her department. But in the media, it wasn't just the men reporters, it was women journalists, too, who felt she was out of her element. They would ignore her when men were around to talk to.

Not Curt, though. He seemed to be hanging on her every word when she talked about the fires and what she could share. She wanted so badly to tell him about the volatile fluid that had caused all the grief. The final death toll had been set at fourteen, most of them at the Cracker Company. There were numerous injuries but little information was being released by anyone as to who the suspects, or suspect was. She knew, if she shared too much, she would get in big trouble. Currently things at work were getting back to normal for her, and she liked that.

Curt had showed up that night in blue jeans and a Chicago Bears tee shirt. They had agreed they just wanted to have a casual evening someplace and talk, so Curt took her to a sports bar on the South Side. Belinda had also worn jeans, and a sweatshirt from her alma mater. She had put her hair in a ponytail, wrapped in a red ribbon, and added some gold hoop earrings. Anyone would have thought she was nineteen and not a twenty-some-years-old mother. Just for tonight, Sam was going to have to drink formula when they got home, because she was going to drink some beer and enjoy the evening. It had been a long time between dates.

They both tired of the shoptalk and talked more and more about their own lives and dreams. She talked about Sam and how much she meant to her, but didn't really talk about the father of her baby. She wanted Curt to know, up front, that she had a little girl, and that she and Sam were a package deal—if it ever came to that some day with some man. Curt seemed genuinely interested in both of them.

He talked about how hard it was for him to break into the reporting business and how cutthroat the competition for scoops and stories had become. But eventually he, too, talked about his parents and his sister—who was a doctor—and what he wanted out of life. For Belinda, it seemed ironic that both of them had a doctor for a sister. That brought up a whole new conversation about how domineering people could be when they had medical degrees.

"If she saw what I ate and drank tonight, she would be having my stomach pumped," Curt smirked. "My parents have her on some lofty pedestal, and she has them drinking spring water and wiping their butts with medicated wipes."

Belinda giggled and said, "My mom's not that bad, but she is bossy as hell." Then they both laughed.

The night flew by so quickly—soon it was last call, and they were turning down the bar lights, putting things away, and the crowd was thinning out. It had been Taco Night at the bar and a mariachi band had come in to play from nine to twelve-thirty. The music was light and had put everybody in a festive mood. She and Curt had tried to dance something that looked like a cha cha with some rumba thrown in and, despite the clumsiness of it, they had fun with it. Now however, with the evening coming to an end, the band members were packing their instruments away and talking to each other in Spanish.

Although Belinda had drunk conservatively, Curt had had too many Tequila shots, and it was evident she would be driving them home, although he protested he was all right. She had no idea how to get to his place and it was way on the north side of Chicago, so she decided, to avoid an expensive cab ride home, she would just take him back to her place, put him in her car, and take him home. He would have to find a way to get his car tomorrow. She called her mother and apologized for the late time, telling her, "Mom, I need you to keep Sam for me tonight." Her mother gave her a sleepy one-word answer, "Okay," and hung up. At least it was Friday night and no one had to go to work in the morning.

David had found a country lane that seemed to be unused. He was going to spend the night, off to one side of the road, in his truck. He was still very tired and very thirsty. He had enough food and water for tonight, but tomorrow he would have to stop somewhere for gas and groceries. He looked in his billfold—he still had almost a thousand dollars, but when that was gone he would have trouble. He could only hope it never came to that.

He slumped down in the seat. It was getting cold in the truck and he pulled an old blanket around him. That was another thing that not having decent skin on his body did for him—he was always cold. He napped for a few hours, but then noticed headlights coming up the lane towards him. He didn't try to hide the fact that he was in there, thinking whoever it was might not stop if they saw somebody occupying the truck. It was obvious he wasn't stuck.

But the car rolled to a stop. An elderly man got out and approached his driver's window. David rolled down the window and spoke first.

"I hope you don't mind, if this is your road, but I'm tired of traveling and just stopped to rest for a while."

One look in the rearview mirror told him someone was still in the car parked behind him.

"No, suit yourself," the old man said. "Don't mind it at all, just wanted to make sure you didn't need help." The old man was diminutive and didn't appear to be overly curious. "Look, if you do need help we're just at the end of the lane. Have a good night and stay warm."

David watched him walking slowly back to his car. He stopped and bent over to look at something in the snow, illuminated by his car lights, but then straightened back up, got in the car and continued up the road.

The old man's name was Herman Spencer, and the other occupant of the car was his wife, Betty. They were retired from farming but still lived on the place, renting out the land in the summer. Both of them were reasonably healthy. They had been coming back from Bingo at the local Legion Hall in town, six miles away.

"Just some drifter," he told Betty. "Said he was tired from traveling and just stopped to rest. Who the hell travels down these roads when they travel is beyond me, but live and let live, I always say."

Betty smiled and touched his arm. "Everybody has to be somewhere, Herme, right?" They both laughed.

"I would have invited him up for coffee but, my God, he stunk, Betty. I could smell him from four feet away. I used to have some old Holstein cows that would get a little ripe from time-to-time, but this character smelled worse than they ever could." He laughed and shook his head.

David was thinking. *What he had said might not have made much sense. If he was supposedly traveling, what would he be doing back in this country? Maybe he should move on. What the hell did that old man see in the snow back there? Maybe he should go check.*

He stepped outside in the cold air, pulling his collar up around his neck. His legs were almost rigid and it hurt a great deal to walk. He cursed the weather, Mike Flanagan, and the Chicago Fire Department. "I wish they were all dead," he muttered to himself.

He stopped where the old man had been looking, and it looked like something had melted a thin line in the snow that headed toward the back of his truck.

David was frantic as he crawled into the back of the truck and uncovered his barrel. It was all wet, and a thin trickle of the precious fluid was leaking near the bottom. The glass liner had cracked. He recalled the truck lurching over a rock in the road when he pulled in. It must have happened then.

He was incensed and screamed, "Shit!" into the night air and shook his fists at the heavens. *What was he going to do now? Why did everything bad have to happen to him?*

CHAPTER TWENTY- FIVE

MIKE'S MEETING HAD BEEN LONG and boring. *More bureaucratic bullshit*, he thought to himself as the meeting dragged on, dealing with red tape and problems. He had daydreamed through most of the meeting because his mind was still back in Chicago, and the events that had taken place there. He was now convinced that his so-called old nemesis was still alive and was now coming back to haunt him again.

Would Bennett come back here? he wondered. *He was easily recognized and would have a tough time staying concealed. He had no friends or relatives that Mike knew of. The police all over the Midwest had the license number of his truck and had been ordered by Chicago Police to be on the lookout for him. But, he wasn't stupid, and he had proved before to be hard to trip up.*

The meeting over, he now sat at his desk and blew the dust off an old manila file folder labeled, 'David Bennett.' He needed to refresh himself, even though the terrible memories of this man seemed indelible.

Back at home at the apartment building, Belinda parked Curt's car and looked over at the sleeping man, his head resting against the window where he had slept since they left the bar. The parking lot light illuminated the inside of the car, and shined off his curly blond hair. *What was she going to do with him? He looked so peaceful. He was handsome in an almost rugged sort of way. Did he have a drinking problem like Jerry had? She didn't need that.*

She was tired, and didn't relish taking him all the way back to North Chicago, but she couldn't leave him in the car either. He could sleep on her couch, but she hoped she wasn't sending him the wrong message by having him up to her home. She thought again about her options, and then said to herself. *What was it going to hurt? He was too drunk to want to try to do anything but sleep it off.*

Suddenly, Curt sat up, muttered something and then, fumbling with the door handle, threw up out the door into the parking lot. *That did it,* she thought. *He was coming upstairs for the night!"*

"I am so sorry." Curt said as Belinda made him a bed on the couch. "I guess I wanted so badly to make a good impression on you that I got carried away with my merriment. This is unusually bad behavior for me. I'm not a drunk."

"Go to sleep, vomit breath," she said smiling. "We'll talk more in the morning. If you need to use the bathroom it's through my room. She kissed him on the forehead and went to bed.

Belinda undressed slowly, thinking about the evening. Despite all that had happened, she liked Curt. She liked Curt a lot, but she had been hurt badly once, and needed to be careful.

David was seething. He knew he had to do what he could to capture some of the valuable fluid now leaking from the back of his truck bed and onto the ground. He carefully opened the door on the passenger's side. He could not create a spark or it would all but be over. He had been so lucky that he hadn't started the engine and tried to drive away. He found a glass jar, full of bolts and nuts from pipe clamps, and dumped them out on the ground. The jar would hold at least a quart of it but he had no acceptable cap for it, just the metal screw cap that would be eaten up by the fluid in short order. He would have to come up with something. There seemed to be nothing else available in his truck that would hold the liquid and no acceptable cap that would keep it from evaporating.

For a long time, David sat on a fallen tree across the road and smoked a cigarette, deep in thought. The night was clear and crisp and not too cold. Somewhere off to his left there was a rustle as a large bird, most likely an owl, took flight—silhouetted against the moon. He would need transportation. There was no way he could start this truck now, it had to be destroyed. It was being drenched in the volatile liquid.

Finished with thinking and smoking he walked back to the truck. The flow of fluid had stopped and the jar was only three quarters full. He picked it up and took it over and hid it under the same log he had been sitting on. Going back, he recovered some clothing, food and water from the cab and brought them back there, also. He would have to light the whole thing off, but first, he needed to get some transportation. He started up the road to the house, each step steeped in such pain that it brought tears flowing down his cheeks. His boots crunched on the hardened snow base, and he shivered in the cold night air. Nothing could happen to Mike Flanagan that would even begin to be payback for how he felt about him right now.

The house was a small, one-story house that sat on the end of the road, at an abrupt dogleg to the left, amongst some old ramshackle outbuildings and discarded machinery. The moonlight, from the almost-full moon, showed everything clearly in its eerie light. The car that had stopped sat next to the house and David went up to it and put his hand on the hood. It was still warm. He walked to the back door and looked through the window into the tiny kitchen. An under-the-counter light gave enough of a glow that it showed the room was empty. The rest of the house was dark.

He just wanted the car right now, and didn't want any other trouble, so he walked over to the driver's door and looked in—no keys. He walked back to the house and tried the doorknob. It was unlocked and, looking inside once more through the doorway, he saw what he was looking for—an old wooden key, mounted on the wall on a cupboard next to the door with hooks on it, full of keys. Quietly, he opened the door just enough to get his hand inside and brought out a ring of keys. They were all padlock or other keys, not car keys, and he threw them in the snow bank next to the door. Once more, he reached inside, and brought out a smaller ring of keys. This looked more promising. There were two keys on a leather tab that said, Cedarville Motors, Cedarville Wisconsin. David walked back to the car and tried the door key first, just to make sure he had the right car—it fit. For a moment, he stood and looked around the farmyard. There was a doghouse with some straw scattered outside of the doorway on top of the snow, but if there was a dog in there he didn't care what was going on. There was a post with a yard light on it but it wasn't lit. He knew the minute he opened the car door there would be a light and some noise. He was starting to shiver violently from the cold—he had to go now.

The car responded quickly and he drove away from the house, the tires crunching on the snow-covered driveway. At the end of the dogleg, he stopped and looked back over his shoulder. The house still seemed to be dark.

Back at his truck, he recovered his belonging and the jar. He packed the top of the jar full of snow and put the metal lid back on. The melting snow wouldn't mix and would stay on top, protecting the metal lid, and he could draw it off later. He moved the car a safe distance from the truck and lit his last cigarette. Carefully, he smoked it down to a butt—it might be a while before he got another. Then, he flicked it at the back of the truck bed.

The explosion knocked him down. It was far more violent than he had expected and now the fire was following the leaking trail towards the idling car and down the road. David moved as fast as he could, getting in the car and heading quickly down the road. The ribbon of fire was following him and was, at times, right under the car, but soon he was clear and out on the highway. Behind him, it was an inferno.

Back at the farmhouse, Betty was sitting up in bed and listening. She had heard an explosion, and outside Duke was barking. She looked over at Herman, who was still asleep, but didn't wake him. She slipped on her housecoat and went to the back door. *It was cold in the kitchen,* she thought. *Why, my goodness, the door was partway open.* She closed it and peeked outside. Duke seemed to be terribly upset and, looking out the kitchen window, she could see flames across the field and down the road. *Oh, that poor man that was down there when they had come in! Was he in a fire?* she wondered. Then she noticed their car was missing.

It was twenty minutes later that the Cedarville Volunteer Fire Department reached the scene and, by that time, the fire had largely burned itself out. Herman stood quietly by while the firemen sprayed water on the remains of the truck. Betty remained up at the house.

The Assistant Fire Chief, Gunner Swenson, walked over to talk to him. The two men were long-time acquaintances, going to the same church, Mount Hill Lutheran. "Yeah, you know," he said in his Swedish dialect, "it looks to me like the truck was empty, Herman, unless the guy burned completely up. We usually have a gut pile left, if nothing else. Takes a lot of fire to burn up guts and assholes." He chuckled at his remarks. "You said there was a man in that cab when you stopped, right?" He spit a long steam of tobacco juice the other direction from Herman and wiped his mouth with the back of his mitten.

"Yup, but now my car is missing too, so it all makes sense, huh? Sons-of-bitches come out here and cause trouble, Gunner. That car wasn't much, but it was all I had."

"Well, I got a call into the sheriff, but they are busy tonight so it might be a while. We got part of a melted license plate from the truck so I hope that provides us with a clue. Judas Priest, that thing got hot! Yah, you bettcha. I never seen nothing burn like that hot before, Herman. Melted the gol dang truck frame right into the ground. Hell, if looks like it even burned the ground—dirt, rocks, and all. Well, we'll let old snoop pants and his deputies figure it out. You might just as well go back to bed and keep Betty warm, if you know what I mean." He winked and slapped Herman on the back. Both men chuckled at the unspoken insinuation.

"Let's wrap it up, boys, and go back to bed!" he shouted to the firemen.

Herman walked back to the house, where Betty was sitting at the kitchen table. "I made some coffee, Herme," she said.

"Well, we might just as well drink coffee and have something to eat, Betty. The sheriff is coming out. Gunner said I should go keep you warm," he chuckled.

"That Gunner has a one-track mind." Betty smiled, put some cookies on a plate and slid them across the table. "Here, you keep these cookies warm instead."

David had some luck going for him. The car had a full tank of gas, and a coffee cake that Betty was going to take into the church bake sale in the morning, was sitting on the seat. It was an old Pontiac sedan and the heater worked good so he was warming up, and starting to smell again. He had gone right through Cedarville and was going to catch State Highway 14 which would take him northwest towards Madison. Then he would work his way west from there. He remembered this much of the directions from when he had studied them last night.

The little town appeared to be mostly asleep, but he did see the door to the fire station opening as he went past it. Two men were rushing to get in an old fire truck that looked almost homemade. Nothing big and shiny, like the rigs he had seen in Chicago. He hated it all the same, and the fire fighters who rode on it.

He was getting weary again. It had been a long time since he had slept, and his mind was foggy and disconnected, but he had to get out of the immediate area. At some point, he would need to think about changing vehicles again. Maybe after he used up the gas in this one. Maybe in Madison where there would be lots of cars—but lots of cops, too, he thought, as an afterthought. *Maybe it was just another bad idea. Oh hell, he was too tired to think about anything right now.*

CHAPTER TWENTY-SIX

The old sheriff's deputy sat at the kitchen table with Herman and Betty, talking so softly they could hardly hear him, his hand cupped around a crockery coffee mug. His eyes were drooping under thick, graying, bushy eyebrows—eyes that had seen too much of the evil in this world, and eyes that just wanted to go home and close, and rest.

His brown jacket was open, revealing a potbelly that had come from long hours of riding around the dusty country roads, and too much coffee and pastries. His brown, sweat-stained uniform cap lay on the table top, next to a yellow legal pad he was scribbling some notes on. His portable radio also sat on the table, and buzzed from time to time with radio traffic.

"We checked the plate on the truck," he said, "and this might disturb you. This truck and this man, whom we believe was in it, are fugitives running from the law in Chicago. Well, not the truck," he added, smiling.

"My lord!" Betty exclaimed. "What did he do?"

"He tried to burn the city down. He killed a lot of people."

Betty gasped and grabbed Herman's hand. "Did you hear that, Herme? We could have been killed."

Herman just drummed his fingers on the table. The guy had stolen his car and that was what he was the most upset about right now. "Son-of-a-bitch," he finally muttered.

The deputy didn't say anything, but wrote down some more things before looking up at both of them. "You need to lock your doors at night. That old hound dog out there is a tight sleeper. We'll get this out right away. He got away from here, but now we know what he is driving and he can't be far away. Thanks for the coffee and the information." He slid his chair back and stood up. "Guess I better get going—nice meeting both of you." He shook hands with Herman, tipped his hat at Betty and was out the door.

"Goddamn world is going to hell in a bushel basket," he muttered as he got back in his dirty squad car and drove off. Duke, on a chain, was growling and snarling at his car.

"Sure, get mad now, you useless mutt!" Herman yelled out the door. "Shut your trap and get back in your doghouse. Let's go to bed, Betty. There are still a couple hours of night left."

By daybreak, David had made up his mind that he simply had to stop and rest or he was going to have an accident. He was south of Madison at a truck stop, fueling up the car, and had given up on stealing anything else for transportation. It was just a vicious cycle. The old Pontiac ran well and wasn't that conspicuous. There was a bunkhouse, across the street from the truck stop, where he could get a bed and a shower; he couldn't stand his own smell any longer. He fueled up the car, got a pack of camels and some junk food, and then drove slowly across the street. David parked between two trucks, where the car would be hard to see, and pushed some snow on the license plate before he went into the bunkhouse.

Belinda and Curt were both up, sitting at the kitchen table. She wore a pair of old sweats and a tee shirt and he was still in his clothes from last night.

"I'm really sorry about all of the trouble I caused," he said. "I better get going."

"Outside of the puking, I thought we had a good time," she smiled. "I would like to see you again, Curt."

"It was a waste of some good Tacos," he grinned. "Maybe I had a touch of the flu." He laughed.

Belinda giggled. "I bet that was it."

They had both stood up and Curt took both of her hands in his. "I would love to see you again," he said.

She reached up and kissed him softly beside the mouth. "Call me," she whispered, as if someone was listening to them.

David had no bags—just the fruit jar with the liquid in it—that he wasn't letting out of his sight. He had tried to be as inconspicuous as he could be, checking in at the desk at the bunkhouse. The woman who was waiting on him was on the phone at the same time, talking in Spanish to someone, and paid little attention to him. She was small, and obviously Latino and, seemingly, doubled as the cleaning lady. She took his twenty bucks and pointed down the hall with a key in her hand that she handed to him.

The room was small and had the bare essentials. A single bed, a small desk, and a wooden chair that sat under a window covered in heavy curtains that were closed. A single light bulb in a porcelain fixture that was in the ceiling glared down at him until he turned on the bedside lamp, and walked over and shut the overhead one off. There was a small mural of a western scene on the wall. No clock or pictures.

David sat down on the edge of the bed and started undressing. He had seen the sign on the wall—on the way to his room—that said, **Showers**. Leaving on his pants, he walked to the door and peered out. The hallway appeared empty and the woman at the end was now gone.

In the shower, he took off the rest of his clothes. His pants were stuck to his legs from all of the puss and watery discharge that had come from his sores. He wanted to scream out as the sores tore back open, but managed to only moan instead. There was a sliver of soap in a tin dish, on the wooden bench in the shower, and he managed to get some lather up and wash himself, as carefully as he could. The soap burned in his sores, but he knew it had to be done or he would die of infection before he ever found Flanagan. Tonight, when he left, he would get some more hydrogen peroxide for an antiseptic. He had been out of it for three days. What he did keep on hand had been left in the burned-out house he had so hastily left in Chicago.

He washed out his underwear and pants. He could dry them on the heater in his room. He had to get some sleep or he was going to pass out.

In his years in inspection, Mike Flanagan had helped convict and incarcerate many arsonists. He had made a lot of enemies, but he knew it went with the territory and it was always in the back of his mind. They knew where he worked—it was hard to keep that a secret—but he had taken measures to keep his family safe. His phone was unlisted and both he and Laura shunned publicity. He seldom let it bother him. Most of them did not want to see Flanagan again.

The rebirth, so to speak, of Bennett was a whole new scenario, though. This was no ordinary crook. He had proven both here, and in Chicago, what he was capable of, and that was proving hard to ignore. It was time to involve the Minneapolis Police.

The Minneapolis Police Department received a constant flow of information, from other departments around the country, regarding people of interest to be on the lookout for. The information on David Bennett had arrived yesterday, and was going to be released to the shift commanders today. It wasn't deemed high priority, but it was out there.

Mike sat across the desk from the Deputy Chief of Operations, talking softly, but candidly, about David Bennett. What Bennett had done previously was before the Chief's time so he had no real knowledge of the man, but he listened intently.

"You think he's headed here?" the Chief asked, his eyebrows raised, while he played with a pencil on his desktop.

"I do," Mike answered. "This guy has a real grudge with me, and with all fire departments, and he doesn't care who or what gets in his way. He is a sadistic pyromaniac, and a callous killer that has taken the lives of a great many people, both here and in Chicago."

"So what makes you think he isn't still in Chicago?"

"It's just a gut feeling, Chief. I got a glimpse of him down in Chicago, and his look back at me said it all."

"How did he get away from you, if you saw him?"

"A long story, but not relevant right now."

There was a knock on the door. A young woman came in and handed the Chief some papers.

"Here's the update you asked for," she said.

He read, and then seemed to reread the sheet of paper she had handed to him. "You might be right, Mike. They found his truck burned out in Southern Wisconsin last night, but no sign of him and some farmer's car is missing. Somewhere near Cedarville, if you know where that is. I'll step up patrols in your neighborhood and we'll get this out over the radio right away. We have a license plate listed here, any description you can help with?"

Mike slid a ten-year-old picture of David Bennett across the table.

"The guy is older now but he didn't seem to have changed that much from what I saw of him."

"We'll be careful, and I'll keep you posted," the Chief said. "We're on it—you can rest assured about that."

"Mike—here." The Chief had gone to a cabinet, dug in a drawer, and now he was handing Flanagan a silver Colt Python 357 Magnum with a two-inch barrel in a worn, black holster.

"I don't know how to use one of these," Mike said.

"Go down to the range and ask for Perkins. I'll tell him you are coming."

When David awoke, it was dark outside, as he peered out a slit between the curtains into a dark parking lot. Checking his watch, it was nearly 11 p.m.. Fourteen hours he'd been sleeping, but now, sitting on the edge of the bed and rubbing the sleep from his eyes, it was past time to get rolling. He reached over and touched his trousers on the heater. They were dry and warm. He would be in Minneapolis before daylight if there were no problems.

David sat in the car, letting it warm up, and looking at a Minnesota and Wisconsin map he had found in the door pocket. He chewed a piece of beef jerky while he contemplated his course. The sleep had done wonders for him.

The trip would take him through a lot of back roads, until he got to Eau Claire. From there, he would go up to Prescott and cross the river into Minnesota, at Hastings.

The rural Wisconsin countryside slid by in the darkness. One darkened farmstead after another, and one sleepy little town after another. To see another car tonight was a rarity.

The car radio was on and tuned to a Chicago station that faded in and out with static—sometimes being cut off by an old-time music station from some elusive source. When it was from the Chicago station, they were still talking about the devastating fires, but there had been no mention of him. The people that had been killed—the buildings that burned—just didn't excite him anymore. What he had planned to happen had not happened and it drove him into a rage, and it was because of Mike Flanagan's interference. What happened in Chicago should have been none of Flanagan's damn business, and now he was going to pay for not minding his business. The drive had given him time to think and plan as he drove, and he was no longer shooting from the seat of his pants. David was rested, more in control, and getting his confidence back.

Ahead, on the shoulder, was a Highway Patrol car with its emergency lights flashing, its spotlight shining on an over-turned car in the ditch. He slowed and pulled far to the left to stay clear. The trooper, standing by the car, was talking on his radio and leaning on the open window, looking at someone in the backseat with the door open. He paid David no attention, but it did get David's heartbeat up.

He had passed through the little town of Ellsworth around five a.m., the last town before Prescott and the Minnesota border. The trip had taken longer than he thought, but that was all right, there was no hurry now. In an hour, David would be in the Southern suburbs of Minneapolis. His plan was to lay low for a couple of days and gather information. He knew where Flanagan worked—now he had to find out where he lived.

CHAPTER TWENTY-SEVEN

Belmont Academy was a prestigious, private high school on the shores of Minnehaha Creek. It was small, by school standards, having less than two hundred students in grades ten, eleven and twelve. Many sought admittance, and the only reason Mike and Laura had been able to get Cindy into it, was her unusual musical talent. The school was a hot bed for the arts and they actively recruited talented students. It was their philosophy that, if the talent was there, they could develop it better than anyone else.

Each day, Cindy would wait on the bus bench on the corner of the red-bricked schoolyard for either Mike or Laura to pick her up. She took the bus in the morning, but most nights there was tutoring after school, so the hours varied. For most of the three years she had been here, she had been watched every day, from in front of two houses down the street, by a middle-aged man in a brown Oldsmobile. He never got out of the car nor did he ever follow her. No one, in either of the houses he parked in front of, paid any attention to him. Parents were always waiting for their kids.

Mason Evans was the mystery man's name and he had reason to have an interest in Cindy; after all, he was her real father. He knew he could never approach, or ever talk to her, and had blown his chance to be a part of her life, but he had never forgotten her, and she fascinated him. Mason had a scrapbook of Cindy's life, filled with pictures he had secretly taken, and newspaper articles from the school paper—picked up from a stand in the entryway. He had seen Laura come to pick her up so many times. They were carbon copies of each other. They laughed the same way and walked the same way. He had witnessed the mannerisms from afar, yes, but they were so obvious. The man had also seen Mike Flanagan on many occasions, coming to get his daughter. He knew Flanagan would recognize him, if he saw him, so he always wore glasses he didn't need, and a derby hat. Mason harbored no ill feelings towards Laura or Mike. He had made his bed and now he was paying the consequences. His life was a mess, and always had been because of the booze. He would only have been bad for Cindy, but he couldn't forget her. Not now. Not ever.

David drove the streets of North Minneapolis, just moseying along, deep in thought and letting the memories wash over him. In one location, a vacant lot still brought back thoughts reminiscent of the night he burned the furniture company that once sat there. *What a great fire that was,* he thought. The car dealership, across the street where he had hidden and watched it burn, was gone, too. Now it was a fenced-in basketball court, where three black men were shooting hoops in the frigid air, dressed in only tee shirts and sweat pants, their backs steaming in the cold air. Minneapolis was much colder than Chicago this time of the year. Cold was something he didn't need.

His plan was to rent some private place, no matter how shabby it was. He wasn't trying to be comfortable. Comfort came in the memories of the fires he had created and the retribution he would be getting when he killed Mike Flanagan. A Minneapolis squad car passed him and turned the corner before he could let it bother him. They had bigger fish to fry—and then—there it was. A small house with a sign out front that said, "**For rent or sale.**"

The house wasn't empty, but looked to be furnished. The sidewalks had been shoveled and, for all practical purposes, it looked as if someone was living there now.

From the front window, you could see through the entire house to the back door—a living room, a dining room and a small kitchen. The bedroom appeared to be off to the left side. There was a phone number written on a piece of paper, and taped to the door, for perspective buyers or renters. It simply said, "Call this number for details." It made no mention of being a realtor.

He drove down the block to a corner market and walked in. "Is there a pay phone around?" he asked.

"You walked right by it, buddy," the old man behind the register said. "It's right there outside the door."

"Yes," a soft voice answered when he dialed the number.

"Is this the number for information on the house to rent on Morgan?" David said.

"Yes, it is. The house belonged to my mother. She recently passed away and I'm trying to rent or sell it myself. Do you have a family?"

"No. I'm single."

"Would you be willing to sign a lease for a year?"

"Sure, that would be fine."

David had no intention of signing anything, or giving anyone any of his dwindling supply of cash.

"Well," the woman said, "I guess the next step would be for you to meet me at the house, and we can work out the details. I have a church meeting this afternoon, but I could come over this evening if that would work. Say, seven?"

"Seven it is," David said.

Amanda Fearing set the phone back down in its cradle. *It seemed strange he never asked the price,* she thought. *Maybe she should call her friend, Addie, and ask her to go along with her.*

Addie's phone rang several times before Amanda remembered. Addie was in Texas, with her son, for a week.

"Oh, well, what could go wrong?" she said to herself. She had to learn to trust people more.

David drove to the library at Webber Park to spend the rest of the day doing some research. On the way, he stopped and got snacks and cigarettes at a drugstore in Camden. He was getting tired again. When he got tired, he got ornery, and when he got ornery, he got careless. *Let's be careful,* he thought.

The library closed at four, today being Saturday. David had found out two things of interest by then. The offices for Fire Inspection for the City of Minneapolis were still in City Hall, and Mike Flanagan was still the Director.

Amanda parked in the alley and walked around the house to the front door. David was leaning on a handrail by the stoop. *Oh,* she thought. *I think I have made a mistake. This man is dirty and unkempt. Her mother would never forgive her for renting to a man like this. She had to worm her way out of this mess. This had been a mistake to even try.*

"Good evening," she said. "I'm sorry for keeping you, but something came up and now I can't rent the house to you, but I thought I owed you some kind of an explanation. You see, another person I had talked to…" The blow from David caught her across the side of her head and, suddenly, she wasn't able to focus her eyes anymore. Then it all seemed to slip away.

The kids had gone to bed and Mike and Laura, also in bed, were talking quietly. Laura had been reading, but now her book lay open on her chest, while she listened to Mike. They had been talking about the day's activities when suddenly, out of nowhere, Mike turned on his side, propped his head up on his pillow and, facing Laura, said, "There is something you should be aware of, Laura. Yesterday I was informed that a certain fugitive from Chicago, who is running from the law there, is headed back this way."

Laura now turned her head towards him, and was looking at him quizzically, but saying nothing.

"I guess what I'm trying to say is there may be a threat against me from this man, but look, I'm being careful, so not to worry."

"Who is it," she asked, "and why?"

"His name is David Bennett, and I thought for the last ten years he was dead, but I know now he isn't. He is very much alive. Look, I have known for quite a few days now about this, because I saw him when I was in Chicago, but I never thought it would come to this."

Laura was looking irritated. "Why, after ten years, would he still be looking for you? Wasn't that the man who was setting fires back here in Minneapolis? Oh, my God!" she exclaimed.

"Look, I don't want you to get upset about this, and maybe it's nothing, but we should be aware of what is going on around us."

"WE! Why we, Mike? Are you saying he would try to harm the kids or me?"

"No, I'm not saying anything, but I just don't know what he is going to do, and I thought you should know what is going on. Look, the police are looking for the guy. He has physical peculiarities that make him stand out in a crowd. He can't hide very well."

Laura brushed a tear from her face. Then rolled over with her back to Mike and shut off the lamp. She thought about the early days of their marriage when Mike had been an active fire fighter and she had wished he would get into something safer. *At least the enemy back then wasn't after his family,* she thought.

She was as light as a feather and the key for the front door was right in her hand, the leather lanyard still wrapped around her wrist. David held her in front of him while he took her hand, inserted the key and opened the door. Outside, and in back of them, cars were going by but no one stopped. The house smelled antiseptic clean and warm. Somewhere, a furnace was quietly running and a cuckoo clock was sounding off.

He had to get rid of her first, and then he would make plans. Carrying her into the kitchen, he saw a door off to the left of the room. Opening it, he was looking down the steps to the tiny cellar. The basement was one stark, gray room—a furnace, a washer and dryer, and one cabinet with some old fruit jars on top of it. That was it.

She moaned and seemed to be having some kind of a convulsion, but then became quiet once more, breathing noisily with blood bubbles coming out her nose. He set her down on the floor and looked at her. *He should just kill her and make everything easier but, for some reason,* he thought, *maybe if she's not hurt too bad when she does come to, she can help me. I need money, if nothing else, and I need to know whom she told she was coming here.*

CHAPTER TWENTY-EIGHT

February in Minneapolis can be a fickle month. You never know what's coming—below zero weather that chills you to the bone, or a January thaw that leaves the streets full of slush from January and December's snowstorms. Today, the weather was mild, but there was a storm predicted for the end of the week.

David had tied poor Amanda up in the basement, just to be safe, even though she had not regained consciousness. The blood that had run from her nose had dried all around her mouth, giving the impression that she had been face down in a cherry pie. Her hands had formed into tiny fists and she had curled into somewhat of a fetal position. Her breathing was ragged, but regular. He had checked on her every hour or so to see if she was going to wake up or not and thought maybe, if she didn't come around soon, he would just have to put her out of her misery and hope no one missed her for a while.

The jar of his chemical, with about two inches of water on top of it, sat in the middle of the kitchen table. If things worked right, he had a fitting finish planned for it.

The Minneapolis City Hall sits on a square block of land in downtown Minneapolis, connected to the Hennepin County Government Center by a tunnel—a dark grey fortress of a building, with its stone walls and green tiled roofs and its towering clock tower. It was a hub of activity and business in the bustling city that never seemed to rest. Finding Flanagan's office was easy enough; there was a directory in the lobby that told you where it was. Finding him might be a more difficult task, however.

David had a different car now. It was one that the police were not looking for, so he could be bolder, more brazen. Unlike the farmer's old rusty Pontiac that now sat in the garage behind the tiny house, this Lincoln was the lap of luxury. Amanda loved her car and it was one of the few luxuries she had allowed herself in her old age. The spinster schoolteacher, now retired, lived frugally, otherwise. She had four hundred dollars in her purse that David had found when he rifled through it. Then he had thrown the purse down the stairs, where it landed in the corner of the basement. He could use the money.

He had no idea what Flanagan drove to work, or where he parked, or which entrance he used. The ramp he was in now had many spots reserved for government officials, on the lower levels, and he scoured the signs as he drove slowly up the concrete ramps. **Reserved for the Mayor,** and the **City Council** and the **Police Chief,** and **Deputy Chiefs**. Then, there it was—reserved for the **Fire Chief.** Five spots, two of them filled already with red squads. He was at the end of the row and, as he turned to go back up again to the next level, the signs continued until he saw **Reserved for Fire Inspection.** There were three spots and one of them was occupied. The good news—it was the end of the reserved spots.

One level up, David parked. It was early, and the level was mostly empty, so he had his choice of many spaces. The one he selected looked right down into the level below and the Fire Inspection slots.

He would wait in the car for a while, pretending to read the paper. He looked at his watch—it was seven thirty a.m.

It had been a quiet breakfast at the Flanagan house. The kids were off to school, and now it was just Mike and Laura, alone in the kitchen. "Mike, I'm sorry," Laura said, wrapping her hands in the towel she had been wiping dishes with. She had a blue terry housecoat on, loosely tied at the waist. Her hair was tied up in a ponytail, with a lot of loose strands hanging out. "I guess, sometimes, I forget that things aren't always your fault when your job has its trials and tribulations. I should be more supportive of you, and look at the big picture." She walked behind him to where he was sitting, his raised coffee cup in his hand. She pulled his head to her bosom and kissed his forehead. "I love you so much," she whispered.

Mike stood and took her in his arms. They fit so well together and their marriage had been an almost endless honeymoon. "You are my life, Laura, and always will be. The family you have given me, the love you have shown for me. Well—I'm just the luckiest man in the world." He kissed her softly. "There was a time when I might be late for work at a time like this," he smiled, and playfully squeezed her butt. "But not today—I have to run."

Back in Wisconsin, at the truck stop bunkhouse David had stayed at, the same Hispanic woman who had been there when he came in, was now talking to a sheriff's deputy who, seemingly, was not the least bit interested in what she had to say. "Look, I am telling you—yes, it is only bedclothes, but smell them, officer, and look at the blood stains—and what are these other stains? Phew. Whoever slept in that bed was a very sick, rotten person and I want him to pay for this stuff. I cannot rent that room to anyone without completely sanitizing it and redecorating it."

"Did he use a credit card?" the office asked.

"No," she pouted.

"Then how am I supposed to find him?"

"I have his license plate," she smirked and handed the officer a piece of paper. "I am not as stupid as you think," she said. "I always write down their license plates."

He looked at the numbers she had written down. Hungry and tired, all he wanted was to get over to the truck stop across the street for breakfast. He would humor her. "I'll check it out and get back to you," he lied.

Outside in the squad, he looked at the numbers once more. Something rang a bell here. He paged through some notes that were lying on the other seat until he found what he was looking for. It was the plate number of a stolen car they had been asked to be on the lookout for. The guy who was in it was very dangerous and wanted by the Chicago Police. *Damn, this could be a feather in my cap*, he thought.

Running back into the office, he told the Hispanic woman. "Lock that room and don't touch anything. The crime lab is coming."

"Okay," she said. "All I wanted was some money for the damages—not that big of a deal."

"Do what I said," he told her.

At eight-fifteen, Mike pulled into the ramp. This thing with Bennett was first and foremost on his mind. The gun the Chief had given him was in his glove box. *Laura would have really come unglued if she saw that,* he thought. He still didn't know how to use it—maybe tomorrow, if he had time. *What was that guy's name at the range?* He tried to recall.

David had seen the movement out of the corner of his eye, and now he saw the black sedan pull in and park. The lone man got out and went to the trunk and inserted his key. He took out a box with some papers and put them under his arm. Then, he looked up at the level above, and David slumped in the seat, but not before he recognized Mike Flanagan.

Looking at his watch, he counted hours. If Flanagan worked a normal day he would be leaving sometime after four p.m. It was too dangerous for him to sit here all day, but he didn't want to lose his space. He got out, locked the car and walked to the elevator. He had to waste a few hours someplace.

It was two-thirty in the afternoon when Mike got the call from the Police Department. Positive identification had been made by the detectives at the scene of the bunkhouse, through fingerprints, and a mug shot that had been shown to the Hispanic housekeeper. "It sure looks like he is heading for the cities," the Chief said. "This information is almost two days old," he added. "He's probably already made the trip."

"Thanks," Mike said.

This only reinforced the gut feeling that he had had all along—that David was coming back to his roots—something he would share with Laura this time. No more secrets.

David spent most of the day in a dark and dreary bar on the city's South Side. It stunk of polish sausage and sauerkraut, and the floor was sticky. He couldn't allow himself to be impaired, so he nursed his beer, and had a hamburger and some French fries. The bartender was washing glasses and cleaning up most of the time. He looked over at him from time to time, but didn't try to engage him in any conversation. He was only one of three men in the bar when he came in but, around noon, the lunch crowd came and the place started filling up, so he left. He walked over to the railroad yards and sat on an unused loading dock and, for a while, watched railroad workmen switching trains. His thoughts went back to the night he had burned the warehouse and the night watchman had been blown out of the building. A grin crossed his face. Then, about two p.m., he started back to the parking ramp. It was too damn cold out here. The Inspector's car was still there.

It was closer to five when Mike finally left for the day. He had made up his mind to buy Laura some flowers, so he went out another door. He stopped at Dayton's ticket office on Nicolette Avenue and picked up tickets for a Broadway show, coming to the Orpheum, he knew she wanted to see, picked up the flowers, then backtracked back to the parking ramp. It was time to go home. Tomorrow was Friday and a well-deserved weekend was coming up. Maybe they could go skiing if the kids were free.

David knew he had to leave first because, if he tried to follow Mike and got delayed at the ticket booth on the way out, he would lose him. The street was a one-way outside the exit, so he didn't have to be concerned with which way he was going. As soon as he saw Mike unlocking his car, he backed out and left. Outside, he pulled to the far left lane and put on his four-way flashers and waited. A stream of cars behind him were honking their horns and gesturing to him to get out of the way—it was rush hour.

A police officer, directing traffic, saw the congestion and leaving his post, started walking towards David's car. Just then, Flanagan emerged on the far side of the street. David put the big Lincoln back into gear and fell in three cars behind him. He gave the cop a gesture with his arms that said, *Sorry, I don't know what happened.* The cop gave him a mock salute.

Bennett was going to have to develop his plan as the opportunities arose. His first thought had been to find out where Flanagan lived, and then figure out how to abduct him. He wasn't going to get into any physical confrontation with him, which would be foolish. David was in no shape for that. He could go get a gun, but that wasn't his style. He had never used guns in his crimes. The man needed to burn to death, and feel the pain and suffering that went with cooking flesh, as David had. *For ten long years,* he thought. His anger came to the surface and he slammed his fist down on the steering wheel, his face beet red.

He had the jar of fluid left for the fitting end to this diabolical deed. It sat under a towel on the kitchen table, in the house he was now occupying, and that would be how he would do it. The only hitch was getting Flanagan into the house. He needed some bait. *I bet if I find his home, I'll find the bait,* he thought.

They drove south on Hiawatha, in almost bumper-to-bumper traffic, until they got to the parkway. Then, the black sedan with Flanagan in it exited and headed west. David had almost lost Flanagan once when he ran a yellow light and Bennett ran a red light behind him to keep up, but nothing had come of it as there was no cross-traffic.

In front of the school, Cindy sat on the bus bench, watching down the street for her ride, as she always did. Her violin was tucked between her feet; her lap was filled with books. She saw her dad coming a ways off and walked across the street to where he would stop at the curb. Mike pulled slowly up to the curb, reached across the seat, and opened the door for her. "Hey, kid," he said. "How was your day?"

"Same old stuff, Dad. Can you stop at the drugstore? I need some lip balm."

David's plan took shape right there. He filled in some of the blanks in his plans. This had to be his kid and he was picking her up from school on his way home. *Did he do it every day?* This could be the bait he was looking for. Tomorrow was Friday and he would get another chance to see if she was waiting for her dad every day, and if it was a regular thing.

CHAPTER TWENTY-NINE

When David got back to the house, the old lady was more responsive than she had been. She opened her eyes and stared at him, but her look said she had no idea where she was or what was going on. No anger and no words—just a blank stare. He gave her some water, and made a mental note to check on her in the morning. He checked the knots on the rope he had tied her up with. There was no room for error now. It was time to get to bed. He was very weary, despite the fact it was only seven p.m.

There were no sheets on the bed but it didn't matter, he just rolled up in the spread and was soon fast asleep.

Amanda lived alone and had told no one where she was going the day she left, but she did have a dog that was now without food, and he had been barking for most of the night. Her next-door neighbor thought it was unusual, so around 11 p.m. he went over to check on her. The house was locked and no one answered the door. He went to the garage and looked in, and saw her car was gone. It was all very strange—she and that dog were inseparable. She would not have gone, and left the dog unattended for a long period of time. Usually, she took the dog with her, unless she was just going for a short time. In fact, he had watched the dog for her on more than one occasion when she was worried she might be gone too long. Maybe in the morning, he would check again.

Amanda was now aware of where she was, and cognizant of what had happened to her. She was just powerless to do anything about it. She had no speech, she could not sit or stand, and her head felt like it might explode if she even moved. He had given her water last night, and she drank noisily, her eyes never leaving David's. Who was this man and why was he doing this to her? She had to go to the bathroom awfully bad after he left. Her bonds were so tight she could hardly move, and finally, she just gave up and wet herself. Then she wept uncontrollably, lying face down, her cheek pressed tight against the cold cement floor.

The next day, David passed the school several times in the afternoon. He had no idea when the kids got out of school, and maybe it was all a bad idea, anyway. On his fourth trip past the school, at four-thirty, she was there but with another girl. He went around the block and parked behind another car that was idling at the curb. A man inside was, seemingly, reading the newspaper. Some other goody dad waiting for his brat, he thought. This was a rich people's school, and full of a lot of spoiled rotten snots whose parents aspired to give them everything in life.

The man in front of him looked at him in the rear-view mirror, but it was only a passing glance. They were both too interested in the girl on the bench.

A few minutes later, a car pulled up and the other girl hugged Cindy and left with the driver. David was too far away to see her features closely but he was close enough to see it was not the same girl Flanagan had picked up the day before.

Then a red station wagon pulled to the curb, and the girl on the bench ran across the street and got into the car.

"Hi, Mom," said Cindy.

"Hi. I wish you would button your coat up. You're going to catch a cold in this weather."

"Oh, Mom. Colds are a virus and you don't catch them from leaving your coat unbuttoned."

David noticed that the driver in front of him had paid particular attention to the girl also, and had left right after the station wagon left.

Could this guy be some kind of pedophile? David wondered. *Well, the freak would not get his hands on her. Not before I do.* He thought about following the girl and her driver, but then thought better of it. *Next week,* he thought. *Next week.*

Why he hadn't gotten rid of the old lady in the basement was confusing even to David. He had killed callously before with no regard for people. For a while, it had even been a turn-on. Was he going soft?

On the way back to the house, he bought some groceries. It was going to be a long weekend.

Amanda's neighbor stood on her steps on Saturday morning, talking with the police officer he had summoned. "She would never have left that dog like this," he said. Looking in the window they could see the dog laying on the floor, looking at the door and wagging his tail. He had heard them outside. There were several poop piles on the rug.

"Well, I'll have a locksmith stop by and open the door, and then we'll take a look inside. I hate to break anything. What did you say her name was?"

"I think her last name is Fearing but I'm not sure how to spell it."

"What kind of car did she have?"

"I think it's a Lincoln Town Car. It's black and big. She looks like a kid behind the wheel." He chuckled.

"Someone will be back here sometime today. Probably won't be me. Keep an eye out. Locksmiths on Saturday are somewhat hard to find."

At suppertime, Mike had told Laura what more he knew about David Bennett. He told her they just needed to be aware of what was going on around them, always. He told her he thought the police would catch Bennett before he could do anyone any harm, but Laura just gave him a look across the table, with a toss of her head that said, *not in front of the kids.*

Cindy had looked up at the conversation with a questioning look on her face but then went back to her food, seemingly unconcerned. They were always talking about things she didn't know anything about.

On Saturday morning, David brought Amanda a doughnut and some coffee. The old lady was starting to grow on him. He could not, for the life of him, figure out why.

She was still not talking, but David knew she wanted to be clean, so he carried her upstairs and set her on the stool. Then, he washed off the blood and sweat from her face. He gave her some privacy for a while, but when he came back she was crying, and that made him angry. He brought her back downstairs and tied her back up, but this time, he did give her a blanket to lie on.

That afternoon, he went to a drugstore and bought a small bottle of chloroform. He had to explain to the druggist why he was using it. David told him that he was using it as a solvent. His chemistry background helped him talk intelligently about the product, and he was allowed to buy some.

He knew that the chloroform was not fast-acting, and he would have to act quickly once he approached the girl. Everything would have to be right. He drove down to the school on Saturday afternoon, and looked at the site once more. The bus bench was right on the street, but shielded from the school by shrubbery. Across the street were private homes, but most of them had enclosed porches that would make it hard for people to see the bench.

David thought to himself. *What were the odds she would be there and alone? What were the odds that no one would be watching? It seemed like a long-shot at best, and something out of a Hollywood script but, as physically crippled as he was, it was his only shot. He would have to quickly incapacitate her, and then drive up and snatch her from the bench. He could park his car across the street, and when he saw her coming down the walk, he would be standing at the bus stop, a few steps from the bench.*

On Saturday afternoon, the police and a locksmith arrived at Amanda's house. It didn't take long, and they were inside. The neighbor, who was concerned about her, walked over and took the dog while the officer checked the house.

Everything, with the exclusion of the mess the dog had made, seemed to be orderly and in place except for the pound of hamburger meat that had been left out to defrost on the kitchen counter and was starting to stink. Something was wrong and the officer knew it.

"I'm going to send an investigator down here," he told the neighbor. In the meantime, we'll put a lookout for her car. You don't know about any relatives or friends she might have?"

"No, her mother used to live over on Morgan, but she passed away a few months ago. Otherwise, she never went anywhere except to church."

"Can you keep that mutt for her until we find out more?'

"Sure, no problem."

"You don't know where, on Morgan, her mother lived?"

"Not really, but it was on the North end here."

The cop shrugged his shoulders and went back in the house. The neighbor took the dog and went home.

The police officer found the address of the house on Morgan in some papers, and decided to drive over there and check it out. In the meantime, an investigator showed up to go over the house.

At the house on Morgan, the officer showed up minutes after David had left for South Minneapolis. The home appeared to be secure, as he walked around it to the back door. Peering into the kitchen, nothing seemed to be amiss. He went back to the garage and looked in the window. There was an old red car in there but it was too dark to make out the plates. He walked back to his squad, passing by the basement window that Amanda was sleeping under. If he had bent over and looked, he would have seen part of her body, but there seemed no reason to look any further.

On Saturday evening, David took a bath. When he had been to the drugstore for the chloroform, he had bought some more peroxide and some medicated salve but, sitting naked in the tub right now, he knew he was in serious trouble. His left leg, from the knee on down, was turning black. He had gangrene, from lack of circulation, and soon it would poison even more of his body. The skin and flesh came off in hunks. He was a walking, talking corpse. The term, "dead man walking," was himself. A low-grade fever had developed and seemed to be getting worse, leaving him alternately cold and hot, and gave him the chills most of the time. David could not get enough warm clothing on, and was drinking copious amounts of water, but never peeing. His body leaked like a sieve.

All of this had an effect on his mind, and he went from seething anger, to quiet resolve. He knew he didn't have a lot of time left. He had to accomplish his mission and fast.

CHAPTER THIRTY

David had come to grips with his own fate; he had no desire to go on from here or to hurt anyone else. His fire-setting days were over. He was only going to use the girl to get to Flanagan. When he had him, he would set both her and the old lady free. There was no hope of him ever recovering from his debilitating injuries, anyway. He was a walking, rotting corpse of a man. Even though he had bought the chloroform, he was now having doubts that it would work; it took too long and he would never be able to restrain her until it took effect. She wasn't going to just sit there and let him put her to sleep and, right now, he would be no match for her struggling. It had been a Hollywood approach, at best. The struggles would also attract the attention of too many people, and he needed to do something immediate to incapacitate her, as he had done with Amanda.

For many years he had managed to function physically, and yes, at times almost normally, but lately, he hadn't had time to take care of himself. This infestation of infection and decay had climbed the ladder to gangrenous sores that would kill him, anyway. He just planned to speed that dying process up once all the pieces fell into place. But time was running short, and he was determined he was not going to die alone.

On Monday morning, the Missing Persons Division of the Minneapolis Police Department issued a search and detain for Amanda's car. It was, simply, the only thing they could do. There was no evidence that anything bad had happened to her, just the fact she had left and didn't come home. The report would be read for the first time at shift change on late Monday afternoon.

David had been on Mike's mind all weekend. He had never felt jumpier and more aware of all of the people he came into contact with, each and every day that he didn't know. He was watching everyone.

What would David Bennett do this time, and was he really in town? Would he start some more terrible fires to terrorize the population of Minneapolis like he had done in Chicago? From what they knew, he had no more fluid. Not unless he had taken some from that barrel that burned up with the truck. That seemed unlikely, because they had evidence the barrel had been leaking for quite some time. But there were other ways to start fires.

On Monday morning, David brought Amanda upstairs once more. He gave her a Danish he had bought, from a vending machine in a Laundromat, and some warm water, and let her use the bathroom. There was no other food in the house. Amanda was now coherent and thinking straight, but still having headaches and dizzy bouts. She chose not to speak and David had nothing to say to her, either, except for some grunts and pointing her to the direction he wanted her to go.

Around one in the afternoon, with Amanda safely tied back up in the basement, David went into the kitchen. He took a large carving knife from a butcher block that sat on the kitchen counter. He wrapped it in a small towel, went out the back door to the car and pulled away. He was nervous and sweating profusely, even though his body was racked with chills. He was on his way to the school. It was almost two when he arrived at the school. He parked about a block away from the school bench, and took up his vigil.

Around three, about a hundred students gathered outside on the sidewalk and the buses came and loaded them up. David could only hope she wasn't in that milling crowd of kids. If today didn't work out for him, he wasn't sure he would be able to come again. He was just that sick.

At four, just when he had almost given up hope that she was going to come outside, she appeared, walking down the long sidewalk to the bench, with another girl. They seemed to be laughing and talking animatedly—totally unaware of what was going on around them. He hated her for meddling in his affairs. Just when he was so upset that he was thinking of trying something foolish, a car pulled up and the other girl left in it.

Mason Evans was late getting there that day but he pulled up in front of David, several car lengths ahead of him, and settled back in the seat.

Who was this asshole, David mused. *He had been here Friday, too, or was it Thursday?* Most likely he had a kid to pick up, too, but if he was watching when David carried out his plan, he would be a witness, and that wouldn't be good. *But what to do about it,* he wondered. *He had to hurry.*

There was no more time to waste thinking about it, he had to act now and to hell with this other guy. He put the big Lincoln in gear and drove over to the bench, parking on the wrong side of the road, and threw open the driver's door. His hand went into the towel for the knife.

At first, Cindy didn't know what had happened, until it happened. David was not that fast, but she had not been paying attention, either, as she was working on some homework. By the time she realized what was going on, he had her by the scarf around her neck and was pushing the tip of the knife under her chin. The more she struggled, the deeper the knife bit into her flesh, and she knew she was bleeding. At last, she screamed with all of her might, but David tightened the scarf and she felt the world going black.

He pushed her into the front seat; face down, her head against the far door. With tires squealing, the big car lurched out into the road and sped away. Angrily, he swept her legs from in back of him, into the passenger compartment, and relaxed his grip on the scarf.

No one at the school saw anything. Cindy's violin still lay on the sidewalk, her books were scattered in the snow behind the bench; one of her mittens was in the gutter. She had simply vanished.

Down the block where he always parked, the only witness to the whole thing put his aging brown sedan into gear and hurried after the black Lincoln. Mason's first impulse was to go find a phone and call the police, but if he stopped, he would lose the car he was chasing, and he didn't have the license number. All he could think was some monster had his beautiful girl in his car, and he was not going to get away with it. He was her birth father, and yes, he had deserted both her and her mother, and he could never make that right. But right now, no one was gong to abduct his daughter.

The red station wagon pulled up and stopped across the street from the bench. At first, Laura wasn't concerned, maybe she ran back inside to get something. Then she saw the violin. Cindy would never have left it there, unattended, for even a second. She got out of the car and walked across the street. Then she saw the mittens and her schoolbooks and papers in the snow. For a second, she couldn't believe her eyes, and then a low moan formed in her throat and her eyes welled with tears. She gathered up Cindy's things and ran for the building, bursting into the front office. "Is my daughter in here?" she cried out.

Wanda Collison got up from her receptionist's desk, sensing something was terribly wrong. "Mrs. Flanagan! What are you saying?"

Laura was crying openly right now. "My daughter's things are scattered all over and she isn't there—that's what I am saying. Are you sure she isn't in here?"

"I saw her leave about fifteen minutes ago. In fact, she waved to me on her way out the door. I haven't seen her come back in, but that doesn't mean she didn't. Let's look around and I'll ask some others to help me. Why don't you go outside and look once more? She might have walked a ways with a friend." Wanda had left her desk and was now hugging Laura. "I'm sure there is an explanation for all of this," she said.

Wanda pushed a button on the intercom that went to all of the classrooms and hallways at once. "Is Cindy Flanagan in the building?" she asked. If so, please come to the office at once.

At the same time, she sent two student workers to check the bathrooms and locker rooms.

Laura, still holding all of Cindy's papers and her violin, walked back outside. She seemed to be a little calmer, but tears were still spilling over her eyes onto her cheeks, and she wiped them away with the back of her hand.

You couldn't see the bench from the front of the school, because of shrubbery, so she walked almost all of the way back to the bench. Then, noticing she had left her car running and the door open, she walked across the street before going to the bench. She deposited Cindy's things in the back seat, shut off the car and closed the door, and went back to the bench. It was then that Laura noticed two drops of blood on the ground. It was now a hysterical Laura who ran into the office, sobbing, and yelled, "Call the police right now!"

David had tried to drive so as not to attract attention, but it was hard because Cindy, now awake, kept trying to get up off the floor where she laid face down. Finally, he slowed for a red light and, pushing the knife into her buttocks, he hissed, "Look, settle down or I will kill you right now. It's not you I want, and I'm not going to hurt you if you do what I ask."

Cindy relaxed. She had no other option than to do what he asked. "Why are you doing this to me?" she sobbed. "What did I ever do to you?"

"Nothing," he said. "But your daddy did something, and he is going to pay. Now shut the hell up."

Mason's old car was overheating, and the engine was knocking. Two red indicator lights were on and lit the dash. He had to keep the black car in sight—they had turned on Broadway and were now heading west. This was his old stomping grounds, and they passed Dumont where he and Laura once used to live; then the offices on Penn, where he had worked before getting fired so many years ago. What a mess he had made of his life and his marriage. Laura had deserved better than him, and she had found it.

Now they were heading north on Morgan. At Fortieth Street, the Lincoln took an abrupt left, and then ducked into the alley before Mason could see where it had gone. Frustrated, he drove around the block, but saw nothing. He went a block in each direction, but no black Lincoln. Then he turned down the alleyway between Morgan and Newton, and there it sat—parked in front of a small garage. He stopped in the intermediate of the alley and shut off his car, but it continued running with the key off, the engine lurching and belching black smoke. Then it gave up with a loud hiss, and died.

CHAPTER THIRTY-ONE

Mike had been walking out the door when the phone on his desk rang. He hesitated for a second, thinking he would ignore it. He was tired and wanted to get home with his family. He had had work up to here, and this thing with David Bennett was taking its toll on him. But, at last he relented, and reaching over the desk from the front, picked it up.

Something was terribly wrong, and he could hardly understand Laura, she was crying so hard. She was at the school, and Cindy was missing and she had called the police, she wailed. Line two on his phone was now blinking, and showing him he had another call. "Laura, I'll be right there," he said. "Calm down, sweetheart." He hung up the phone.

He looked at the blinking light. *He didn't have time for this,* he thought. Mike had to get to Laura, *but maybe it was the police on the other line. She had said she called them.*

Mike punched the other button on the phone and then froze in place.

From the first words said by David Bennett, he knew his worst fears had been realized.

"You listen, and listen good," David said. "I have your precious daughter and, if you want to see her alive again, you need to do what I'm going to tell you. First, if you call the police, I will slit her throat. It's you I want, not her. I'm not going to say it again. No cops."

He could hear Cindy's muffled sobs in the background.

Mike was furious. "Look, you son-of-a-bitch. You harm one hair on her head…"

"Shut your Goddamn mouth and listen!" David was shouting into the phone. "No more talking," he hissed. "You go north on Morgan to Fortieth. Then take a left, and come in the alley to the third house down on the left, where the black Lincoln is parked. Come to the door, alone and unarmed." He hung up the phone, and the connection was lost.

Mike's head was spinning. Laura had already called the police but they knew nothing about this call. He had to talk with Laura first before he went for Cindy. He dialed the school and Wanda answered.

"This is Mike Flanagan. Is my wife there?" he asked.

"Yes, she's right here, and she's very upset, Mr. Flanagan."

"Please put her on the phone," he said.

"Mike," Laura sobbed, "Where are you?"

"Look, honey, I know where she is and I'm going to get her. Wait for the police and then go home, Laura. I can't tell you anything yet, but give me fifteen minutes and I'll call you."

"Where is she," she wailed. But the line was dead.

Laura handed the phone to Wanda and slumped in the chair. Just then, two Minneapolis police officers came through the door.

After he had called Flanagan from the kitchen phone, David had literally dragged Cindy down the stairs, by her scarf again, almost chocking her to death. Once in the basement, he told her to sit down. When she didn't respond as quickly as he liked, he kicked her legs out from under her, and she fell clumsily to the floor. He rolled her onto her stomach, and quickly tied her hands behind her back, with the ropes he had already cut and left lying there, for just that purpose. Cindy moaned and screamed, and he grabbed her hair from behind and jerked her head back. "What did I tell you!" he yelled. "Shut your mouth and do what you're told to do." He banged her head down on the floor. Just as he finished tying her feet, he heard footsteps upstairs.

Cindy could not see the old lady, lying across the room, very well. She was on her side, in an almost-fetal position. She appeared to be dead, and this unnerved her even more. *This guy was a vicious killer,* she thought. *How many others had he killed?* He was using her to get to her dad and then he would kill both of them.

Mason walked around the house outside, seeing what he could see under the window shades, but the house appeared to be empty. He heard muffled talking and screaming, but from where? He went to the back door and tried the knob—it was open. Cautiously, he walked in. The door to the downstairs was closed when he walked in, and he went right past it into the rest of the house. He peered into each room but the house appeared empty. Then, coming back, he went to the downstairs door, studied it for a moment, and then opened it. Before Mason knew what was happening, David plunged the knife, from out of the darkness, into Mason's chest and, spinning him around, threw him down the stairs. He slid down the stairs on his back, headfirst, and crashed into the wall at the bottom of the stairs. He lay, spread-eagled, on the floor. Motionless, the knife still buried in his chest, a pool of blood spreading out under him. For a moment, David peered down after him, thinking, *"What the hell was happening? This wasn't Flanagan! Where did this guy come from and why? Was he a burglar that just stumbled in?"*

Mike was speeding up Lyndale Avenue in his patrol car, the red light and siren on. He had the radio microphone in his hand and he could ask the police to meet him there if he wanted to, but he remembered David's words. 'If I see one cop I will kill her.' He reached over and punched the button on the glove box. The revolver lay right there, on top of some papers. He took it and stuffed it behind him in the waistband of his trousers. Now he wished he had gone to the range and taken the lessons he had been offered, but how tough could it be? Squeeze the trigger, and bang!

Mason had come to and was moaning. The blood puddle was from the cut on the top of his head where he had hit the cement wall. The knife wound had penetrated his chest, to the point that about half an inch of it had come out his back, under his shoulder blade. It had cut through his lung, and each breath hissed with escaping air from his chest, but surprisingly, it was not a fatal wound. He had been lucky; it had missed all the major blood vessels, and yes, he had been lucky, too, that his flight down the stairs was on his back, or the knife would have torn him up terribly.

Cindy had pulled herself up into a sitting position, and was staring at Mason across the room, her wide eyes still filled with tears. She had been conscious when the man's body hurtled down the stairs, and she had heard his head hit the wall. For a few minutes, after the door upstairs had slammed shut, he appeared dead, but slowly, his feet were moving back and forth. Then he raised his head and looked at her.

"Cindy, can you come over here?" he gasped.

She was petrified! Who was this, and how did her know her name?

"Take the knife from my chest and cut your ropes," he gasped. "Go upstairs and run for your life!"

She still couldn't see his face very well. The shadows of light from the only window were fading fast, and he made no attempt to come to her, but laid his head back down into the pool of blood.

She was scared, so much had happened in such a short time.

"What's your name," she asked, her voice quivering.

He didn't try to raise his head again. Moaning, he said, "Mason, Mason Evans."

Laura had told Cindy her real father's name, but that was when she was twelve and they had told her, her real past. The name, Mason, had stuck with her, but not the Evans. She had never seen a picture of him or ever met him.

"Are you my father?" she asked.

Cindy started crying again, but still had not moved.

David heard the voices downstairs. The bastard was still alive and they were talking—or was the old lady talking to her. Flanagan could be here any minute, but the intruder had to be dead, and he had to make it fast. Down the stairs he went, his stiff legs making the steps so difficult he almost lurched from side to side with every step. He had switched the light on so he could see the man clearly. He stopped two steps from the bottom. The man appeared to be dead. There was blood everywhere. He stepped over him and walked partway over to Cindy, a few feet from Mason's body.

"Who were you talking too?" he asked. His back was to Mason.

Cindy did not answer and, before he could ask again, Mason lunged for his legs and pulled him down to the floor. One of David's rotten legs snapped like a broken stick and broke, mid-way between his knee and his ankle. Suddenly, before David could recover or realize what was happening, the knife was in Mason's hands and he plunged it into David's chest over and over again, and then collapsed on top of him.

Slowly, he sat up and said, "Cindy, it's over. Come here."

She slid across the floor on her butt, and Mason cut her hands free, and handed her the knife. "Cut your feet free and go call the police."

Mike roared up Morgan Avenue, and slid around the corner and into the alley. The alley was blocked by an old brown sedan that was leaking fluids, so he stopped behind it, and got out of his car. Then he saw the black Lincoln, parked in front of the garage. He felt for the gun in the small of his back, just to reassure himself, but he didn't take it out. Just as he reached the car, the back door of the house burst open, and Mike looked up to see Cindy leaping off the steps. She screamed and ran to her father's arms. They were both crying now, and he held her at arm's length and looked at her cuts, then pulled her back to him.

"Let's get to the car," he said.

Once inside the car, he checked her injuries once more, but not before he called the police. A squad was just minutes away.

Cindy was sobbing, but in between her crying she told him, "Dad, there is another man down there in that basement, and he saved my life. He's my father, Dad."

"Mason?" Mike asked. "But how did he…is he okay?"

"No, he's hurt bad, Dad, but he killed that evil, stinking man. It was so bad, Dad, and there is an old lady down there, too, but I think she might be dead. Just then, two squads pulled in and the police ran for the house, their guns drawn.

Mike needed to call Laura and fast. He got back on the radio, and asked the dispatcher to patch him through to his home phone. He hoped she was home by now.

THE CONCLUSION

Laura was on her way to the scene, in the back seat of a Minneapolis squad. Mike had reassured her Cindy was fine, so she seemed to be composed, but would tear up from time to time when she thought about what could have been. She had no idea what had happened there, only that Mike said, he had her with him and she was okay.

When Laura got to the scene, she saw Cindy sitting in the front seat of Mike's squad. She ran to her and embraced her. There was an ambulance, and a Minneapolis police car, there. The Medical Examiner's station wagon was just pulling onto the scene.

After Laura and Cindy had talked and cried things out a bit, they walked, tentatively, up to the house. She wanted Mike to know she was there, and they were together. She could see him in the kitchen, talking to a police officer. Mike looked up at her and walked outside, taking them both in his arms. "Look, Laura, there's no sense in you two hanging out here," he said, holding them at arm's length. "Just take my squad and go home. I know the city frowns on that but we are going to just have to make an exception, aren't we."

He walked to the car with them. "Leave the lights and siren alone," he laughed.

Laura looked out the driver's window at him after starting the car. "How will you get home?" she asked.

"Cops will bring me."

"David Bennett?" she asked, with a question on her face.

"He's dead," Mike said. "When I get home, we have to go see someone in the hospital," he said. "All three of us."

Laura looked puzzled.

"Cindy can fill you in. I've got to get back inside."

When they brought Bennett's body up the stairs, Mike unzipped the bag so he could see his dead face. He wanted to be sure this time, and he could only stare at the man who had terrorized so many people over the last ten years. *What created this monster?* He wondered. *What made him act the way he did?*

Mike found the jar of liquid on the table before he left. *He had saved some,* he thought, as he examined the contents. He shuddered, when it dawned on him what David was going to do with it. *I hope I never see this fluid again.*

Amanda was doing well in the hospital, after surgery to remove a blood clot on her brain. As for Mason—he, too, recovered. The meeting at the hospital Mike had talked with Laura about, was just the first of many meetings, with Cindy and her birth father. As for Mike and Laura, they preferred not to get involved in his life, but had no problems with their daughter seeing him. They would always be grateful for what he had done.

Back in Chicago, Belinda and Curt were in love, and engaged. She now worked full-time in a private lab, away from the sexual harassment she had put up with from all of the men in her former department. She had never been happier in her life. She found that elusive man of her dreams, in Curt. The city had recovered from the damage David Bennett had inflicted, and they were wiser for the experience. However, they knew it could happen again because every day brings more David Bennett's to this world, and they were ready for them.

Jerry and Noreen Marten were a happy family, once more. Jerry had become an advocate for alcoholics, everywhere, and he was president of his local CHAPTER. Noreen told him that, on his one-year anniversary of sobriety, they would go tie the knot once more. She was so proud of him.

On a beach in Jamaica, Mike Flanagan lay on a beach towel, under a cabana, on the fine white sand. Soft, turquoise waves gently lapped the beach, and the sound of calypso music wafted in the air. Laura arrived, and knelt in front of him with two fresh margaritas, handing him one with a mischievous smile.

"What you been thinking about, buddy?" she asked, bending over and kissing him softly.

"Oh, nothing much. I've been lying here looking at the night sky, and trying to match each star with a reason why I love you, but I ran into a problem."

"What's that?" she giggled.

"I ran out of stars," he smiled.

LaVergne, TN USA
02 November 2010
203109LV00002B/5/P